JESSIE

The Adventures and
Insights
of a
Nineteenth-Century
Woman

A Novel by
Dean Robertson

QUAKER CONTENT

Copyright 2017 by Dean Robertson

"What do we live for, if not to make life less difficult for each other?
(George Eliot/
Mary Ann Evans)

—

Author's Note

Jessie: The Adventures and Insights of a Nineteenth-Century Woman is a work of fiction. The main characters, the story, and the dialogue are entirely products of the author's imagination. Because the story is set in a particular city at a particular time in history, a few of the people, places, and events that provide the backdrop for Jessie's story are real.

Society Hill is one of the oldest neighborhoods in Philadelphia. Except for the predominance of the style of domestic architecture known as the row house, all details about Society Hill are imaginary.

Doctor Thomas Story Kirkbride's groundbreaking work with mental patients at the Pennsylvania Hospital for the Insane is well documented and easily available from several sources on the Internet.

The Arch Street Meeting House of the Society of Friends plays a prominent part in *Jessie*. It is real. It existed during the period covered in this novel, and it is still open today, both as a historic landmark and as a Quaker Meeting House. All details in this novel about what occurred at the Arch Street Meeting House are products of the author's imagination.

The Battle at Antietam Creek, Lee's surrender to Grant at Appomattox, the assassination of President Abraham Lincoln by John Wilkes Booth, and the surrender, by Cherokee leader Stand Watie, of what are claimed as the final forces of the Confederate Army are actual historical events.

Philadelphia, the city founded by Quakers with their tradition of peace, did have two military hospitals during the Civil War. The "medical stations" that figure prominently in the relationships among Jessie, Warren, and Patrick, are entirely imaginary.

Philadelphia's prominent position in two areas is well documented. The city was, at the time in which this novel is set, a center of medical research and training in the nation. It was also a hub of the movement known as The Underground Railroad.

Evidence supports the claim of considerable conflict within the Society of Friends on the subject of war.

Any errors in fact or mistaken assumptions about a time and a place about which much has been written are entirely the responsibility of the author.

—

Chapter One
Philadelphia, Pennsylvania
1840-1862
Jessie

Jessie Augusta Brynley Ashmore found herself in a familiar situation, one of many that made her realize how badly she wanted to change her life. These occasions usually involved doing something she didn't want to do, which had the immediate effect of reminding her that she needed to figure out what she *did* want to do. Today, for example, Jessie was on her way to the dressmaker, and she would rather be doing almost anything else. It was time to make some decisions. Unfortunately, she wasn't a very decisive person when it came to decisions about giant leaps into unknown territory. She was fine with the giant leaps. It wasn't the leaps that stopped her; it was all that pondering. No doubt about it: Jessie was a bit of a ponderer.

She wasn't an anarchist. She wasn't Joan of Arc. She couldn't cut her hair and go off to fight Rebels. And like most women who were twenty-two and unmarried, she lived at home with her parents. It wasn't unusual; it was just that Jessie, being Jessie, was finding it unusually unsatisfying.

She was brave enough to attend lectures and help out at the large Arch Street Meeting House of the Society of Friends (commonly called Quakers), brave enough even to prepare food or roll bandages for the soldiers coming home from the war down south or to bring meals and what she could offer of comfort to the widows of those who didn't come home. But she never quite had the courage to go against her father's wishes and work with the Quakers on behalf of the abolitionist movement that had spread like wildfire throughout Pennsylvania.

He had sat her down one day, taken both her hands in his, kept his pale blue eyes a little averted, as he always did, and said,

"Jessie Augusta, you must listen to me and do what I ask on this one thing. It is a dangerous world out there right now. You are the light of my life, and I could not bear it if anything happened to you. Make tea at the Friends Meeting House and wipe the sweat from our soldiers' faces. Don't put yourself at risk trying to help slaves come up from the South; feelings are running high and people are getting hurt. Do I have your word?"

"Yes, Father, you have my word."

The conversation ended, and the subject was never brought up again.

Jessie had never played any part in helping a runaway slave to escape capture, had never worked with the near-mythical Underground Railroad, that finely-tuned system by which a man who had fled his slavery in one of the southern states was passed from person to person and house to house and, finally, to safety and freedom.

The problem, and one that had prompted her to promise, without argument, to do what her father asked of her, was that along with the growing support for the slaves there seemed to be increasing—sometimes violent—opposition to the slave owners. Some of them had been hurt by Pennsylvania abolitionists when they came looking for their slaves; Jessie had even heard that one slave owner had been killed. Working for the Underground Railroad was now a risky business.

Franklin and Augusta Ashmore were typical of a large part of the population; they supported the idea of abolition but had never harbored a runaway slave or helped to "discourage" a slave owner in pursuit of his runaways. Franklin had a family and a business, and those were his priorities. He knew that he had asked Jessie to stay clear of a completely justified and very popular cause; he also knew it was dangerous, and Jessie was his oldest daughter and his favorite.

This was, of course, terribly frustrating for Jessie and, in her more frivolous moods, Franklin Ashmore's favorite daughter sometimes dreamed of running away altogether and joining up with one of the travelling theater companies. There were the medicine shows and the minstrel shows although, honestly, she thought that selling phony tonics and making up in blackface sounded equally distasteful, and what there was of the burlesque was mostly in New York and was, she had heard, more than a little racy.   Although she longed to break the restraints she felt were binding her, Jessie had been brought up in a particular way and, in spite of her resistance to its rules, she couldn't help believing that proper young ladies didn't go into show business of any kind.

Besides, when she thought seriously about what was possible and about what she wanted—about what suited her best--Jessie realized that she probably wasn't cut out for hiding runaways or fighting their owners. What she was doing wasn't just some second-rate activity she'd adopted because she lacked courage. She was actually happier setting up the Meeting House for visiting speakers; she was excited about her first few times sitting with returning soldiers. She was just listening to them right now, or writing letters if

—

they asked, but it was a start, and she liked it. And occasionally, she had the chance to talk to a grieving widow. She thought she might be good at it. There weren't many people doing those jobs and none that she knew of who were doing them with a sense of their importance. Although she might not understand yet who she would become, without realizing it, Jessie was discovering who she was.

Jessie Augusta Brynley Ashmore was named after her mother (Augusta) and a distant cousin of her father (Brynley Walter Ashmore), who had run off with the pastor's wife and was seldom mentioned at family gatherings. Jessie's mother (called Gus) had just liked the way "Brynley" sounded, and he really was a very distant cousin.

From Jessie's Journal
What I Like About my Mother
I like that my mother has chosen to be called "Gus," a man's name, really, rather than the very proper "Augusta," and my favorite thing about her is that she chose to add "Brynley" to my string of names, when she knew perfectly well that "Brynley" was that wild cousin of Father's who did something terrible—I heard the rumor that one

day he just up and left town with the preacher's wife, and has never been heard from again. And she gave me his name for no better reason than she wanted to do it. I overheard Father grumbling about it once when he and Mother were having one of their infrequent disagreements, but I've never heard a whisper since.

My mother, Gus, is a quiet woman who never talks much or offers a strong opinion except to lecture me about the dressmaker, but it's funny. No one ever seems to want to cross her. She's smart, and not too beautiful, and she got a husband and he loves her and she pretty much does what she wants.

So I'm still trying to figure out that whole situation. Meanwhile, I can tell you that I don't think nearly as much about getting married as I do about having an adventure. And so far I haven't seen any evidence that it's possible to do both.

No one seemed quite sure how they had come up with "Jessie," but the name stuck and the older she got the more entirely it seemed to suit her. As for having three given names, it was a tradition in certain branches of her family, and not uncommon among her friends. At least two of the girls she knew in the neighborhood had a string of names just as long, but Jessie was secretly proud of the history of "Brynley." She felt it set her apart, even if no one else knew about it.

—

She was born in 1840 in the Society Hill neighborhood of Philadelphia, Pennsylvania. Philadelphia was a city of neighborhoods, and Society Hill was one of the oldest, dating back to the beginning of the eighteenth century. The Ashmore Family lived in one of Philadelphia's signature row houses. The house had been a gift from a relation of Gus's father, when Gus and Frank married.

Society Hill was a wonderful place for a child to grow up—street after street of the brick rows, two and even three-story houses that gave the place a delightful look that Jessie described one day when she was five as "just like a painting."

The thing she didn't like was that name, "Society Hill," which the more well-heeled residents liked to think meant exactly what it sounded like. They would have been disappointed to know the truth.

Jessie, on the other hand, was delighted when her father told her the real story. Society Hill was started in the eighteenth century when a group of merchants who called themselves the Free Society of Traders obtained a piece of land and started building; people around the city called it "The Society's hill." For Jessie this meant it wasn't entirely a place for people with money. In fact, Society Hill was really a neighborhood laid out in layers, much like those huge cakes with icing in the middle that her mother was teaching her to make. Her house was more-or-less in the middle, and she was curious. Finally, she asked permission to explore.

"Now, Father, you know I can be trusted to go exactly where you tell me I can, and nowhere else. I will be happy if you give me a small number of streets I've not visited before, then I'll set out one morning and walk around and I will come directly home once I've seen those streets. Maybe then you would consider giving me a few more streets on another day."

Jessie did not have her sister Alice's way with their father, in fact wouldn't have even considered tilting her head and looking up coyly from under her eyelashes—a little performance Alice had already mastered at the age of seven. At eleven, Jessie's accomplishment was the development of a slightly exaggerated sense of her own dignity. Alice's wiles would have been beneath her. So she stated her case, folded her hands in her lap, and waited for her father's response. Of course, he said yes.

So Jessie set out to investigate, and even with the limits her father had set, she found some of the back streets and alleys with their much smaller houses and a few of the free-standing mansions of the truly wealthy. And she began to realize that there were many different kinds of people in Society Hill. It was a bustling neighborhood with just about anything anyone might need, including the large clothiers that her father owned. She knew that all the most prominent men in the city came to Franklin's for their suits and shirts.

Jessie knew they must have plenty of money, although her mother always told her it was best not to mention such things. Mentioned or not, they had enough for a small staff of servants to take care of the house and to maintain the gardens. And the Ashmores were known for parties in which the candles were lit, the rugs were rolled up for dancing, and supper was served late.

She could recall the conversations overheard from her parents' bedroom before every party, "I hope everything is the way you like it for the party," Gus would say quietly, followed by some grumbling from Father about this or that not being as nice as the last time. Then Mother's firm, clear voice, "I gave the money that the five additional servants would have cost—the exact amount—to the Society for the Care and Support of Young Women with Children." And with what Jessie knew was her sweetest smile, Gus would say,

"I'm sure you will agree dear, since you have always been in the lead in collecting the funds to maintain that program.

"Now button me up in the back, and let's go down to greet our guests. Oh, Frankie, for heaven's sake. You will ruin my hair and get me too flustered to greet anybody. Stop it now!"

And they would laugh quietly, then the door would open and they would walk down the staircase to be, once again, the best host and hostess in Society Hill.

As a young girl, although she was never interested in these parties, or in the almost identical ones held in her friends' homes, Jessie had considered them a harmless kind of entertainment. But when she was a bit older she had begun to notice people on the streets outside her neighborhood who seemed not to have proper coats in winter or wore shoes with soles that had pulled loose and were flapping, and she had found herself becoming more and more disturbed by those parties. She didn't understand why her parents weren't disturbed, as well. They cared about the poor.

They donated money to groups that helped them; they volunteered at some of the places that gave out free food on holidays. It was too confusing, and she finally decided just to ask someone. One morning after breakfast she went looking for her mother. She finally found her in the scullery, an unusual place for her to be when Cook's girls were clearing up. Gus was scratching her head and looking frustrated and tired.

"Mother, do you have a few minutes for a talk?"

"Of course I do. In fact, let's make a pot of tea and sit in those very comfortable chairs in the

—

morning parlor; the sun should be coming through the windows right about now. And I must admit I could use a break." Great pots of tea, mugs filled liberally with milk before it was poured, were essential for any serious discussion in the Ashmore household. Whether those discussions took place in the parlor or in the kitchen, they seldom occurred without tea. After they had settled into their armchairs and Gus had poured, Jessie—feeling a bit self-conscious—began.

"Mother, have you ever noticed the people on the street right around the corner when we leave the neighborhood—the ones who don't have very good clothes or have shoes that are falling apart or sometimes don't look very clean? Have you seen them?"

Gus was very quiet for what seemed to Jessie like a long time before she answered.

"Yes, Jessie, of course I have seen them, I have *noticed* them. Yes. Did you want to ask me something about them, because I probably don't know much, just that they are very unfortunate."

This time it was Jessie who waited to speak. "I know you and Father give money to help poor people, and I know you sometimes go down to hand out free food. I know that."

"Yes. We do." The conversation stalled, but Jessie picked it up.

"Mother, do you like the parties that you and Father give. I mean, do you enjoy them? Do you think you'll go on having them or—I guess I mean do you want to go on having them?" Jessie was aware that her mother had gotten very still.

"Jessie, where are you going with these questions? I'm happy to answer them, but they do seem random and I can't quite understand what it is you want to know.

"I guess it doesn't matter. Here are my answers. I sometimes enjoy the parties, but I often don't. The house gets uncomfortably warm with so many people, and they do talk a great deal, not always about anything interesting or important, and all that talking makes a terrific noise. I frequently have a headache after everyone has left. In fact, sometimes I slip upstairs to bed while they are all still here. I don't believe anyone has ever noticed."

"And will you still have them, Mother, since you don't like them much?"

More silence. It seemed to Jessie that there was a great deal of silence in this conversation.

"I expect we will, Jessie. Your Father likes them very much, and as long as he wants to have them, we will have them."

Gus knew exactly what Jessie's questions meant; she was aware of the terrible discrepancy between her own life, with its lavish parties, and the lives of the people Jessie was describing. It made her weep with anger and, since she couldn't do anything about it, she had made it a habit to take a different route out of the neighborhood.

And that was that. Jessie sensed that talking about the parties had upset her mother, and so she stopped. But after the questions, and the answers, she went away still unhappy, still with no understanding as to why her parents, who cared very much about the things one should care about, didn't see that all the money spent on all those parties could be given to people who needed it. She also went away with a rush of anger about those long tables laden with food, perfectly balanced at either end with cut glass punch bowls reflecting candlelight, and the house suddenly filled with unfamiliar servants. She knew this wasn't the right time to say that. She was afraid it might never be the right time.

Jessie Ashmore was not a beauty, by any means, but she was a wholesome-looking girl, dark-haired, a bit shorter than the average, with good legs and an ample bosom. In spite of what many called her "eccentricities," people liked Jessie, and Jessie liked people. She was easy to please in everyday matters, not inclined to fuss over chores or to complain about small inconveniences. Granted, she was a bit stubborn when one of her pet "causes" was the issue, but still everyone who knew the Ashmores was surprised that Jessie was still single and confident that any day now she would marry, and marry well.

Not that marriage particularly interested her. Although she would never have dared tell her mother, Jessie sometimes imagined herself as an entirely independent woman, and she knew there were ways of accomplishing that. She didn't have a sum of inherited money to start her off, and people generally assumed you couldn't make it without that. But Jessie had some ideas. Her first choice was to become a writer, a real one, who turned out brilliant essays on the political topics of the day or clever observations about the society around her. Perhaps she could write a novel. She would even be willing, for an adequate salary, to write sentimental pieces for *Ladies Home Journal* on subjects like the purity of a mother's love or the beauty of a baby's toes. Jessie was willing to compromise.

Naturally, she would rather not, and there was always the dream of writing for *Godey's Lady's Book*, the most popular monthly magazine in the country, published right in Philadelphia. She had heard they had a policy of hiring women and the current editor, a woman, published three issues a year that were entirely written and illustrated by women. Thinking about *Godey's* gave her hope, even though she suspected getting work there wouldn't be as easy as it was in her dream.

Educated in all the subjects thought suitable for a young lady, Jessie had learned to play the piano, to sing, to do needlepoint or turn a hem. She could dance. She knew how to arrange cut flowers or make a centerpiece for the table. But what she loved was to use the chalk or paintbrush and to see a picture emerge on a piece of paper or a small canvas.

A well-bred young lady was supposed to be educated enough to carry on a conversation in polite company, talented enough to be entertaining, but never an expert, never an intellectual, never too serious. Above all, never a bluestocking. Fortunately, though Jessie was reasonably intelligent, she had never been much of a scholar. Unfortunately, there were other impediments to her finding a suitable husband. Although she did manage to keep her most outlandish ideas safely tucked between the covers of her journal, she could sometimes be too outspoken. The men in Jessie's world wanted a woman who at least appeared to be a little fragile and in need of their protection, and Jessie's attempts to appear fragile and needy were unconvincing at best. They had been known to inspire uncontrollable laughter from her family.

In spite of her best intentions—and Jessie's intentions were almost always the best—she simply could not be counted on to curb her tongue. Many a prospective suitor had shied away when challenged by her strong opinions on slavery or the war or women's suffrage. And she was especially daunting when she got started about her ambition to roll up her sleeves like Florence Nightingale, bathe half-naked soldiers, and wring out bloody bandages.

How often had she heard,

"Jessie, my dear child, there are plenty of ways to help the war effort without that kind of thing."

Her main problem seemed to be that, all things taken into consideration, she was just entirely too serious. Everyone was concerned about the war, especially since the Confederate army had gotten closer to Philadelphia than anyone had thought possible, but Jessie seemed to take everything a little too much to heart.

From Jessie's Journal
A Brief Note on Spinsterhood and Marriage
I am twenty-two years old and, if I say it myself, an unusually thoughtful and serious person for my age, and yet I often find myself behaving and being treated like a young girl. I wonder if it can really be just because I am unmarried. The spinster occupies a peculiar place in the world I inhabit. She is at once seen as a shriveled-up old maid and a perpetual girl—always a virgin. Admitting I don't exactly know who I want to be, I am sure it is neither an old maid nor an adolescent. Somewhere in between I believe there lies a whole country where a woman is just herself.

My mother often asks me, in an exasperated tone of voice, "Good heavens, girl! Do you not want to find a husband?" My answer, were I to answer honestly, is that I don't know if I want to find a husband. <u>I think the truth is that a husband will have to come and find me.</u>

—

Like any young woman of two and twenty years, however, Jessie Ashmore wasn't all Worthy Causes and Lofty Principles. She did sometimes dream of falling in love – really in love, with a splendid, dashing young man, at least just once. Her heart longed for a little bit of romance. She was not yet resigned to the prospect of its never happening. She just didn't want to end up like every married woman she knew, and sometimes they did all seem just alike. It wasn't that she had anything against being married. She just didn't want to be married like *that*.

There had to be a way to have it all. And she paid close attention to the stories about women like Mary Ann Evans, who was publishing novels under the name George Eliot, and who now lived openly with her lover right in the thick of Victorian England. Evans really did seem to suffer from every possible obstacle to romance—she was too intelligent, far too serious, extremely talented, and physically unattractive. Yet hers was one of the great love stories of the century. Jessie couldn't quite see herself flaunting the conventions to that extent, but she did feel she was prepared for a bit of adventure, should it come her way.

Today, she had a busy day planned. There was this dreaded visit to the dressmaker, and then, much more inviting, a lecture at the Quaker Meeting House. Unfortunately, it was beginning to look as if she might be late to both.

"So, madam," she said to herself quite loudly, "Do you really believe you're going to do anything about changing your life? Anything at all? I, for one, wouldn't bet on it!"

Jessie hated it when she scolded herself. Her mother did quite enough of that. And, besides,

"I expect if I just wait, that adventure will come looking for me one of these days."

Chapter Two
A Day in November 1862
Jessie

Jessie tapped her fingers on the seat beside her and swung her foot back and forth as she sat impatiently in her parents' beautiful four-horse carriage, late for the dressmaker's appointment. Jessie was always late for appointments with the dressmaker, because Jessie didn't want to go to the dressmaker at all. As her mother never tired of pointing out, she managed to arrive everywhere else on time. The truth was that Jessie resisted the whole idea of getting dressed up. It felt to her like putting on a false face, and Jessie had very strong ideas about being truthful.

Jessie had strong ideas about a good many things. Never much interested in the rules for what young women of a certain class should wear, since she had started spending most afternoons at the Arch Street Meeting House, she was trying to slowly adapt her wardrobe to their plain dress. And besides, Jessie knew—as did everyone else—that she was past that magic age of twenty-one when she could ever be called a "young woman" again. She had recently turned twenty-two. Jessie was a spinster.

"If I became a Quaker, then the whole problem of choosing just the right dresses would be solved.

"Since I've become a spinster, the whole problem of choosing just the right husband should be solved!"

Jessie was pleased with the thought, and with her own wit.

"But not only am I already late," she complained, "but there is a speaker at the Meeting House this evening and I promised Eleanor I would meet her there to help set up tea. I can already hear Mother holding forth, 'Jessie Augusta, have you still not realized that you are too intelligent and not beautiful enough to be able to afford to ignore your looks. Good Heavens, girl! Do you want to find a husband, or not?'"

Jessie tapped a little faster. "By the time I've stood for this fitting, then listened to Mother, I probably will miss the speaker altogether. Will I ever be able to do what I want to do? It's hardly fair!"

All this time, Jessie had been talking right out loud, occasionally gesturing with her hands to make a point. This was a habit of hers. Warren Griggs, who had been driving for her family for as long as she could remember, turned around finally and, to Jessie's embarrassment, responded,

"Well, Miss Jessie, I'll tell you. I love to see a young woman like you dressed well, make no mistake about that. But I think those Quakers are

—

doing some very important work. I believe they volunteer at our two big military hospitals even though they are against war, just because they want to help those young soldiers who come home from fighting down south. And for the boys who aren't in hospital, they set up these places where they can get a plate of food or just sit down and have a bit of a rest when they've nowhere to go. Do you know some of those men come back here and have nowhere to live? And they are down there fighting for us. Not right. Not right at all.

"And the Underground Railroad—I have heard about it, of course, but have never been able to figure out how it works. I'm sure someone you know at the Friends' House could say more."

Jessie could have answered Warren's questions about the Railroad but, for once, she held her tongue. Warren was inclined to deliver speeches instead of just talking to you, but Jessie was used to him and, to be honest, she made her fair share of speeches, so she answered him briefly and lightly.

"Warren I agree with everything you say about the Quakers and I especially like the part you left out—no more trips to the dressmaker!"

From Jessie's Journal
Talking to Myself; Talking to Warren
I was up to my old tricks today, talking at the top of my voice—like there was somebody there besides Warren and me. I would love to know what Warren thinks about me. He has always seemed to me like a

very wise man, and I guess I would like him to think well of me. Recently I have started to think about Warren. Warren Griggs. His name is Warren Griggs. He has been driving for my parents since before I was born and the only thing I know about him is that he lives in an apartment over the stable. I don't know if he's ever been married, or had children. Probably not, since he's lived over the stable for as long as I can remember. I wonder if he would ever let me come to visit him. Mother, I believe, would absolutely forbid me to do that, but would also wish just a little bit that she'd thought of it herself.

They had stopped and, pulling herself out of her daydreams, she saw they had arrived at the dressmaker's and, as Jessie had feared, there were her mother and her sister, Alice, waiting impatiently for her in the doorway. They had been calling on a friend, and she had been kind enough to drop them off at the dressmaker's at the appointed time. Jessie was more than half an hour late. They were both accustomed to this, but that didn't mean they liked it, and it didn't mean that Gus would refrain from saying so.

Before her mother could start, Jessie beamed on them both, gave her mother a warm hug, and touched her cheek to Alice's. Her sister had begun insisting on being addressed by both her first and middle names, she felt it gave her a certain

—

dignity and sounded elegant. In an attempt to smooth over the potential conflict, Jessie took both her sister's hands in hers, and positively cooed,

"Alice Morris, I do not know how you do it. I'm away from you for a few hours and you mange to look more beautiful! Why, if I didn't love you, if you weren't my sister, I might be just a little jealous." Alice Morris was clearly pleased and Jessie saw her impatience lift.

Her mother, less easily pacified, immediately began the familiar scolding.

"Jessie Augusta, can you not have the common courtesy to get to these appointments on time? It's quite embarrassing. We had to make your excuses to Madame Prous."

Jessie started to apologize, but her mother, looking more like an "Augusta" than a "Gus," interrupted. "Jessie, let's go in now before she's convinced we aren't coming at all."

Jessie hung her head, acknowledging her mother's criticism, but inwardly still defiant. Really, what did it matter what she wore, when there was so much suffering and turmoil in the world? She was determined that one day she would make her own rules.

The evening before, Jessie had chosen two of last year's dresses to have Madame Prous rework and restyle, as was the custom even among Madame's wealthiest clients. Jessie had decided on a shot silk day dress in alternating stripes of dark teal and pale gray, with the wide pagoda sleeves that were still in fashion. It was one of her favorites. Jessie's second choice, on which her mother had frowned severely a year ago when it was made, was something much closer to the plain dress of the Friends. She had tried to choose an attractive fabric and to describe what she wanted so that it sounded much like her usual dresses, but her mother was having none of it. When Jessie had first reached for the pale gray thistle-print cotton, Augusta had burst out at her.

"Jessie Ashmore! Don't think for one minute I don't see exactly what you're about. That fabric, and the dress you're describing, is something the Quakers would wear, and don't expect me to be fooled because you're altering it a bit."

"Mother, if you would just let me . . ."

"There's no use explaining, dear girl. I am not going to dictate what you wear as long as it's decent, so you go ahead and get this dress made and we'll just see what everyone thinks of it. But *I* am not going to like it. You should be getting dressed in the finest, not trying to look plain."

In the year since the dress was made, Jessie had not asked for any more "plain" dresses, but just seeing that her daughter was having the dress reworked to wear for another year had reminded Gus of how angry she had been in the first place.

—

By the time they had finished with the fitting and pinning, gotten everything together and made it home, Jessie had to skip dinner and hurry as fast as possible to get to the Meeting House; and, even with all that rush, she was still too late to be much help to Eleanor. But her friend reassured her.

"Jessie, just your being here helps me. I am neither comfortable nor very good at greeting guests. You'll be able to charm this one before I start my official job as his guide, and I'm counting on you to do it. Anyone can make the tea!"

Jessie was immensely pleased that her being there was important to Eleanor.

Chapter Three
Later the Same Day
Meeting Eleanor (1861)
Meeting Clarke

From Jessie's Journal
Arch Street Meeting House and Eleanor
One Year Earlier

I remember the day I walked into the Arch Street Meeting House for the first time. It was a year ago, and it was the day I met Eleanor Harrison. I don't think I will ever forget opening the heavy door—being ever so careful to close it quietly—and, walking on tiptoes into that front room. It was all light and empty space. I've never seen such wood—the floor was yellow pine planks, oiled and spotless. The walls were free of any ornament. The whole room shone in the late afternoon sun.

I felt free, and I believed that I had come home. In a strange building, in an alien landscape, a stranger, knowing not one soul, I was sure I had found my place. And then there was Eleanor, a woman I didn't know at all and with whom I exchanged no more than a few pleasantries. I felt, in a split second, possibly before we spoke at all, maybe even as early as seeing her across the shining room, that I had found my best friend. I was completely certain that she was the person I'd been looking for. On that cold November evening in 1861, Eleanor was the smartest, liveliest, bravest, most reasonable, and most beautiful person I had ever known.

—

That was a year ago. Tonight I met Doctor Clarke Stanbury.

Jessie Ashmore had been known to be impulsive and perhaps too easily passionate.

Eleanor had spread the tablecloth on the battered oak table that the Arch Street Meeting always used for refreshments when they had a speaker. This time a physician, just back from the battlefields, was coming to talk about what was happening just south of them where the fighting was the worst. In spite of an uncompromising rejection of war that was a founding principle of the Society of Friends, several of the members of the Arch Street Meeting had sons fighting in the war against slavery, and everyone was eager to hear any news this stranger might bring. There was considerable contention between those in the community who held fast to their fundamental peace tradition and those who felt that slavery was the worst kind of violence.

Nevertheless, when there was danger to any member of their own Meeting, all differences were set aside.

"Could someone please direct me to Miss Eleanor Harrison? My name is Clarke Stanbury and, if this is the Arch Street Meeting, I believe I will be speaking here tonight."

Eleanor and Jessie, and the handful of other women who had come in and were busy setting up the tables, were briefly stunned into silence first by the voice, which was low and soothing and, then, when they turned to look at the stranger, by both his youth and his very good looks. Dr. Clarke Stanbury was an exceptionally handsome man.

"I believe I'm scheduled to speak here tonight," he repeated, "but I can't find anyone to tell me where to go. Can one of you ladies help me?"

Jessie was the first to come out of her trance and actually attempt a response to the doctor's questions. Fortunately she had a clearer head than she gave herself credit for.

"Doctor Stanbury. My name is Jessie Ashmore, and I am so sorry you have been inconvenienced."

Jessie held out her hand and exchanged a firm shake with Clarke Stanbury, who looked a little surprised then smiled and took her hand. Jessie's mother had told her, time and again, that young ladies did not shake hands; that was a gesture reserved for the men. This unwritten rule, like so many others, made little sense to Jessie. She made a point of breaking one of them whenever it was possible without causing a fuss. Besides, Jessie was secretly proud of her firm, no-nonsense handshake. And, in this case, she was pleasantly aware of the warmth of the doctor's hand.

—

"And please allow me to introduce you to Miss Eleanor Harrison, who will see to it that you know where everything is and have an enjoyable evening at Arch Street." Eleanor stepped forward.

"Very pleased to meet you, Dr. Stanbury. I am eager to hear your news from the war. I'm your official guide today. I'll show you around first, then you can let me know what you need."

They walked away together, talking as they went, and Jessie stood looking after them for a minute or two before she turned back to the tea table. She had been reminded of what Eleanor had said earlier—that she was not very good with guests. She felt a hint of discomfort at the obvious contradiction, but it was gone almost before she recognized it.

From Jessie's Journal
Doctor Clarke Stanbury: First Thoughts
Well, Doctor Stanbury was a shock, and I believe he paid me just a little extra attention. Life certainly has a way of surprising us just when we think nothing will ever change. I wonder if Doctor Clarke Stanbury is . . . I had best not even speculate on what Doctor Clarke Stanbury might be. Realistically, I expect he will be no more than last night's guest speaker at the Meeting House. But, then, when was I ever realistic?

The evening was a success. Jessie did her job—which, besides helping set up the tea table and introducing Dr. Stanbury to Eleanor, consisted mostly of being sure that the urn was full and that all the guests had everything they needed. There were always visitors from the larger Philadelphia community when Arch Street had speakers, but when the speaker was someone who had seen the war, like Doctor Stanbury, they could barely provide seats for everyone. Whatever was the truth about her own social skills, Eleanor was right about her friend. Jessie was exceptionally good at paying attention to people, and she saw to it that each one felt welcome and noticed. It was perhaps her very seriousness and, at least when among strangers, her quiet, self-effacing manner, that caused everyone she encountered to feel somehow singled-out for special attention.

So she charmed the mostly middle-class Philadelphians at Doctor Stanbury's talk, but her mind kept returning to something she had seen this afternoon on her way to Arch Street. She had been leaning back in her seat, catching her breath after the rush from the dressmaker, and she turned her head to glance out at the street as they drove by. What she saw caused her to sit up straight and ask Warren to slow down.

By the side of the street was a couple—it was impossible to tell their ages—with three children, all young, holding hands with each other and anchored to the two adults by the oldest of them, who was holding the mother's hand. They had been dressed in filthy rags, the husband of the pair wearing a stained and tattered army uniform. There was nothing she could do.

Jessie shook her head to clear it. Someone was tugging gently at her sleeve and asking if she could bring more tea.

Eleanor, as usual, did her job with near-perfection. She was efficient and practical, and she knew everything there was to know about the Society of Friends, the Arch Street Meeting House, the particular speaker in her care on any given day, and how to get that speaker settled, with enough of an introduction to the Meeting House to be comfortable. She knew every problem that might arise in the building, and she could solve most of them herself. She was always pleasant and attentive. As the war heated up and the Arch Street Meeting House became the center of the wave of patriotism that swept the city, Eleanor's position grew in importance.

She was not only of help in practical matters but, because of the status of women among the Friends, she usually sat in the Minister's Gallery during their services. Although the services were silent—there were no sermons or speeches—anyone, if moved, could stand to speak. The seats in the Gallery were reserved for those known to be talented speakers, and Eleanor had been seated there for over a year.

Two years older than Jessie, Eleanor, too, still lived with her parents, but she intended to move out in the coming year. She was an inspiration to Jessie who hadn't really gotten beyond the vague wish for some kind of change, and the two women had many conversations about the way they imagined their lives would be.

"I'm awfully close to being able to do this," Eleanor said one day after they had been friends for several months.

"I have a close friend, a few years older than I am, who has rented one room in a boarding house for as long as I have known her and would love to find a suite of rooms that we could share. I have a small inheritance to get me started and sustain me until I find work, and my friend is a writer at one of the women's publications. I will confess to a bit of no doubt premature shopping for somewhere to live. I've seen two lovely places—both suites of rooms, one near the Meeting House."

"I'm impressed, and I'm also feeling pretty ridiculous. I hadn't thought about any of that." Jessie was not happy.

"I'm not at all sure I even have a friend close enough to ask and, honestly, most of my so-called friends are just acquaintances and they are very—well—traditional, I guess I'd say, in the way they think. I don't imagine the idea of getting some kind of independent life would have entered their minds. What do you think, Eleanor? Do I even stand a chance of doing something different, or am I just trapped?"

Eleanor paused before she responded.

"Oh, Jessie, I don't think we're ever trapped unless we choose to be. You'll find your way out—a way that's right for you, that suits you—and you will know it when it comes along. Don't be impatient." As it turned out much later, Eleanor knew a good bit about being trapped, possibly not in the way Jessie meant it.

And with a grin she said,

"In the meantime you can meet my friend, Sarah Portman, and then you will come to us often. We will drink cocoa or milky tea and have all kinds of outrageous conversations about your life. We'll pretend you're going to run away to California, to the goldmines, or move to the South to stir things up. We probably won't come up with a real plan, but we will have a great deal of fun!"

Jessie was always cheered by these conversations. Eleanor seemed genuinely hopeful and optimistic about life in general while Jessie believed she had a tendency to look on the gloomy side. But Jessie didn't recognize the hope she often brought to others, and she tended to idolize Eleanor.

The two had met on Jessie's first day at the Arch Street Meeting House, almost exactly a year ago. Jessie had come in timidly, having heard that a poet, a woman, was to give a talk and read some of her poetry. She had no idea what to do once she had gotten up her nerve to walk through the door.

Did she have to sign anything? Let somebody know she was a guest? She knew she would have to find out where the talk would be, and that meant approaching someone and asking.

So she glanced around—and there was Eleanor, looking as if she knew just about everything, and quite attractive besides. She was tall, only two or three inches under six feet, slim but large-boned, and with that black hair that looks almost blue when it catches the light. Sometimes, just briefly, it was possible to believe she was Iroquois or Shawnee, but then she'd turn and the illusion would fade. She was smiling at people as they came in and, in a few cases, walked right up to the men and held out her hand for a shake. Jessie told her a month or so later that she had thought she was the only woman who did that.

Jessie took a deep breath and, appearing a good deal more confident than she felt, walked right up, held out her hand, and said,

"Hello, my name is Jessie Ashmore, and this is my first time here. You look as if you can tell me what I need to do."

That all came out in a great rush and Jessie felt foolish, but Eleanor took the outstretched hand, shook it firmly and smiled what surely was her brightest smile,

"I am Eleanor Harrison and I'm very pleased to meet you, Jessie. I expect I *can* tell you what you need to know, but why don't we walk around together and I'll show you where everything is. Then when you come next time, you'll be able to manage on your own.

And I do hope you'll come back."

Two things of importance happened to Jessie Ashmore that day in the late fall of 1861. She pushed open the door to the Arch Street Meeting House of the Society of Friends, stepped inside, and saw a world. And in the very middle of this world stood Eleanor, smiling, waiting for her.

It was a critical time in the life of the Philadelphia Friends, and especially at the Arch Street Meeting House, which had become the center for discussion of causes like abolition and more rights and, ultimately, independence for women. The war was getting worse and moving closer, and the plight of the colored people in the South had become evident as soldiers returned with stories about the conditions in which they lived. The Quaker women responded, in that concrete way that was so well suited to Jessie's temperament, by organizing sewing societies. The clothing they made was sent directly south and somehow made it into the hands of those with the greatest need.

Jessie was happy. She had learned to sew early and well. It was one of the skills a young woman acquired, and it was a skill she had considered frivolous until she was able to put it to use in the service of a good cause. Little by little, she became more involved with the Friends at Arch Street, and she and Eleanor began their friendship. The work at the Meeting House and the strong Quaker principles suited her well.

Jessie was soaking up new information and throwing herself passionately into this newly discovered life. She was learning; she was preparing herself for a time that was still ahead. But, for now, she was simply content.

Chapter Four
Doctor Clarke Stanbury

In November of 1862, when he spoke at the Friends Meeting House on Arch Street in Philadelphia, Doctor Clarke Edwin Stanbury was thirty-four years old, six feet tall and possibly a little too thin. He was clean-shaven (having removed an impressive beard to make himself more comfortable among the soldiers down south). His abundant hair was a deep brown, as were his eyes. The eyes were noticeable because they often seemed to be either far away in thought or crinkled at the edges with some secret amusement.

Doctor Stanbury sometimes appeared to be laughing at something and, if you were a young woman who had already noticed how handsome he was and how wonderful his voice sounded, had already felt the warmth of his hand in yours, then you most likely were hoping that "something" wasn't you. Jessie wasn't exactly thinking these thoughts, but she did feel a bit uncomfortable when, after his lecture and the many questions that followed, she saw him in conversation with Eleanor, occasionally glancing her way and chuckling.

Yes, it was a bit worrying. As things turned out, Jessie wasn't to think about this again for a very long time.

Doctor Stanbury, as diplomatically as he could, was asking Eleanor about Jessie, whose firm—and daring—handshake he couldn't seem to get out of his mind. When Jessie spotted the two of them, and the doctor laughing, the conversation was going something like this,

"So, Miss Harrison, how do you think your friend, Miss Ashmore, would react if I just walked right up and asked her to tell me about herself? I assume that still runs counter to those unwritten rules young ladies grow up with."

Just briefly, Clarke felt Eleanor's smile was a little odd, almost flirtatious, but he was sure he had been wrong. Her response was charming and geared to appeal to his sense of humor *and* to put Jessie in a very good light.

"Doctor, I can only tell you that my friend, Jessie, devotes several hours every day of the week, Sundays included, to thinking up ways to break those rules. I believe her goal is to break at least one a day. I hope I'm not violating any confidences here, but I can tell you that, of my own personal knowledge, her current record is four."

With that, she looked down at her shoes, and it was at that moment that Doctor Stanbury burst into the appreciative laughter that Jessie saw and that was so much of a concern to her. Although Miss Jessie Ashmore tried to limit her private monologues to the family carriage, this was one of those occasions when the pressure of the situation just got the better of her.

—

"Well, Jessie girl, I don't know quite what it is you've done this time, but it was clearly foolish enough to have earned you the ridicule of a very attractive man. Good work again!"

And she stormed into the kitchen to help with the cleaning up. As she started stacking plates and taking them to the sinks full of sudsy water, it suddenly occurred to her,

"Oh, goodness. I suppose that's it! Of course it was because I held onto his hand too long. How embarrassing. How forward of me, and mother warning me at every turn that men like women who are shy and behave properly. I'm sure if she ever finds out about tonight, I will be hearing about it for a very long time. Why, oh why, can't I listen and take advice?"

Since several of the Friends were moving around in the kitchen, it was fortunate that Jessie at least didn't say any of this last out loud.

Meanwhile, Doctor Stanbury and Eleanor had finished their conversation and the doctor was looking around for Jessie. He didn't see her anywhere in the big room, but he wasn't ready to give up yet. It did seem as if this opportunity might not come again. And, as he wandered through the few rooms that made up the Meeting House, he considered that handshake again.

"There are several aspects of that handshake that intrigue me."

This thought was silent. Clarke Stanbury was unconventional in many ways, most of them probably due to the amount of time he had spent in unconventional situations, like battlefields, but his particular eccentricity didn't extend to talking out loud to himself in public.

"Yes, Miss Ashmore is attractive in more ways than just her appearance—although I find her appearance very appealing, indeed. I like the boldness of her offering the handshake in the first place. I like her firm grasp of my hand and the fact that she didn't pull away when I held on a bit too long; I could almost imagine that she was holding on as well. And, oh my goodness, that is a very soft, warm hand."

With that thought, he came upon Jessie in the kitchen, her forearms exposed and up to her elbows in soapy water. He took one deep breath, walked over to her side, rolled up his sleeves, picked up a towel, and began drying and stacking the plates as she washed them. Neither of them said a word, but both were smiling as they washed and dried those dishes. The job could most likely have been done more quickly, possibly there were even one or two plates that weren't completely clean, but they were in no hurry and were, to be honest, a little distracted.

It was late when Doctor Stanbury handed Jessie into her parents' carriage, and she had to endure a mild scolding from her mother when she got home. Unfortunately, she didn't hear most of it. She was thinking about the question the doctor asked just as Warren was about to drive away. "Miss Ashmore, would it be acceptable to you if I called on your father to ask his permission to see you again?" Jessie was speechless and could only nod before Warren drove away. Neither she nor Warren uttered a word on the drive.

When Clarke Stanbury turned twenty-one, he decided he wanted to be a doctor. He knew that one of the best schools of medicine in the country was at the University of Pennsylvania, and in the Fall of 1848 he enrolled for lectures in infectious diseases, surgical pathology, and nervous disorders, little suspecting that before he was thirty-five, he would be using that early training on the battlefields of a bloody civil war that was threatening the outskirts of the city where he acquired them.

Clarke was born in New York, but had moved to Philadelphia when he was five years old. His father had died early that year, of tuberculosis, and he and his mother had made the trip to Philadelphia to live with his aunt. His mother had eventually gotten work as a seamstress and, working in a sweatshop, under the worst possible conditions, had succumbed to the same lung disease that killed his father. Clarke had just turned twelve. His aunt, a wonderful woman but frail and not always in her right mind, raised him until he left home at eighteen. He had been living in rooms, picking up odd jobs wherever he could find them, when he suddenly knew he wanted to study medicine. He couldn't have chosen a finer city to do it. By that time, Philadelphia was the center of medical research and training in the country.

After he had completed his studies, he spent two years learning as much as he could about a wide variety of illnesses, but he finally chose to practice with the Quaker physician, Dr. Thomas Story Kirkbride, who had recently been appointed to head the Pennsylvania Hospital for the Insane. As his enrollment in that first lecture in infectious diseases had been inspired by the deaths of his parents from tuberculosis, so his aunt's mental problems sent him to Dr. Kirkbride and, finally, to the war in the South where many young soldiers were having emotional breakdowns that often were punished rather than understood.

Kirkbride's years at the Hospital for the Insane saw the implementation of his pioneering idea that the insane should be treated humanely, and he presided over a hospital where patients were not chained, where they were given time outside to exercise, where—as often as possible--they slept in private rooms. Perhaps most radical of all, Dr. Kirkbride believed there should be no distinction between the treatment of the wealthy and the treatment of the poor. Doctor Clarke Stanbury was in his element and, without knowing it, was preparing himself to be the perfect physician for those young soldiers in 1862.

This combination of a painful childhood, a few years of aimless wandering, the finest medical training possible, and a life that was largely celibate due to the growing demands on his time and energy, had produced—by the time he approached Miss Jessie Ashmore—a decidedly eccentric man. He seemed the ideal match for Jessie. And he certainly thought so as he watched her pull away from Arch Street that night. Although it would be improper for a young lady to be thinking along the same lines, still one must admit that the thought did enter Jessie's mind. It should come as no surprise that the equally eccentric Jessie should be entertaining improper thoughts, nor that she was waiting at Arch Street the very next day when Eleanor arrived.

"Eleanor! Oh my goodness, Eleanor. Come and sit down with me. I will explode if I can't talk right now, and you are the only possible person. Can you take just a few minutes?"

Eleanor put her arm around Jessie's shoulders and walked her into the kitchen where she put water on for tea. She moved a few things from the large kitchen table, then pulled out two chairs and sat down across from Jessie.

"Well, Jessie, it sounds as if you might have something exciting to tell me. And since I saw you just last evening, I can't think what could have happened in so short a time."

Eleanor already had a fairly accurate idea about what Jessie's news might be, since she had spoken with the doctor, had watched him searching for Jessie, had seen them both go into the kitchen, and had seen them walk out together. Jessie all but fainted with the thrill of describing, perhaps more than once, the washing, drying, and stacking of the dishes, the way the soapy water felt on her hands and arms, the question through the carriage window, and her anticipation and doubt. Eleanor listened with some interest to the predictable story of infatuation. Jessie was a friend, after all, and Clarke Stanbury had seemed a nice enough man. Jessie had discovered the sensual life in a basin of warm soapy water and, goodness, she had lovely things ahead. And as for Doctor Stanbury—well, why on earth not?

Exactly one week after his talk at the Arch Street Meeting House, on a bright, chilly afternoon, Doctor Clarke Stanbury knocked on the door of the Ashmore home, having first visited Mr. Ashmore at his place of business to ask for permission to call on Jessie.

Chapter Five
Frank

Franklin Lucas Ashmore was only eight years older than Clarke Stanbury. At forty-two, he was just shy of six feet tall, with light brown hair and a short beard and moustache, trimmed neatly, also a light brown. His eyes were pale blue under eyebrows that were turning a premature gray. He had the beginnings of a receding hairline, but altogether he was a handsome man. He was two years younger and more conventionally attractive than his wife, but not nearly as captivating. He didn't catch the attention of passing strangers as did Augusta. When he was younger, his friends called him Frank. For many years now, he had preferred Franklin. His wife had always called him Frankie.

He never had much of a relationship with his son, Franklin Lucas Junior, who was called Luke. When Luke was small, Franklin was working long hours, and when he finally had more time to build a relationship with his now nearly grown son, the opportunity seemed to have passed. When the war started, Luke signed up and went south to fight. A young soldier who had come home wounded brought them a message from Luke six months after he left, and that was the last time they'd had any word. They didn't talk about this at home.

Franklin was closer to his daughters, although that closeness was not without complications. His younger daughter, Alice, had learned how to manipulate him and, because he was susceptible to flattery and disliked any kind of conflict, he almost always gave her what she wanted. She was an uncommonly pretty girl, and he was proud of her looks and her little charms, but he found he was often annoyed after she had coaxed something out of him. He knew he was being "handled," and he upbraided himself for giving in.

It was Jessie, his independent, opinionated, strong-willed, crusading daughter, who wouldn't stoop to manipulation or coaxing or feminine wiles to convince him to do anything, who had his deepest love and his genuine respect. He was sometimes afraid for her, especially because she seemed too often to have no fear for herself.

At the same time he envied her willingness to stand up for what she believed to be right. He had never been a hundred per cent convinced that her association with the Quakers was a good idea, but he knew much better than to cross her on something that she embraced so completely. And there was no doubt that the people in the Society of Friends, and especially those he had met from the Arch Street Meeting, were very good people. He had no worries on that score.

As for Augusta Morris Ashmore, his wife of a quarter century, she amazed him every single day. It was as simple as that.

From Jessie's Journal
My Father's Stories
I have always loved Father's stories, he has so many and he's a great storyteller. He likes to talk about the jobs he's had, and I could listen forever to the stories about when he worked at a big stable—which was what he was doing when he met my mother. After that, and after they were married, he worked for a year as a tailor's apprentice and he says that was the hardest year he's ever had. But the result of it was that he became a great tailor and now he owns his own shop that is probably the best one in Philadelphia. But my very favorite thing is hearing about when he met my mother. They still act like sweethearts. It's very encouraging.

Franklin worked hard, made good money, and enjoyed it. He gave large parties, went out of his way to do favors, and treated his employees more than fairly.

"Ah, Frank lad, admit it. You were ever so much happier every single day when you were sitting long hours on an uncomfortable stool, pricking your fingers until they bled, praying for the calluses to grow, and getting a rap on the head every time your stiches weren't straight or didn't hold. You have never felt that satisfaction with yourself for even one day since you opened your own business and became the boss over young boys about the age you were when you signed on to learn how to sew. Maybe you just don't have the temperament for being in charge, though it's too late to think about that now."

His son was off in the war; his daughters had busy lives and were seldom at home. And he seemed to spend less and less time with his wife. He was lonely.

Frank Ashmore was not quite eighteen when he married Jessie's mother. Marriage was not in his plans, although he certainly found Gus Morris very attractive. He liked her down-to-earth good looks—her thick dark hair and full bosom. Their meeting each other at all had been unlikely. Augusta Morris lived in an odd sort of arrangement with a maiden aunt, in which she seemed free to come and go as she pleased while the aunt stayed at home, mostly crocheting doilies. They lived this strange life in one of the wonderful old row houses in Society Hill. Gus and the aunt apparently shared this enormous place with two elderly servants, who saw to their basic needs.

It was all decidedly eccentric, as was Gus, a fact that had become clear to him in a variety of ways over the decades. But Frank Ashmore had been in love with Gus Morris from the first day he saw her and it was her eccentricity that fascinated him the most. She was, at a time when young ladies were dedicated to being young ladies, a perfectly straightforward, honest woman. He adored her for it.

That meeting happened on one of the rare days when Gus had been able to talk the aunt into leaving the house, and they had gone for a carriage ride in the park. A wheel broke when they hit a large rock; the driver, an old man himself, was unable to do anything except sigh and shake his head; and both he and the aunt were near hysterics when Gus spotted a stable on the other side of the park. Hiking up her skirts, she walked over and asked the first person she saw for help. That person was a devilishly good-looking stable boy named Frank Ashmore. Twenty-five years later, Frank still recalled nearly every word of that first conversation. He felt sure that Gus had forgotten at least the details, which indicates that Franklin didn't know his wife as well as he thought, even today.

"Hello there. My name is Gus Morris and I'm in a bit of a pickle and could use some help."

"Well, miss, as you can see I'm in a bit of a pickle myself here getting this poor horse shod on one hoof before he throws another one—which he seems determined to keep on doing until they're all off."

"Oh, dear. It looks as if we're both having a rather bad day. I wonder if we might make a deal and improve the prospects for us both."

Frank was immediately suspicious. Even at seventeen he knew not to make "deals" without a thorough investigation. However, he was beginning to notice Gus. She was quite good-looking, and he was considering rethinking his position on deals.

"It would have to be a pretty good one, because this horse is in trouble and I'll be in worse if I don't get all these shoes on and have him back to his owner before dinnertime." And he waited.

As she had managed to do over the years, with an impressive success rate, Gus had a solution.

"My trouble is that my elderly aunt, and her equally elderly driver, are sitting across the park in a large carriage that has a broken wheel. My aunt is beginning to panic, and the driver isn't far behind her. Obviously, they can't fix the problem."

Frank was still waiting.

Well – may I know your name, seeing that you know mine?"

"It's Frank, miss, Frank Ashmore."

"Part of our deal, Frank, will be that you stop calling me 'miss.' Can we agree to that part first?"

"Don't see why not."

"Then, here's the rest of the deal. If you will walk back with me and see what you can do about that wheel or, if it's hopeless, let us borrow a vehicle from the stable here to get these two old people home . . ."

She didn't get out another word before Frank interrupted her,

"Perhaps you don't understand, *miss*, but I don't exactly own the stable. I am in no position to be sending carriages out on loan. Good Lord, what can you be thinking?" Frank huffed with impatience.

—

"Oh, for heaven's sake, Frank. Of course you don't own the stable. Could you allow me to complete my thought? As I was trying to say, if you will solve my problem, in whatever way you see fit, I will send a friend who is an expert at shooing horses, right over to the stable the minute I get home and with the two of you working together you should have that horse in fine shape long before dinner."

Frank took a deep breath, walked the horse back into his stall, turned around, gave Gus Morris one look, and said, "Are you coming or not?" And he headed toward the road. She ran to catch up and walked beside him the rest of the way.

Miss Augusta Morris showed up at the stable at least twice a week from then on. She didn't talk much, just hung around, asking him occasionally to show her how to do something. She learned fast, and she was strong. She could do most things around the stable, and she was willing to work. Frank was finding it pleasant to have her around.

Then one day she came very early in the morning. Before lunch, they were in one of the back stalls, one that Frank had fortunately mucked and covered with clean straw just the evening before. Frank had heard all his life that women didn't have sexual urges, but whoever said it hadn't met Gus. He was sure she enjoyed it just as much as he did. As he had sat down and settled himself in the straw, Gus had stood up and put her hands on the buttons of her blouse, and looking him straight in the eye, she asked—in her matter-of-fact voice,

"Well, Frank Ashmore, will you be embarrassed when I start unbuttoning this blouse, when I let it drop to the floor, when I unfasten the skirt and let it slide down, when I stand here without a stitch of clothing? I left home this morning without my corsets and without my petticoats. In fact, I came away without undergarments of any kind. I have discovered in this short time that being without them is the most luscious sensation and I'm considering never wearing them again."

As she talked, Gus unbuttoned. The blouse—a dusty pink cotton with long sleeves and a pattern of small, pale flowers—was in the straw before he had a chance to answer her question. It didn't seem to matter. Frank was staring at Gus's breasts; they were beautiful, large, like melons, and firm, with pink nipples that were stiff with excitement. Did she expect him to say something?

"No, Gus. No, I won't be—I'm not embarrassed. I've never seen anything as wonderful as you are at this minute." And Frank stood in front of her, close enough to reach out and cover her breasts with his hands.

"I can feel your nipples getting harder, Gus. Is that because I'm touching them?"

"It certainly is."

And so the afternoon passed slowly and the two young people made love, rested in the straw, and made love again. During the next few months, they made that stall their home, and sometime toward the end of the third month, Gus told Frank she was pregnant.

"Guess what, Augusta Morris. I'm glad. We will get married right away, and we will have a baby. Maybe will have two or three more babies. We will make love as often as we can—with all those babies running around. And we'll be happy. And, by the way, I love you."

And all Frank's predictions came true. They had those babies. They made love often and with great enthusiasm. They were happy. It hadn't been his first time, but it was the one he still remembered because it wasn't like anything that came before it and he was certain it was better than anything else out there if he were ever stupid enough to go looking.

And he knew, without knowing how he knew, that Gus would never go looking either. They both had what they needed, and more, right at home. Frank had known that day in the stable that he'd landed in heaven and he wasn't really upset at all when it turned out that they needed to get married. And Gus had been proving all the experts wrong about women and sex for two decades and counting.

She was smart, much smarter than he was. At first he hadn't realized just how smart, but it didn't take him long, and the funny thing was he never resented her for it, never was jealous. Gus was just in a different category altogether. He knew he had accomplished a great deal since those early years, but he had worked hard and sweated to do it. It seemed to him that Gus was successful just by being herself. People were drawn to her, adored her, and came to the house to ask her advice.

Even his daughters, when they had a problem they couldn't solve or a question they couldn't answer, went directly to Gus. He couldn't remember one single time, in all the years since Luke had been born, that either of them had asked his advice about anything. He suspected part of that was just that he was a man, but he knew that a larger part was simply that he wasn't Gus. Nobody was Gus.

He recalled a terribly awkward conversation with Jessie not so long ago, when he had not been able to understand what it was she expected of him. He often tried, with Jessie, to figure out what she wanted him to say so he could say it and impress her. He was seldom successful, but he never stopped trying. The topic of this particular conversation was the parties that he and Augusta gave. She had come upon him dozing in his favorite armchair and had sat down on the ottoman directly in front of him, watching him and waiting quietly. That silent stare from his daughter was not conducive to peaceful napping, and he was by this time wide-awake.

When she had asked, with no tension or pressure in her voice, the innocent question,

"Father, could I ask you about something?" he had responded quickly,

"Well, of course you can, Jessie. Anything at all."

"How do you feel about the parties you and Mother give? I mean, do you enjoy them?"

Franklin Ashmore did not hesitate even long enough to take a breath before he smiled at his daughter and said,

"Oh I feel wonderful about them, Jessie. Why, I not only enjoy them, but I am very proud of them. Your mother sees to it that the house is decorated beautifully; the food is always superb; the additional servants are carefully chosen to blend in with our regular staff so they seem to have been with us forever; and I believe I am safe in saying that everyone has a lovely time. In fact, many have told me so."

Jessie was emboldened to confront this disappointing answer, delivered in such a cheerful voice, and she continued,

"Did it ever occur to you that what I imagine is quite a lot of money spent on those parties could be put to better use? Why, it could be given to any number of programs around the city designed to help those much less fortunate than we are. You could even have half the number of parties and give just that much money."

And now Franklin did take that breath. He was, at the same time, puzzled at this odd attitude his daughter seemed to have about parties, and furious that she felt she had the right to question how he spent his money. Jessie, for all that he loved her, could behave in such an outrageous way and say such unacceptable things that he almost believed she couldn't be his daughter. Goodness, where could he begin?

"Well, Jessie Augusta, you certainly have a different idea than most young women about what it is appropriate to say to your father. That is my first thought."

Jessie was just opening her mouth to respond, when her father cut her off,

"My second thought is that you have no idea about the finances in this household, either what kind of money I make, what our regular expenses are, or how much we spend on those parties. So I fail to understand the basis on which you ask these questions. I have usually found you smarter than this.

"Believe it or not, you have succeeded in making me angry, so if you will excuse me, I will go out for a walk before dinner."

And with that, Jessie's young, healthy father made quite a show of pushing himself slowly out of his chair, groaning a little, and holding his back as he actually limped out of the room. Franklin was feeling exceedingly sorry for himself. He was also aware that he had made a poor showing with his daughter.

—

Franklin Ashmore sometimes wondered if life needed to be this complicated.

Chapter Six
Gus

Gus Morris was not a bad girl the day she seduced Frank Ashmore. And seduce him she certainly did. What else could you call it when a girl walks into a stall in a public stable, takes off all her clothes and lets a boy she barely knows, two years her junior, put his hands all over her, and laughs and screams and generally makes such a racket that it's a wonder they weren't caught and hauled off to jail? Gus Morris seduced Frank Ashmore, then she kept on doing it until she got pregnant and married him. Frank co-operated fully, but Gus started it.

She scouted out the stable, then studied the week's schedule for the days and times when owners were coming in to either leave or collect their horses. She marked out, in her mind, the two days when the place would be empty for the longest. And then she rolled the dice, accepting the strong possibility that someone would come by unannounced. All things considered, Augusta Morris was quite a young woman.

She knew perfectly well that what she had done did not fall into any category of ordinary, acceptable behavior. But then, Gus had never been ordinary, nor could she have been, given her upbringing. The only thing ever known about her parents was that they were gone, and as far back as anyone could remember, Gus Morris had lived in that big row house in Society Hill with her aunt, a woman who was never referred to as anything other than "Aunt Morris," which would suggest she was Jessie's father's sister, but nobody knew that for certain. To take care of the two of them, and everything else, there was one very old servant, who clearly couldn't handle the house and gardens himself, so he hired young house servants and a gardener from somewhere in the city. There was never anything resembling a permanent staff, but there was a more-or-less regular group of them who showed up several times a week. They were pleasant enough, the house was always immaculate, and the gardens were a showplace. It was, over all, a good place to grow up, but not particularly exciting, and Gus Morris was restless.

Frank Ashmore was something entirely new, and Frank Ashmore was a challenge.

Gus hadn't changed all that much from her eight or ten or twelve-year-old self.

She was a thoughtful child, always older than her years, but with occasional moments, even whole days, of a kind of reckless and brilliant joy that made her irresistible to some and absolutely terrifying to many. On those days, she was just the kind of girl to have gotten herself pregnant with a boy who was barely old enough to be out of short pants, who had no family that anyone could find, who had not a dime in his pocket and who was, when she met him, cleaning up after someone else's horses.

At nineteen, Gus still had all those qualities that adults value. She was mature, she was thoughtful, she was cautious, but those reckless days came around and caution never had the appeal of jumping in with both feet and getting muddy right up to her knees.

She realized that this situation was a bigger mess than muddy knees, but she felt pleased with herself that they hadn't gotten caught in the stall; her planning really had been impressive. Still, it did look like a disaster, and Gus couldn't quite figure out why she was feeling more thrilled than anything else. If Frank was exciting, and he surely was, then think what a baby would be! Right now, though, she needed to get her feet back on the ground. She had to talk to her aunt.

"Aunt Morris, do you have a minute to talk?"

"Oh, of course, Gus. I'm just sitting here making more of these damned doilies that no one, including me, will ever use; I've never much liked doilies. Sorry to interrupt."

Gus was getting confused, as she often did right at the beginning of a conversation with her aunt. Fortunately, things seemed to clear up as they went along. Whether Aunt Morris suddenly got her thoughts sorted out or Gus just got used to her chaotic way of talking, Gus never figured out, but in this case she hadn't the patience to wait and she just blurted out,

"Well, Aunt Morris, I suppose you ought to know that I am going to have a baby and I will be getting married soon and I hope you will come to the very small wedding. In fact, if you attend, you will be the only guest."

Gus's Aunt Morris looked her squarely in the eye for a minute, and she started to laugh.

"Why Augusta Morris, I just had no idea that you knew anything about—well, no need to get into details, and you clearly don't need me to explain about any of that now, and goodness gracious, child, we are going to have a baby in the house! There is nothing lovelier than that. I am delighted! Now, I expect it's this young stable boy? What did you tell me his name is? No, do not remind me. Frank. Frank Ashmore. I don't suppose he has any family to speak of. No. Well, nothing less important, really."

"Aunt Morris, maybe you don't understand me. I am pregnant. I am not married. I am getting married, but I got pregnant first."

She paused, to be sure she had made her point. "Does that make sense?"

"I believe, Augusta, that it is perfectly clear. Whether it makes sense you must decide for yourself."

"Aren't you upset or angry with me about this?"

"For the Lord's sake, I do lose patience with that kind of question. You have an excellent brain, Gus. Use it. What possible good would it do for me to be angry or upset? Let's think about what we have to do. I will provide whatever money you need and you will take the carriage and go shopping for everything that is required for a well-appointed nursery. And I do not intend you to stick to whatever you think are the essentials. I will expect at least half your purchases to qualify as essential just because they're wonderful.

"You know, I might even go with you. Heavens. Well, we'll have to see.

"I believe I need to lie down. Congratulations, young lady, and of course I shall attend your wedding."

Aunt Morris, more sensitive than might have been expected, realized that the newly married couple needed some time to themselves, and so she waited. It was only after several weeks that she summoned her niece and sat her down for what turned out to be a long and life-changing talk.

"Augusta, I have enjoyed all these years with you, and I haven't said that enough. You know, this place will be yours and Frank's when I'm gone, and I am pleased to think of the two of you here, making a life, raising your children."

"Oh, goodness, Aunt Morris. I am very grateful. You know I love this house as much as you do, but you don't need to be thinking about all that now."

"Well, dear, I believe I do need to be thinking about it. First of all, loving it and taking care of it are two different things. This place requires a great deal of hard work. Possibly you will enjoy caring for some of the flowers, and you tell me that Frank is very good with his hands and he could certainly do some of the work around here, but I imagine you are going to have a houseful of children, and whatever Frank decides to do, I expect he'll be busy doing it, so the two of you will already have plenty to keep you occupied. But, busy or not, I expect you to maintain this place just as I have, and that is going to cost a great deal of money."

"Aunt Morris, please don't worry about all this. Frank and I will find a way to do it all. We will."

"Gus, please listen. I am setting aside a large sum of money specifically for the maintenance and improvement of this house and the gardens attached, for as long as you and Frank—or any of your children, or their children—choose to live here. You will use the interest that accrues as often as you can, but when a big job needs doing you are to take whatever you need from the capital. I want this house kept in good repair. You will not need to cut corners. Are we clear?"

"Yes. We are clear." Gus was looking a little overwhelmed.

"One more item here, Gus. Can you pay attention?"

"Yes, I'm fine and listening, Aunt Morris."

"I am depositing a much larger sum of money for you and Frank personally. The interest on that money should be more than enough for all your regular living expenses, with a good amount left over every month. However, should any kind of emergency arise, the same dictum applies: go into that money and take whatever you need to be certain that you and Frank and your children are taken care of. Are we clear on this?"

"Aunt Morris, of course we are clear, but this seems all too much. I don't know how much money you're talking about, but it sounds like a lot. Do you have all this?"

"You're correct. It is, in fact, an enormous amount of money, a truly vulgar amount of money. And of course I have it. And what else am I going to do with it? I haven't any cats to leave it to. Be reasonable, Gus. I'll be dead. You are the only family I have, well you and Frank and this baby and any babies that come along later. I will also, if you don't think it too high-handed, make specific arrangements for the division of the money among your children when you are done with this life."

Dead silence. And, as she often did, Aunt Morris just stopped talking and appeared, Gus always thought, as if someone had hit her over the head with something heavy. She stood, looked at Gus and said,

"As usual, I have worn myself out talking. I am exhausted and I'm going to lie down. I'll see you at dinner."

—

Gus was unable to say one word, but she walked over to her aunt and, for much longer than she ever had, she put her arms around her and buried her face in the old neck, and held on.

She wasn't much better able to express herself the next day when she sat down to try to explain to Frankie (who was becoming more insistent by the day that she call him simply "Frank").

"Frankie—I'm sorry, Frank—I have something to talk over with you and it really does seem to be a rather large piece of news, or information, or whatever we're going to call it. I'll need your full attention—the kind of attention one is only able to give if one is sitting down rather than pacing around the kitchen, opening and closing all the cupboards."

"Gus, I really will be with you, but I haven't eaten since breakfast, I am starving half to death, and I don't see one thing in the cupboards that holds out much hope."

Gus resisted rolling her eyes, got up from her chair, and without a word began preparing dinner for her husband. Frank sat down and, by the time Gus was ready to put the food on the table, he had nearly fallen asleep in the chair. It wasn't unusual for him to be tired after a long day at the stables, but this looked to Gus like more than tiredness.

"Frank, what's wrong? You look worried." For a minute Frank didn't respond, didn't even lift his head, but finally, "Gus, I'm not so much worried as I am just worn out from worrying too long before I decided to do anything.

"You know I've been thinking hard about what I want to do since we're going to be a family and I can't settle for being a stable hand for the rest of my life. I've been thinking more and more about tailoring, and a few days ago I saw a sign in the big shop right here in this neighborhood. They have an opening for an apprentice. We have to talk about that because of course it doesn't pay anything. I'd be there for a year learning the trade, and from everything I've heard the man who runs this shop is the best teacher in town."

Gus tried to interrupt, "Frank, listen, we'll be just fine about the money." But Frank needed to go on.

"So I took off from the stable at lunchtime and hurried over to the tailor's shop to ask about the position. I have to say, Gus, it looks good. I mean, well, it looks actually pretty terrible. It's a small-scale sweatshop and the guy was yelling at an apprentice when I walked in, but I looked at what the apprentices were doing and, Gus, it was beautiful work.

"Anyway, to make a very long story as short as possible, I got back to the stable late, ran right into the owner—who never comes to the stable—got a thorough dressing-down in front of stable boys and a couple of our regular customers,

—

then stayed late to finish up, which is why I'm so tired. But it sure got me to thinking, Gus. I got yelled at and had to work over my time, but at the end of the day I got nothing but a sore back, some sweaty clothes, and a bad attitude. I'd probably have a lot of those days at the tailor's but I'd walk away every day with a little more knowledge and skill."

Gus didn't talk for a long time. Frank ate as much of his dinner as he wanted; he was really more tired than hungry. Then he looked sheepishly at his wife. "So that's my sad story, Gus. I don't know what we're going to do. We're expecting a baby and right now we need the money I bring home. But if you think further ahead than just right now, that job at the stable doesn't get us anywhere. I don't know."

Gus felt a rush of happiness and she leaned across the table and once again took her husband's hand. "Oh, Frank. I have such a story to tell."

And only twenty-four hours after Gus had listened to Aunt Morris's unbelievable plan, she and Frank sat down together at the kitchen table and, by the light of the lamps they had lit sometime in the after-dinner dark and then by the light of dawn, Gus told Frank about Aunt Morris's tremendous gift. She told him every single detail she could remember about her conversation with Aunt Morris and finally she told Frank that Aunt Morris had offered to set him up in his own business, any business he chose.

Frank only had to think about that for a couple of minutes.

"No. Nope, I don't think so, Gus. I think I need to go in tomorrow first thing, quit my job at the stable, and be there to apply for that apprenticeship. I need to put in my year. Then I'll see how things look and what I want to do from there. I have to do this by myself, Gus, in my own way, with the money I've got in my pocket. I'll talk to Aunt Morris as soon as I'm back from the tailor's. Then I'm going to need to go to bed and sleep."

He sounded so sure, stronger. She almost started to argue, but then thought better of it. Frank sensed her hesitation and, before he went up to wash up and change clothes to start a very different kind of day from the one that was ending, he looked at her and shook his head slightly, almost as if he didn't believe she was there,

"Gus, Miss Augusta Morris, Mrs. Ashmore, I am crazy about you." And, unusual for the quiet Frank Ashmore, he continued.

"Listen, Gus, you and I are going to be married for a long time. Forever. And I need to know as the years go by that I am the main support of my family. I am more grateful than I can say for Aunt Morris's generosity; it is going to make everything easier and a lot of things possible that weren't within our reach no matter how hard we worked. I am also scared to death of her generosity. If I let Aunt Morris and her money take over our lives, then I will just gradually shrivel up and you won't have a husband at all."

Gus just nodded. Frank went up to get ready for his day, which was going to a challenging but exciting one. Gus sat for a few minutes more, then got up and got on with her own day. Six months later, Frank Lucas Ashmore Junior was born and he was his parents' great joy.

Two years later, in September of 1840, Aunt Morris and the midwife who had delivered Frank Junior, helped Gus into a sitting position while she gave the last push for Jessie Augusta Brynley Ashmore's triumphant, and early, entry into the world. Four years after that, the youngest and last of the Ashmore family, Alice Morris Ashmore, was born, and the Ashmores of Society Hill had a full house.

And much, much later, in the fall of another year, Aunt Morris departed this world. She had thought to live out her last days alone. But instead they had been filled with all the noise and activity of a happy marriage and three children, every one of whom she had helped deliver. When she breathed her last, Aunt Morris's room was crowded with Ashmores, and Gus was certain that Aunt Morris chuckled and winked at her right before she died.

Chapter Seven
The Doctor Makes a House Call

Benjamin, the Ashmore's oldest servant, made it to the front door just as Clarke Stanbury was knocking for the third time. The doctor had felt a little uneasy when no one had responded to his first knock, and by this time he was barely tapping. It was a wonder that Benjamin, who was nearly deaf, had heard him at all. It was likely he had been listening with extra attention because he knew that Miss Jessie had a caller. However it was, the old man pulled open the heavy door, not without considerable effort, nodded, and said,

"Good evening, Sir. Who may I say is calling?"

Stanbury liked him immediately and refrained from holding out his hand to shake only because he knew that ignoring the customs that governed his world would almost certainly make Benjamin uncomfortable. So he smiled broadly and responded,

"You may say that Doctor Clarke Stanbury has come to call on Miss Jessie Ashmore, as arranged."

Benjamin nodded and stepped aside to allow Stanbury to walk into a beautifully appointed entry. "If you will excuse me for a minute, Sir." And he walked down a long hallway, opened a door on the right, and announced,

"Doctor Clarke Stanbury for Miss Jessie," and again stepped aside so that the doctor could walk past him. Clarke turned to face Benjamin, smiled again, and said,

"Thank you, Benjamin. Thank you very much." Benjamin returned the smile and responded,

"You're very welcome, Sir, and we'll hope to see you again soon."

Clarke was certain that Benjamin winked before he turned and walked off down the long hall.

Clarke Stanbury, arrived to spend an hour with Jessie Ashmore, stepped into a remarkably lovely room, filled with the sun of late afternoon as it drifted in through the panes of beveled glass and bathed everything in a dusty gold light that was constantly in motion. The room's décor was typical of a house of this type in this age of Queen Victoria; it was too full of furniture—elaborately upholstered couches and armchairs, and tables of all shapes and sizes, each one covered with at least one of everything it was possible to collect in miniature.

Added to the furniture, also predictably, were at least five very large ferns, perched on Greek columns and anchoring the four corners of the room. The fifth fern, precariously placed in front of the largest window, drooped slightly as if it knew it was one too many. Stanbury, who had spent the past two decades either living in bare student accommodations or camping near a battlefield, was no longer accustomed to all this clutter and found he didn't like it very much.

In this particular room, however, someone had been possessed of the good sense to offset the crowding with color and light. The drapes and the carpet were a soft green. The faded floral prints on the chairs and loveseats looked as if they had grown there in this pale green garden. And incongruously, but perfectly at home, in the midst of it all was a large, slightly battered chesterfield, the usual coffee-colored leather worn over the years to a paler hue. The effect was altogether soothing and Clarke could feel himself relaxing after the wait at the door and the encounter with the unlikely Benjamin.

He was distracted only briefly by the room itself before he walked directly over to Mr. Ashmore and held out his hand. They shook and the doctor spoke first,

"Mr. Ashmore, it is very good to see you, and let me express again my gratitude for your permission to call on Miss Ashmore today. It is an honor, Sir."

"We are pleased to have you, Doctor, and allow me to present my wife, Mrs. Augusta Ashmore. She is really the guardian of the gates here, so it is to her that you should express your gratitude. If Mrs. Ashmore says no, then no it is," and with a chuckle Mr. Ashmore put an affectionate hand on his wife's shoulder. Gus held out her hand and shook the doctor's with a firm, warm grasp that felt very familiar. He wondered if she had taught Jessie.

—

"Mr. Ashmore was kind enough not to say that I am the *dragon* at the gate, but in this case I admit I found Jessie's description of you sufficiently interesting to relax my usual fierce refusal of all access to my daughters." And, in spite of the circumstances, Gus indulged in what Clarke would learn was her signature belly laugh. It was terribly un-ladylike and very appealing.

"And please call me Gus."

"Mrs. Ashmore—Gus--I realize that what I am about to say will sound like flattery of the very worst kind, but I must take the risk. You are a most extraordinary-looking woman. I am going to assume you are aware of that?"

Under any other circumstances, Gus would have been rolling her eyes and thinking to herself what utter nonsense this was. It was a rule of thumb with her never to trust a man who resorted to such cheap tactics. But somehow this doctor inspired a different reaction altogether. She knew from Jessie that Doctor Clarke Stanbury had seen the pain of patients in mental hospitals and on battlefields and she suspected he no longer had time for anything much beyond the simple truth.

"I am aware that some people think that about me, Doctor Stanbury, but as I seldom have time to spend in front of the looking-glass, I cannot of my own experience confirm it.

"Please let me hand you over to Jessie's good care while I slip away to take care of a few details below stairs. I realize this is a bit unconventional, Dr. Stanbury, but could I persuade you to join us for an early and very simple family dinner? We seldom have guests when we eat early, so it will be just the three of us. My youngest daughter, Alice, is visiting some friends and won't be home until later. If you won't be too bored with that limited company, we would love to have you. I am eager to hear more about your work with mental patients and with the soldiers down south." She stopped at that.

It was entirely unconventional to invite Doctor Stanbury to share the normally private family dinner. It was almost scandalous to invite him, on the spur of the moment, as an extension of his clearly defined hour with the unmarried oldest daughter of the house. There were very few among their circle of friends and neighbors who would have approved.

Clarke Stanbury thought that, had he not already grown fond of Jessie Ashmore, he might well have fallen head-over-heels in love with her mother.

"I am flattered beyond words, and I accept your generous invitation. However, I am hoping that this early dinner won't be ready too soon. I do still want to claim my hour with your daughter," and he grinned at Jessie, who forgot all the rules governing the behavior of young ladies with young men who have come calling, and grinned right back. They must have looked very happy.

Within minutes Gus had gone to check on those "few details" and Franklin, after an awkward attempt to talk to Clarke about the study of medicine, ambled across the room and, mumbling something about his afternoon walk, slipped out and closed the door behind him. No one seemed to be thinking clearly, and Jessie and Clark found themselves alone together in a parlor where the afternoon was moving toward darkness.

Just as Jessie was getting visibly agitated—mostly about the possibility that one of her parents would realize and would come back to correct the situation--a young maidservant knocked softly then walked in and lit all the lamps. The shadows were chased into corners, and Clarke thought to himself that this room was made for light. Once the fire was blazing, Clarke realized he could imagine spending long, contented hours there. He didn't know if he would ever get used to the presence of people whose purpose seemed to be to do for him those things he could very well have done for himself.

The young girl, whose name Jessie remembered was Angela, asked if there was anything else she could do and Jessie and Clarke said together, "No!" Then Jessie continued, less eagerly,

"No thank you, Angela. And thank you for coming in and rescuing us from the dark."

"You're welcome, Miss Jessie, and if that is all, I'll go down to help with dinner." And just before closing the door, she smiled.

"I heard we were having an important guest."

Without a word spoken they turned and looked at each other. Neither of them broke the gaze. Clarke Stanbury knew that he was falling in love with this unusual young woman. For her part, Jessie found she was having some trouble controlling her breathing.

More intensely than in the kitchen at the Arch Street Meeting House, Jessie felt that melting, shimmering sensation all over her body and she really was getting concerned about being able to take a breath without passing out or just looking foolish. She didn't entirely understand what all these sensations were—although she was beginning to suspect—but she liked them. In fact she liked them quite a lot.

"Jessie—I hope you are still agreeable to my calling you Jessie—I want to say how grateful I am that you agreed to this visit. I was certain I wanted to know you better but wasn't sure you felt the same."

Jessie was unable to respond with more than a nod.

"Although you and I had little opportunity to talk, I did gather from your friend Eleanor's enthusiastic praise of you that we might, in fact, have a great deal in common. I hope we share the same ideals, believe in the same causes, and even enjoy the same sorts of entertainments."

Jessie felt that her corsets, never comfortable in any situation, might actually choke her to death on this couch.

"Oh, dear," she thought. "There must be some way to slip out for just long enough to take them off."

She had forgotten that she wasn't able to remove them without help. Maybe she could ask Clarke; he was a doctor.

"Oh, dear goodness, I believe I am losing my mind and I am certainly going to faint," this mercifully to herself. But then she turned to Clarke—forgetting completely that he had become "Clarke," and said in an uncharacteristically plaintive voice, "I wonder, Dr. Stanbury, if you would be so kind as to find me a large glass of water."

By the time Clarke had returned with the water, Jessie—the cause of her spell having been removed—was feeling much better, but Clarke, still concerned, sat next to her while she drank the water slowly as he instructed.

"Jessie, you are gulping that water, and it will only make you feel worse if you do."

Jessie had started panting, and he could see she was dizzy.

"I am going to arrange these pillows behind you at this end of the couch, Jessie, and I want you to very carefully lie back and try to relax against them. And you must let me help you; I don't want you exerting any effort—not with that breathing."

He put his arm around her shoulders to steady her, lowered her head onto the cushions and, finally, lifted her legs so that she was reclining on the buttery-soft leather of her father's chesterfield.

"Now, Jessie, take some slow deep breaths and tell me how you feel. Does that help at all?"

Jessie not only didn't feel better but her head was spinning and she felt hot and wildly out of control. She put her hand over her mouth not quite soon enough to contain a peal of laughter.

What happened next was out of Doctor Clarke Stanbury's experience and, although several years later due to events in his own life he did come finally to understand Jessie's "spell" a bit better, he and Jessie—odd as it may seem—never discussed it. There in the familiar surroundings of the Ashmore's parlor, Jessie, perspiration running down her cheeks, her breath coming in ragged pants, began to tremble. At the last minute, she lifted herself into a partial sitting position, holding onto the back of the sofa with one hand, and looked straight into his eyes. With an expression that Clarke read as some combination of fear and pain, Jessie shuddered and with one loud moan seemed to collapse.

"Jessie. Jessie. Speak to me, my dear. Can you hear me? What are you feeling? Is there pain?"

With her eyes closed now, Jessie whispered, "I believe I am just fine." And she chuckled quietly.

Clark had reached the end of his store of medical knowledge. He stood carefully so as not to disturb her, and started toward the door.

"Jessie, I have to confess that I can't diagnose what has been happening to you, and I think it wise at this time to seek further medical help. I am going to find your father and send him off to the University to explain the situation and locate someone who can be of some assistance. I won't be gone for long."

From Jessie's Journal
Going On and On About Clarke
I have been busy, to say the least, but I should write when my emotions are engaged because as even a few weeks pass, I tend to forget the details of highly charged events—like what happened the first time Clarke came to the house. It is odd, I suppose, but Clarke and I have never talked about it. In fact, neither one of us has so much as mentioned it.

It really is like it didn't happen, because every time since then—starting with a visit only two days later—we have gone back to the way things were when we were washing those dishes. It's hard to explain it, but when we sit side by side, with a reasonable space between us, I feel my breathing getting faster and that kind of gooeyness—I'm sure that isn't a word—and I start to get sleepy. And somehow, each and every visit, before he leaves, we manage to actually touch each other—accidentally bumping each other when we sit down or stand up, hands brushing when I'm pouring the tea and handing his cup, once he actually just reached over and put his hand on my arm when he was talking, but he seemed to be alarmed that he'd done it and it hasn't happened again. It's been puzzling to me since I rather enjoyed that first visit and do hate to feel we're losing ground.

It has all been very exciting. He comes to the house at least once a week. The first few times he went by Father's work to get his permission, but Father finally asked him to please stop interrupting him at work and said he could just assume permission was given as long as he didn't come too often. I don't know when Clarke asked Father about the carriage ride, but he did and asked me later if I would go. He plans to pack a picnic lunch—pack it himself. Well, it does sound delightful, but for some reason I am feeling a bit nervous about it. You see, I have not forgotten that first visit. In fact, I remember every single detail. Every one. But, I refuse to worry. That picnic can't happen until spring and the warm weather, so until then I suppose I'll put it out of my mind. I can make one decision, though, without much thought at all. If we do go on a picnic, I intend to leave my corsets at home. No one will know and I will at least not suffocate should Clarke decide to touch my arm or take my hand while we're there.

—

Jessie looked up at him, her face now drenched with sweat, her hair that had been pulled up high and beautifully coiffed falling loose to her shoulders, her breath finally slowing down but still ragged. She looked rather frightening and the way she gazed at him made her appear almost mad.

"No, Clarke, I don't need another doctor. I truly believe I will be completely well without any further assistance. I am so very sorry to have alarmed you, and I hope this unfortunate incident won't keep you away. Will it, Clarke? Will you never return once you have escaped this madhouse today?" Jessie was sounding distressed.

"Quite the opposite, Jessie. Quite the opposite. I intend to stop much more often now, just to be certain that your recovery continues. And thank you for trusting me to care for you today."

For just a fleeting second, Jessie's face wore the satisfied smile of a cat after a large bowl of milk. And as Clarke was pulling on his coat against the February cold,

"Of course I trust you, Clarke, and I've an answer for you about that picnic when spring arrives. I would be delighted to accompany you, if you still want me."

This time it was Clarke who smiled, "Oh, I still want you, Jessie Ashmore. I do indeed."

He leaned over and kissed her lightly on the top of her head and turned toward the door. He thought that Jessie had never looked so beautiful.

From Jessie's Journal
On Missing Eleanor

I suppose I found out today exactly what might be too much to tell even your best friend. Would it be possible, in any situation I can imagine, to describe to Eleanor what just happened to me? I would, first of all, be completely embarrassed. This isn't even the kind of thing you could tell your doctor. Well, unless your doctor was there. Oh, my goodness.

But how could I tell any of this to Eleanor? I don't actually even know if it was normal. Clarke seemed alarmed, and he is a doctor. There could be something wrong with me.

And look at Eleanor, all that tall elegance and self-contained beauty. It is not possible that she would allow herself to have any kind of experience this undignified. I was sweating, my hair was all about my shoulders, I was feverish, I was laughing very loud and could not stop, everything about me was a mess. No, that wouldn't be Eleanor and I can't imagine that what happened to me could happen while everything stayed tidy.

All that aside, I miss my friend. I realize it has only been a week, but it feels as if I have crossed a bridge or something and am way on the other side of a river and can't get back to Arch Street, can't get back to Eleanor. This can't work at all if it means I can't see Eleanor, and that's just that.

—

Chapter Eight
Part One
Alice

On her seventeenth birthday, Alice Morris Ashmore, known for the first sixteen years of her life simply as "Alice," stood up in the drawing room after dinner, and announced,

"Starting today, I would like to be called 'Alice Morris' rather than just 'Alice,' and I would very much appreciate it if all of you would make a special effort to address me in the new way."

Not even Jessie was willing to risk a scene by asking the obvious question, 'Why?" But Jessie, being Jessie, was not entirely able to curb her tongue, and she did look her sister straight in the eye, and with only the slightest hint of an attitude of any kind in her voice, said,

"'Alice Morris.' It sounds very sophisticated. I, for one, am delighted with the change. It is terribly creative of you, and I applaud you for your appreciation of the aesthetics of names."

Alice looked at her sister with barely concealed anger. Of course she didn't understand one word of what Jessie had said and of course Jessie knew that, but for once Alice thought it best not to respond. The family would support her in this, as in everything else, and that included her insufferably conceited sister, Jessie.

The actual change to "Alice Morris" after so many years was an awkward adjustment for the family, but they worked hard to accommodate her. Although Jessie occasionally created a ripple of discomfort with her various causes and the relentless questions that sometimes felt like an interrogation, she could be counted on to step back short of serious disruption.

Alice Morris was the one person in the family who seemed to have no hesitation at all about creating a full-blown crisis in the service of having the fabric she favored for her new day dress—in spite of the fact that it cost nearly double any other bolt of cloth in the shop. On the day of the discussion about the fabric, Alice Morris actually stomped her dainty foot and growled at her mother right out on the street,

"You are just an awful person. I *need* to have it!!"

And rather than block her way, Gus stood down. The fabric was ordered and the dress was made. Alice, as she still was then, received many compliments the day she wore it for the first time.

The members of the Ashmore family generally did their best to keep the peace and, by age eighteen, Alice was firmly established as Alice Morris. This was accomplished with her usual combination of a winning charm as she asked for whatever she wanted and the unspoken threat that all hell would break loose if she didn't get it. When the entire family was at risk, they pulled together to be sure she wasn't denied.

Who was she, this Alice Morris Ashmore, this much-feared presence who held her family in thrall? She was petite, only a few inches over five feet, and very slender--one of those women whose waist—even without her tightly laced corsets—was almost small enough for a man to get his hands around. She had bright blue eyes, and ash blond hair, which she wore elaborately coiffed, usually with at least a few curls falling on each side of her face. She had a sweet smile, and she was smiling most of the time when she thought anyone was looking. Her voice was one of her finest qualities; it was low and she spoke with a kind of breathlessness that made it necessary to lean toward her to hear. When she was angry, it was rough and almost menacing, but this was a sound that very few outside the family had ever heard.

Alice Morris was an exceptionally pretty girl, in an exceptionally ordinary way. There was nothing unusual or irregular about her looks. Her nose was small and nicely shaped; her blue eyes were clear and set at just the right distance from her nose. She had a rounded chin and her teeth were white and straight. Her hair was possibly a little dull, but she had found just the right way to wash and brush it to bring out a shine. She dressed in pastels and ruffles, sometimes changing her costume two or three times a day. She was a large item in her parents' budget as she often summoned Warren to take her alone to the dressmaker. Her mother knew about these trips—Warren told her—

but she never interfered. Gus knew they could afford it; she liked to think of the money as an investment in Alice's marital prospects; she couldn't work up much interest in her younger daughter's wardrobe; and, in any case, it certainly wasn't worth one of Alice's temper tantrums.

From Jessie's Journal
On the Difficult Subject of Alice Morris

Alice Morris is a thorny subject. I have known my little sister since the day she was born and in this incredibly sweet, pretty, smiling way, cause one major disaster or another. It's as if she gets bored with the normal tone of life and decides to change things.

It is very hard to describe this because Alice is so sweet, so pretty, so uninterested in anything other than how she looks or what parties she is invited to or, recently, flirting and finding a man, that anyone who meets her would naturally assume that she is an ordinary pretty girl, a bit spoiled, who likes the expected things and is fairly happy with life. I have suspected for a very long time that Alice is miserably unhappy and desperate to run away and make her life here just disappear. And I think that's why she keeps making trouble, somehow hoping it will be something so bad she'll be forced to leave town and never come back. She needs help and I don't know how to help her.

—

Alice Morris' temperament did not always match those lovely looks. She was entirely self-absorbed and never gave a thought to other people unless they had something she wanted. She appeared to have a very high opinion of herself and to feel that she was generally misunderstood and rather badly treated. She was terribly afraid of looking foolish and could never understand Jessie and her way of asking embarrassing questions and making scenes about things like slavery. As if anybody could do anything about that, so why on earth go on about it? She tried to be condescending to Jessie but she didn't quite pull it off. Alice Morris secretly admired her older sister and wished she could be more like her, but this was not something she could admit even to herself.

Chapter Eight
Part Two
Luke

On 17 September 1862, in what would later go on record as the single bloodiest battle of the American Civil War, Union and Confederate soldiers faced off near Antietam Creek in Sharpsburg, Maryland. They fought from sunrise to sunset. The combined deaths exceeded twenty-two thousand men—one in every four who fought. Among the dead that day was a young soldier from Philadelphia, Luke Ashmore, age twenty-five. His death notice, when it was written some months later, said he was survived by his parents-- Franklin Lucas Ashmore and Augusta Morris Ashmore, and his two sisters—Jessie Augusta Brynley Ashmore and Alice Morris Ashmore. What could be found of his body was only shipped to Philadelphia in late December. By then, the ground was frozen solid, so Luke wasn't actually buried until April of 1863.

It was not until the first week in December, in the early morning hours of an exceptionally cold day, that the front door shuddered from a heavy knock. The Ashmore family had just sat down to breakfast and Jessie, responsible for the Bible reading that day, was fumbling to find her place while Alice straightened the long sleeves of her dress and admired the fabric. When the knocking thundered into the room, Alice let out a startled shriek; Gus and Jessie looked at each other across

—

the lace tablecloth that Gus had said was made by an old aunt of Frank's who had died long before Jessie was born. Their look wasn't alarmed, just alert, waiting.

Gus was silent for only a moment.

"Franklin, would you mind answering the door? I can't think who would be calling at this time of the morning."

And Franklin Ashmore, a man who usually seemed in a bit of a rush, stood up slowly and dropped his napkin next to his plate, which was still empty because Jessie had not yet read from the Bible and only then did the family ritual permit them to walk to the sideboard to serve themselves. Having stood and put down his napkin, Franklin turned to his wife and, for so short a time that Gus wasn't ever sure she had seen it, a look of pure fear crossed his face.

He closed the door of the dining room behind him, and they could hear his boots on the oiled pine planks as he crossed the wide center hallway and approached the door. They heard the muffled sounds of two voices, speaking quietly, then the door closing. They waited and, after what seemed a long time, they heard Franklin crossing again. When he came in, he held a small, wrinkled piece of paper and a sword that was caked with mud and something else, something darker. In his clear voice, he said "It's Luke."

From Jessie's Journal
Jessie Says Her Goodbyes

It seems as if I've tried to write about Luke hundreds of times since he died. We will never know what time it was on the 17th of September 1862, when Luke was knocked from his horse by a Rebel soldier who ran him straight through with his sword. I don't know why, but not knowing the time continues to bother me. We only know as much as we do because his Captain told us the day he made a special trip to knock on our door, talk to Father in person, and hand him Luke's sword and a piece of paper someone had found in his pocket—before the dogs got to him—that turned out to be part of a letter he was writing to me. And, by the way, the Captain didn't say anything about the dogs, but I heard people at Arch Street talking about what had happened to the thousands of corpses (a terrible word) left lying around that day.

Anyway, by the time the Captain brought that letter, it was wet and wadded up, with some pieces torn out, and as hard as I've tried I haven't been able to make out more than a few words. That makes me laugh since, knowing Luke, he wouldn't have had more than a few words to say anyway. Lord, I loved him. Two years older, he was my star, and always the best and the kindest man I've ever known. I can't get it out of my mind that Luke got knocked down and killed because he didn't fight back, wouldn't have drawn a weapon against

—

another man, and that man probably younger than he was. I was surprised when he even went to the war because he didn't believe in it—all the killing. He's the one who should have found the Quakers.

I believe he went to the war to get away from here. Even as much as he loved me, it wasn't enough. He was so out of place in the city, even—if I'm really honest—in this house. I know Mother adored him, but she couldn't let herself get sucked inside his darkness or she'd have been too sad and dark herself to take care of the rest of us. And we needed her; she was our anchor. And Alice just didn't understand Luke at all and she isn't a very nice person sometimes and she'd tease him and try to get him upset. He never did get upset, at least not where anybody could see him, but he told me once that it made him feel hopeless that anybody, let alone his own sister, was that mean-spirited and just plain cruel. Luke really did want to believe that people were good deep down. Alice makes it hard to hang onto that kind of idea.

But the fact of the matter is that Luke Ashmore is gone from this earth, and in spite of everything our Methodist minister tells us about heaven and hell, I personally don't have even one single idea about where any of us will be after we die. I expect there's a good chance we won't be anywhere, which sounds pretty peaceful to me.

Luke Ashmore--firstborn of Gus Ashmore, age nineteen, and Frank Ashmore, age seventeen--was a difficult baby. Plagued with stomach gas and leg cramps, refusing the breast early and still often unable to hold down milk or later the sweet mashed fruits and vegetables that Gus prepared, he cried constantly. By the time he was five, Luke had become the person he would remain his whole short life. He was painfully shy, withdrawn from everyone except Jessie, and even she couldn't always get through to him. He was a recluse by nature. To most people, he almost always seemed unhappy.

"Talking to people just wears me out, Jess," he would say, trying again to explain it to her.

"It isn't that I don't like people. I really like most people a great deal. It's just that I can't figure out how to be around them without feeling upset all the time, and then I get terrifically tired and I have to get away."

He went on long, rambling walks around the neighborhood, soon around the whole city. He would get lost, sometimes for an entire day; then he started being gone all night, then several days and nights. Jessie pined to go with him, and a couple of times she followed him for several blocks, but when he turned and saw her, he walked her right back home and gave her what was for Luke a long lecture about the dangers of the city and her responsibilities at home.

"Are you paying attention here, Jessie? Can you even imagine what it would do to Mother and

Father and, bless her, even Alice, if something happened to you? Can you imagine?"

Gus, meanwhile, had made up her mind to stop worrying, because it did no good, nor did talking to Luke, first about the danger of his behavior, then about the anxiety it caused his family. None of it had any effect because whatever you called those shadows inside Luke they had convinced him that he just wasn't that important to anyone. Once when he had been gone for two days, he came home to find Gus at the kitchen table, weeping, and he was shocked and distressed that he had been the cause of that. Luke was uncannily silent and he didn't do much in the way of hugging, or even touching, but that night he pulled up a chair and sat down facing his mother. He wrapped his arms around her and they sat there, Gus's head on Luke's chest, for a long time.

"Ah, God, Mother. How can I keep on doing this to you? If I just could be a little further away so you didn't have to watch it every day."

But he just couldn't seem to help it, couldn't stay in that house for long. His job down at the Market, loading and unloading the produce wagons that delivered and picked-up the finest fruits and vegetables in the whole county, saved his sanity, maybe his life.

Jessie always thought it was a terrible shame that Luke hadn't run into Clarke Stanbury there on those battlefields because Clarke, with his compassion and his training in mental illnesses, had made some strides in the treatment of soldiers who had that darkness, that kind of fundamental melancholy that was like Luke's. When she and Clarke were just sitting together on the front steps and he was talking about all the things he'd done, Jessie was most interested in what he had to say about mental problems and sat fascinated as he told her stories from his days with Doctor Kirkbride. Jessie also knew what even Clarke had not considered—that the wives of these soldiers had their own anxiety and fear and unrelenting sadness. Some days she felt sure she could help them, and especially now, knowing about Luke, she wished she had the courage to just get out there and do it.

The days passed slowly after Luke died, but they did go by. There were those months when they seemed to do nothing except think about the funeral in the spring. Jessie was a great help to Gus during those first months when Gus, usually able to pull herself up from anything, could barely get out of bed in the morning. It was hard to say they missed Luke, since even when Luke was at home he wasn't there, but they missed something, maybe just that space Luke's body had inhabited, even when he was lost in the city or walking around the neighborhood, or just lying on his bed staring at the ceiling, sometimes with tears streaming down his face. Sometimes they even missed his darkness.

"I miss him, Mother," she said one day as they sat in the kitchen so Gus could help Cook without seeming to interfere.

"I mean I miss every bit of him, even the terribly sad bits."

"I miss him, too, Jessie. I miss him, too, some days so much I think I will die from it. You know how much I love you, and I imagine you know that of all of you, you have always been the one I love the most. But Luke was my firstborn, my only son, and there's something in just that simple fact that sets him apart. I think your father misses him, as well, but he has always felt so much guilt about not spending any time with Luke when he was growing up, that I believe Frank feels some relief that the burden of Luke's pain is finally gone. I hope you understand what I mean."

And Jessie understood exactly. And what they both understood too well, and didn't see any point in mentioning, was that Alice had taken a reasonable amount of time to go into hysterics, then she went right upstairs and started dressing for a party at a friend's house later that evening. She actually said, just before she left,

"I think I won't mention to anyone what's happened to Luke. It would just make everybody sad, and you don't want that at a party."

But in the months ahead, Jessie talked to Clarke and to Eleanor and Gus talked to Frank and both of them talked to Jessie, and so Luke Ashmore, who made such a light footprint in his world, was remembered with great affection.

Although Gus Ashmore, Luke's mother, talked to them all, sat comfortably for hours with each one and with all of them together, swapped stories, shared her memories and listened to theirs, there were a few memories, and there was one story that she didn't share. Franklin knew it already, but it wasn't the kind of story Franklin would tell; Gus knew it embarrassed him. And so she sat and remembered the story of how Luke began, and she knew absolutely that it was a story Luke would have loved, a story that would have cut right through that darkness, if only for a few minutes, would have had him holding his sides and laughing until the tears ran down his face. Yes, it was a Luke story in every way. And in every way a mother's story.

Chapter Nine
Two Sisters and Two Men
(Spring 1863)

In the world of Jessie Augusta Brynley Ashmore—as in the larger world-- the early months of 1863 went by and spring arrived. After Luke's death, it was a long time before Jessie could get interested in her life again. The exception was those evenings with Clarke on her father's chesterfield. The new sensations in her body whenever she was with him were a temporary distraction from the deep darkness of Luke's absence.

In early April, Jessie, her father, her mother, her younger sister, and Clarke Stanbury gathered near a freshly dug grave in the new Laurel Hill Cemetery. Its location five miles north of the city made for a long day, getting there and back, but once he had seen it, Franklin insisted, and the decision was made. And in that beautiful garden spot, the Ashmore family stood silent as the coffin carrying the torn remains of their son and brother was lowered into the recently thawed earth. It was still cold in Philadelphia, and their heavy coats didn't keep them from shivering. Jessie's father had wondered if it might be best to wait, until the cold weather had completely passed and they could be sure of thawed earth as far down as they needed it. But they decided to go ahead. They had waited long enough and needed to put Luke and their grief to rest. They were ready.

"I'm not sure I have told you, Clarke—I certainly haven't said it enough—how very much I appreciate your presence during all this time since Luke's death. I have felt just paralyzed, except for these afternoons and evenings with you, and it has meant the world."

Clarke took her hand and held it between both of his. For once, Jessie felt only comfort; the excitement of his touch had given way to her need to just have a friend next to her. And, in fact, Jessie and Clarke were becoming friends. They spent a great deal of time together and in the course of it they naturally talked about themselves, about all the beliefs that Clarke was so pleased they shared. And it is in that kind of talk, over time, that friendships—and other intimacies—are formed.

"Jessie, it has been nothing but selfish pleasure for me to have so many hours with you. It is I who should be expressing my gratitude. If I have been of some help to you along the way, I am glad of it. But every minute I am in your presence is an unexpected and undeserved joy."

"Why, my goodness. I am flattered, Doctor Stanbury," and Jessie, who usually took a strong stand against that kind of behavior, tilted her eyes up at Clark from under long dark eyelashes and smiled her most flirtatious smile. She was feeling mischievous, but she was also—although she might not have realized it—carefully moving the conversation away from the seriousness with which Clarke sometimes spoke of their relationship.

"Before you distract me with that look, young woman, I am going to say what I intend to say, whether you are ready to hear it or not. I love you, Jessie. I have loved you for some time now. It is real, deep, thoughtful, and committed love, and it can only lead in time to marriage."

Jessie was getting restless, but Clarke was going to be heard, "I am not going to ask you to be my wife, Jessie. Not now. It is too soon and I think you are not ready. If I asked you today, I believe your answer wouldn't be the one I want. So, I am going to wait. But I am not going to wait forever. I am putting you on notice."

"You give me a great deal to think about, Clarke. But I cannot think about anything today. I am tired and a bit irritable, and I think what I most need is an early bedtime. I hope you won't mind if I slip away."

From Jessie's Journal
Thoughts about a Marriage Proposal
I expect that no matter what I had said or done, this day was bound to come, but I can't help feeling that it was my expression of gratitude for Clarke's friendship and support, his understanding, since we learned that Luke was dead, that brought it to this point today. Luke's death has been devastating and has changed not just our family but every one of us individually. And Clarke has seemed to understand just what that is like. But the thing for which I owe

him the greatest debt, owe him everything really, is that he took the time to look way deep inside me and he saw that not only was I in pain but that the pain was turning me to stone. And he held out a hand and little by little, slowly and without any dramatic gesture he saved my life. It is as simple as that. He saved my life.

And now he has said those big words—love and marriage—right out loud, looking me in the eye in that direct way he has. Has said them, and has made it clear that the two things belong together. He said precisely that—I love you and that can only lead us to marriage. And goodness of course I love him; he is a best friend just as much as Eleanor is a best friend, and I need them both.

So, very soon I'm going to have to ask myself: Do I love Clarke Stanbury and, if I do, what is the nature of that love, and does that love lead me inevitably to marriage?

I do love Clarke Stanbury. He is a part of my family now. I see him almost every day. If he weren't around, it would be like losing Luke again. I can't imagine not seeing him. It hasn't been all that long but it does seem as if he's been here forever.

And there is the physical attraction, which is another thing altogether, a different kind of warmth, sometimes heat that has also played a part in keeping me alive. And I'll say this bit right out: I would like to make love with Clarke Stanbury.

Now, that's on the table. But, truly, I hadn't really thought much about sex at all until that first time on Father's chesterfield, but since then I have thought about it constantly.

I would do just about anything to keep Clarke Stanbury in my life.

Anything except marry him.

I know this subject will come up again because Clarke, for all that he is easygoing, is persistent about anything that matters to him. And I matter. And so I know I am not through with thinking about this. I know it is important, not just to Clarke but to me. But for today I believe I have written down all the thoughts I have. I love Clarke. I love him as much as I love anybody I know. And on top of that I find Clarke almost irresistible physically and being around him has me actually thinking, for the first time with any seriousness, about what sex would be like, what sex with him would be like.

And all that sounds like the perfect combination for a marriage, right—love, sexual attraction, trust. How could I not want to marry him? The only answer I have today is, "I don't know."

"I will mind very much, Jessie, but I see I have made you uncomfortable, so you go right ahead. But I am not going to let you escape entirely. We discussed this in the winter, and now that winter is over, I am bringing it up again. You agreed to the general idea. Now let's set a date for that long carriage ride with a picnic at the end. I will provide the lunch."

Jessie was suddenly wide awake. Here was adventure, a possibility that interested her much more than marriage. And she remembered the anticipation, the fear and the excitement when the idea of the picnic had first come up. And here it was, come round again, and with no excuse not to do it.

"You know, I believe you're right. Picnic season has arrived and I say we plan one day in the next week or two when the sun is shining and the roads are dry. I will let you choose the day, Clarke, and I will accept your offer to pack our lunch, as well. I shall dress comfortably and devote myself entirely to pleasure. I hope that will be acceptable." And again, that smile.

Doctor Stanbury went home that night a contented man.

Miss Jessie Ashmore went to bed tingling with excitement.

While Jessie grieved for Luke, and spent all her spare time with Clarke, Alice Morris had not been idle. Ready for anything that involved going out into the world beyond Society Hill, Alice had attended an exhausting number of parties, receptions, weddings of friends, wedding of friends of friends. In short, Alice Morris had managed to obtain an invitation to every event at which it was even remotely possible that she might meet eligible men—eligible for marriage, of course.

She was not without standards, and in conversations with far too many women she barely knew, she had been heard to say,

"I am very selective. I do adore men, but when it comes to considering candidates for marriage, there are certain qualities I will insist on."

And whatever particular acquaintance happened to be on the receiving end of this litany would look fascinated and gush,

"Oh, goodness, Alice Morris, you must tell me right away what they are. I am always looking around for a man who might suit me and I could make good use of a list like yours. It must clarify the whole process."

At no point in any of these conversations, or during her frequent, sometimes unwelcome appearances at social events where she knew almost no one, did it ever occur to poor Alice Morris that she was making herself an object of ridicule. It is a cruel truth that it is seldom possible to force yourself into a group of people who either don't want you or don't know you exist, and forcing herself was exactly what Alice Morris was doing. She was getting a reputation for it. Too often, at one of these large, anonymous parties, Alice could be heard introducing herself to a group of women who were giving each other the kind of looks that said,

"How can we get away from her without being rude?"

"Alice Morris Ashmore. I live in one of the Society Hill row houses. My sister and I keep begging Mother and Father for one of the lovely free-standing houses; there are only a few and we would all love it. But they inherited the row house from a slightly batty old aunt and she wanted so badly for them to stay there forever. So they are just sentimentally attached to our house and my sister and I really do despair of ever changing their minds."

Alice paused long enough for one of the women to respond.

"I have always thought that those old row houses are just about perfect--so much personality, and history; why I understand that some of them have been there nearly a century.

"Those free-standing 'mansions,' as I believe their owners call them, are just not quite— oh, I'm not sure of the word I want. I suppose I mean they aren't quite in good taste. And they are relatively new."

Another woman in the group, especially attractive—taller than average, slender, wearing a simple black dress, with the minimum number of petticoats and an almost too revealing neckline, and with hair just the bright shade of blond that Alice

Morris longed for, looked at Alice blankly and said,

"I am so sorry, dear, but tell me your name again."

And for just that split second, Alice Morris understood everything that was happening, and she had the presence of mind to turn on her heel and walk away.

It was then that Alice met Jack Crestfield, an exceptionally handsome man, cut from the same beautiful but conventional cloth from which Alice Morris was formed. Jack had dark blond hair, shading to red and what could only be described as "piercing" blue eyes. The hair on his forearms looked nearly white, as he had taken off his coat and rolled up the sleeves of his pale blue handmade linen shirt in order to help an attractive woman bring down the contents of a cupboard. As it turned out, the item for which she was searching wasn't in this cupboard, only a great many old books covered with dust. It was possible that Jack's expensive shirt and the silk vest he was still wearing were ruined. While Jack's clothes and his attitude, the way he carried himself, suggested a wardrobe at home filled with these linen shirts, the shirt Jack was wearing the evening Alice met him was the only one like it in his apartment.

Had he believed he could get away with it, Jack would have stolen shirts from the homes of the men in this higher circle, men with whom he played poker a night or two a week, men who had won a princely sum of money from Jack. He felt they owed him. It was in those weekly card games, where he had lost the bulk of his inheritance from his beastly mother, lost it to men who were even more beastly, that Jack began to lose the last shred of hope. He now believed that his choices boiled down to suicide or marriage to a wealthy woman.

He had been watching the scene unfolding in the small group of women at the other side of the room and was especially aware of Alice and her situation. He knew precisely what was happening, having had the same experience, and he watched her turn and walk away, a look of humiliation and distress on her pretty face. Very carefully, he approached.

"Please forgive me if I am intruding, Miss."

Alice whirled around toward him and through a clenched jaw she said, "Please step back out of my way, Sir. You are certainly intruding and how dare you approach me? I don't know you."

Jack took a small step backward, but he showed no signs of walking away, and Alice was becoming more agitated. Jack stood very still, hands in his pockets, and looked calmly but steadily at Alice's face. She started to cry.

"Now do you see what you have done? I am not accustomed to having a scene in public."

But unaccustomed or not, Alice's crying was getting louder. Jack came only a half step closer, raised his hand just a fraction in her direction, and spoke so softly that Alice had to lean slightly forward to hear him.

"I am so sorry, Miss. Would you consider taking my arm and allowing me to accompany you out of here? My name is Jack Crestfield. May I possibly know yours?" Jack had moved another step forward and Alice's rapid breathing, along with most of the tears, had stopped.

"It is Alice Morris Ashmore, Mr. Crestfield, and I must thank you for your offer—and for seeing my distress from across the room. There aren't so many men who are sensitive to a woman's feelings."

Alice was regaining some of her confidence and had finally noticed that Jack Crestfield was a handsome man. She took her own step forward, put her arm through his, held on perhaps a bit more tightly than was strictly proper, and—as promised—he walked with her out of the large room where she had recently suffered such social defeat.

They had reached the entry hall of the large house and Jack asked if she would allow him to summon his carriage and see her home.

"If my driver is a reasonable example, then I imagine yours might be the same. If Oliver ever drove me home in an embarrassing condition or spotted me saying goodnight to the men I play cards with, he would have informed my mother before the sun rose on a new day. Perhaps you would rather not have your own driver asking too many questions. And your eyes are still red and swollen from all the crying. I am happy to oblige if that arrangement would suit you."

So Miss Alice Morris Ashmore arrived at her door, earlier than expected, in a very fine carriage that Jack Crestfield had borrowed for the evening in exchange for one of his rare victories at the card table. The man he defeated, a Mr. Charles Worthy, was a sullen loser but cheered up immensely when Jack told him he would take two hours' loan of his vehicle in lieu of payment. Thus several people ended the evening quite pleased with themselves.

From Jessie's Journal
Concerns About Alice
While, honestly, I don't usually pay much attention to Alice Morris, in the past several months I have not been able to avoid noticing her. She is not herself at all. Oh, she is still obnoxious, completely self-centered, obsessed with her clothes, sneaking out when she thinks she's getting away with it and ordering extra dresses from Madame Prous. I realize, and I hope I am not just being a snob, that Alice isn't brilliant, but even she can't be so utterly lacking in brains as to believe that Warren wouldn't go straight to Mother about those drives to the dressmaker. In short, in many obvious ways, Alice is just Alice, no changes at all. But I am her sister, just four years older, so we mostly grew up together, and she has tormented me most of my life, so I know her inside and out. And I am certain that something is wrong with her. I wish I could be

more specific. She appears to be terribly excited for no particular reason; never one for long periods of sitting with a book or her needlework, she now seems unable to sit for much longer than five minutes before she is up and pacing.

I have a theory. Alice has been attending more than the usual number of parties—receptions, buffets, book discussions, whatever one calls them these days—and she leaves here dressed either like a princess or—it's frightening even to form the thought, let alone write it down—like some
creature of the night. It's subtle, not as if she's wearing dark red lip polish or her hair down around her shoulders. But, sometimes when she's leaving for a late party, her outfit has that feel to it. And she is always nervous when she leaves the house for these gatherings, she acts as if she's about to go on stage and is afraid she'll forget her lines.

I have asked her twice if she was all right, if I could help at all, and with her voice at its highest pitch, she always answers with something like, "Why would you think you could help me, Jessie? I don't think you even can imagine the wealth and glamor I am seeing and becoming a part of on these outings. Goodness, there are eligible men everywhere. It is just a matter of time."

I will just write one more time that I am worried!

Alice went to bed in a high state of excitement. "Oh I do wonder if he will call on me. I do wonder." She even managed to wring her hands a few times. Being mostly a person not inclined to long periods of worry, however, Alice Morris fell asleep quickly and slept late into the next morning. By the time she was ready for her coffee, the morning was full of dark clouds and occasional fits of rain. As mid-afternoon approached, the clouds had grown darker and there were heavy storms, accompanied by loud peals of thunder that rolled down the hills around the city of Philadelphia on the heels of bright flashes of lightning. This weather was typical of late April and May in this part of Pennsylvania, but Alice, even though she had grown up with it, never got over her fear. She hated these thunderstorms that not only seemed to arrive earlier every year but lasted until the end of the summer. After that, there was snow. Alice often felt that her life was a trial.

In any case, the rainstorms made a postponement of Clarke and Jessie's day out unavoidable, and for the week it took to dry the ground sufficiently for Clarke to declare it "safe for horses, carriages, and those hardy souls who venture into the wild," the two could be seen playing two-person pinochle (always confusing to Jessie) or Old Maid in a deep window seat or reading aloud or nodding off on the chesterfield, which they had now claimed as their own. They both enjoyed novels (although Clarke would periodically, already primed for defeat, bring in one of his medical books), and they took turns choosing. It was Jessie's turn and, having recently discovered the new genre of mysteries, she had selected *The Woman in White* by Wilkie Collins, whose earlier books she had liked.

On the Thursday, Clarke stopped by, as he did most days. He waited for Jessie in the front hall and when she came in he swept downward in an elaborate bow, then in an unnaturally formal voice and with not a pause to take a breath, he announced:

"Jessie Ashmore, I have come to issue a formal invitation to accompany me tomorrow morning for a ride in my less than perfectly elegant carriage to be followed by a picnic lunch. We will drive to the Woodlands, which I believe will be new to you. There we will spread out our lunch, eat our fill, then take a long walk to aid digestion. You will see a variety of trees and shrubs and flowers greater than you could have even imagined, all with a glorious view of the Schuylkill River. It is Paradise. I recommend then a short rest, after which I will deliver you to your door at a time to be designated by your parents."

He gave a low bow and smiled up at her.

Jessie was delighted with this performance; she was fairly jumping with excitement. What an unexpected and unusual treat Clarke was providing. At that moment, she could almost believe herself falling in love.

She was up early the next morning, going through her entire wardrobe in an effort to find something to wear that was both attractive and comfortable. She settled on the gray thistle-print cotton skirt and blouse that Madame Prous had recently reworked, the one her mother suspected was some attempt on Jessie's part to become a Quaker. The outfit had continued to be a subject of conflict with Gus, who was still unhappy with the plain style and unfashionable fabric. But today, Jessie felt sure that Gus was so pleased about the outing with Clarke that she wouldn't have much objection.

Jessie's decision to go without her corsets was an entirely different matter, and if Gus had known about that Jessie would have spent the day at home. But Gus didn't know, and Jessie walked down the stairs to greet Clarke, luxuriating in the unfamiliar sensation of her linen chemise lying lightly against her skin. She felt weightless and could fancy herself as a beautiful bird, lifting right up off the ground and flying free, flying anywhere she wanted to go. Later, on the ride, Clarke took her hand and said,

"You know, Jess, you look more peaceful than I have ever seen you. I could almost imagine you as the Madonna."

—

It is worth noting that in the months during which Clarke Stanbury had become a regular guest at the Ashmore home, spending his time with Jessie, he also enjoyed frequent talks with Franklin about his business and was known to sit as much as an hour at the kitchen table with Gus exchanging quiet confidences about Jessie and listening to Gus's concerns about her younger daughter's lack of direction. In short, Clarke had become a regular and trusted member of the household and so, on the day of the picnic, neither Mr. or Mrs. Ashmore had any reservations about giving Jessie their permission to accompany the doctor on an adventure here in the city.

The carriage packed and Jessie wrapped in a warm shawl that Clarke had purchased especially for this day, they were on their way not much past ten o'clock.

Not too long after Clarke and Jessie had lost sight of the house, a visitor arrived, unannounced, and knocked on the front door. It was the gentleman who had rescued Alice from the awkward situation at the party, had listened to her somewhat modified version of events, and had seen her safely home.

Jack Crestfield had waited the week so as not to appear too eager and to allow for as many chances as possible for another win against the unpleasant Mr. Charles Worthy. Then the evening before, just when he had given up hope, Jack had turned over his cards and, once again, was in possession of Mr. Worthy's carriage.

As usual, Benjamin took his time getting down the long hall, then another long while pulling open the heavy door, but at last he managed it and stood face-to-face with Mr. Jack Crestfield. Benjamin frowned slightly; he didn't quite take to Mr. Jack Crestfield. But he had no doubts about his duties and he nodded respectfully and asked,

"Who may I say is calling, Sir?"

Jack was a little out of his element, but he was familiar enough with the stage to recognize Benjamin as the butler and he rallied quickly.

"You may say that Mr. Jack Crestfield is calling for Miss Alice Morris Ashmore."

Benjamin hesitated just long enough for Mr. Crestfield to notice, then asked, allowing a trace of doubt to sound in his voice,

"And are you expected, Mr. Crestfield?"

Benjamin knew perfectly well that Mr. Crestfield was *not* expected, and now felt entirely justified in letting him experience the full force of his skepticism. Benjamin took seriously his obligations to the family.

"Well, Mr. Crestfield, I am sorry to have to send you away when you've just arrived, but Mr. and Mrs. Ashmore do not make a habit of allowing

—

their daughters to receive gentlemen who have not first sought out and obtained permission from Mr. Ashmore himself.

"I can tell Mr. Ashmore that you called, and possibly you could call on him and explain your business with Miss Alice."

Jack was checked. But not for long. Jack Crestfield had been around for more years than his appearance suggested, and in the beginning it had been a struggle, until he had figured out that everything—the whole business of life--was a game of cards and you just had to learn to deal from the bottom of the deck without getting caught and to recognize when the other man was doing the same. Most often, Jack looked for a quick cash settlement, but in a situation like this, he was willing to take a chance on a longer-term investment. Miss Alice Ashmore presented some real possibilities.

"I do know that my calling unannounced is inappropriate, and believe me when I say that my dear mother, the Lord rest her soul, would be appalled by my apparent disregard for the traditions with which I grew up. I repeat ---could I know your name?"

"My name is Benjamin, Sir, and I will really have to insist that you return to your carriage and call on Mr. Ashmore at his place of business on Monday when I am sure he will be glad to hear what you have to say."

Benjamin, who was an old man, with the stoop and the shrunken frame of the elderly, could nevertheless and inexplicably be a rather frightening presence when he stood his ground. And stand his ground he would as long as there was breath in him. Why this man was obviously some sort of scoundrel, and Miss Alice not yet eighteen years of age. Scandalous, if you asked him, scandalous and dangerous.

"Look, Benjamin, this is a bit urgent, really. I last saw Miss Ashmore one week ago, at which time she was in considerable distress. She was, in fact, so upset that I brought her home, right to the door here, in my own carriage. I am not a doctor, but I have studied the medical sciences, and I cared for my sweet mother for years before her passing; and I know the signs of an approaching fever. I am convinced that Miss Ashmore is at some risk; you know these things often appear weeks after the precipitating event. She ran into a rather unpleasant group of women at a social gathering and was treated shabbily. It was obvious that her reaction was intense; she wept and trembled and all but fainted. I was just grateful to have been there to help."

Benjamin glared at Jack Crestfield with venom, but he turned toward the house as he muttered,

"Wait here."

Jessie was determined not to lose control of herself as she had done the night Clarke had become so concerned about her, but from the moment they pulled away from her house she was nearly undone by a flood of new sensations that really were almost too much. First, Clarke leaned over to pull the soft cashmere shawl more securely around her shoulders and to ask, when he saw her hands held tightly in her lap,

"Are they cold, Jessie? I'm going to take my gloves off—no, now, Jessie, I wouldn't do it except that they have become a bit overheated for me—and, if you look, you will see they are rabbit fur on the inside. Put your hand in here; I'm afraid they will be far too large, but they will keep your hands warm."

And he leaned across her to pick up the far hand and slide it into the deliciously furry glove that still held the heat from his larger hand.

"Really, Clarke, I am fine and I am certainly able to put the gloves on without help. I am afraid I am not much of a success at being a helpless woman."

Jessie could hear herself beginning to chatter in an effort to hold off the deluge that was coming on in spite of her efforts. As before, only this time it did not come quite so unexpectedly, the tingling started below her waist and seemed to move, as if it were in no real hurry, down to her feet and upward to her breasts and shoulders, seemed in fact to spread itself so completely over every surface of her skin that it was impossible after a few minutes to tell arm from foot or shoulder from calf. In spite of her best intentions, Jessie was not able to control the first shiver, but after that she breathed slowly and deeply and concentrated hard on remaining calm. It wasn't easy and she felt quite proud of herself.

She did, however, realize the necessity of avoiding contact with Clarke for the rest of the ride, so she slid a little away from him and made a great show of straightening her skirts and pulling the shawl even more securely around her. Clarke simply moved with her, covered her gloved hand with his and held it there in her lap. Jessie thought about this after many details of the day had faded from her memory—the weight of Clarke's hand, holding hers, resting high up on her thigh. She never understood how it was that she had not cried aloud. But she didn't. And they arrived at their destination and for a while Jessie was distracted.

"You were right, Clarke. You didn't exaggerate one bit. I have never seen anything so glorious. Even at a distance, I can hardly believe the colors and sizes and shapes all grown together in that great flowering. I can't wait to walk closer after we've eaten."

"I am very glad you appreciate it, Jess. The first time I saw this place I really thought I now knew what the Garden of Eden must have looked like. There most likely wasn't such a place, but I'm happy to settle for this."

"Are there signs or something that tell you what each tree and flower is, or do you just wander in blissful ignorance?"

"Well, dear, blissful ignorance doesn't sound such a bad state on a day like today, but yes there are small plaques that identify each by its Latin name and its common name. I expect you will enjoy having all that information."

Jessie felt a rush of the old insecurity of being too smart and not pretty enough, but then she looked at Clarke who was looking at her as a man wouldn't look at a woman with those handicaps. Today, Miss Jessie Ashmore felt very pretty indeed, and she turned to Clarke with a glimmer in her eye.

"Must a girl wait forever to eat, Sir? I come, I believe, from hardy peasant stock—or so I'm told—and I have appetites to match. So, let's unpack that basket and see what you've made for us."

Clarke missed entirely the double meaning in the use of the plural "appetites," and he nodded at Jessie and turned back to fetch the large picnic basket. He spread out the "squares" that were really something else entirely and when Jessie realized that they were very large, slightly frayed sails she was delighted.

"Yes, they're sails all right. I have a friend with a large two-master that he docks down on Boathouse Row, and he is meticulous about keeping his sails in top shape. Lucky for me, I happened to be looking for something that would keep us dry out here only a few days after all that rain just when he was getting rid of these frayed sails. So, here we are, with a better-than-expected arrangement for sitting. There is plenty of room for the both of us and the basket with space to spare to lay out the food."

So, for the better part of an hour they sat in the sun as the day grew warmer, ate the lunch that Clarke had spent nearly two days preparing, then discovered that the combination of all that food and all that sun had made them terribly sleepy. Clarke fully intended to gather up the food, repack the basket, return it to the carriage, then take that restorative walk over to the gardens. Jessie had already folded her shawl to make a pillow and, with her arms flung over her head she was sound asleep. Clarke sat looking at her and began to reason with himself.

"This is out of your experience, old man. This is not one of the women you sought out in those years when the need became too great. This is the woman you intend to marry. Of course, there's no real danger here of anything improper, but she does look almost impossibly lovely. Just the woman to spend your life with."

But Clarke, too, was growing sleepy and, thinking that a few minutes beside the woman he loved, here in this beautiful place with the sun now high above them, couldn't do any harm, he piled the food carelessly into the basket, pushed the basket out of the way, and lay down next to Jessie. He reached over and, certainly meaning no harm, put his hand very softly on her breast. And Clarke, too, fell sound asleep.

It could only have been a few minutes before Jessie stirred and was immediately aware of Clarke's hand. She had never felt anything like it and she shifted slightly in an attempt to increase the pressure. He woke with a start, knew that he must pull his hand away before Jessie woke up and became alarmed, then understood that she was awake and was moving against his hand.

They really had no chance after that. Clarke resisted the longest and the hardest, reasoning with Jessie, explaining why it was impossible, appealing to her best instincts, to her intellect, to her belief in certain fundamental rules by which everyone understood they must live. But Jessie was lost in the fine land of her body and, once again, she was panting. She guided first Clarke's hands and then his body, lifted her skirt, and turned to face him.

Though Clarke was plagued with guilt and apologized over and over, Jessie Augusta Brynley Ashmore never had one moment of regret.

While Benjamin was thinking how he could safeguard Alice and get rid of the horrid Mr. Crestfield without admitting that Mr. and Mrs. Ashmore had gone out calling and would almost certainly stop for lunch with neighbors, Alice had come downstairs to fetch a book she had left in the parlor, had overheard enough of the conversation to recognize Jack Crestfield's voice, and had been doing a bit of thinking of her own. In her most imperious voice, she summoned Benjamin.

"Benjamin, please tell Mr. Crestfield, who is a particular friend of mine, that I will receive him."

Benjamin knew his place, but he had known Alice since the day she was born and his concern for her welfare outweighed his usual deference. He was just about to object, when Alice shook her head.

"I assume you were not about to question me, Benjamin. Please do as I've asked, and tell Mr. Crestfield I will be ready just as soon as I can."

Unfortunately for Jack, Alice hadn't quite remembered to indicate that he should be taken into one of the parlors, so Benjamin at least had the satisfaction of making him wait in the hallway.

It took Alice Morris nearly an hour, with the help of her own maid and Jessie's, to get her corsets laced tightly enough to suit her and to choose just the right day dress—a lovely silk in a blue that exactly matched her eyes and boasted a widely split skirt over a pale yellow petticoat and that on top of a gold petticoat with traceries of flowers in gray that showed plainly through the paler fabric. After that, there were shoes and a hat to be considered—and a great deal of consideration they did require. Eventually, however, even Alice Morris had to descend, and she did look irresistibly lovely as she came down the stairs to meet her caller, who was accustomed to waiting for what he wanted.

At the slight rustle of petticoats—a sound with which he was familiar—Jack Crestfield rose languidly from the bench in the corridor to which he had been directed by the deplorable Benjamin, and turned like a dancer to greet Alice. He approached as she stepped onto the floor, took her hand, bowed a little too deeply, touched her hand with his lips, then stepped back with a look of pure amazement on his face.

"Good heavens, Miss Ashmore, you are almost too lovely for mortal eyes to bear. Some of my close friends—I don't believe you know them as they were travelling when you and I met--are having a garden party. They are lovely people, very top tier in this city, and I am certain you will like them. The wife, especially, has very fine contacts. I hadn't planned to go, but I would be honored to escort you, if you will permit."

So quickly that it might not have happened, a look of alarm crossed Alice's face, and she turned to Benjamin, who had entered the hallway quietly and was standing, hands crossed behind his back, watching and listening. Alice's agitation wasn't yet noticeable to Jack, but Benjamin knew her well and once more he tried to intervene.

"Miss Alice, I wonder if it might not be wiser—even though you will miss this particular event--to postpone your drive for a few days. Mr. Crestfield could go to your father's office and arrange a day when he can call on you and then have a chance to spend a bit of time with your parents."

He looked at her with his head tilted and an inquisitive eyebrow raised as high as could be reconciled with his position. As long as she was in this house, Alice Ashmore was in his care. In this case, however, Benjamin was outmaneuvered. Mr. Crestfield knew exactly when to appear to surrender. He began very slowly to gather up his things.

"Miss Ashmore, I believe Benjamin is correct and has offered a much better plan. Sadly, I will be leaving the city in a few days and am not certain of the date of my return, but the first thing I shall do when I am at home again will be to call on your father. You may count on it. I only hope that the business on which I am travelling doesn't delay me longer than I expect."

Poor Alice hadn't the experience necessary to mount a defense, and she turned on poor Benjamin, "Benjamin, I will be going out with Mr. Crestfield. It will be fitting. Jessie and I will be riding out in carriages and having picnics on the same day.

"Mr. Crestfield, if you can give me one more minute, I will fetch my coat and a warmer hat than I've chosen, as the day I believe has gotten chillier. Benjamin, tell Mother and Father that I will be home for dinner."

And with that, and before Benjamin could think of a way to stop them, Jack Crestfield and Alice Morris had climbed into his carriage and were on their way. It was then that the loyal Benjamin realized he had no idea where they were going.

Crestfield, normally the most patient of men when it came to matters of seduction, especially where a sum of money was almost certainly involved, found that he was really almost angry with the insipid Miss Ashmore who was too ridiculous even to recognize danger when it came knocking on her front door. He could countenance almost anything in a woman except stupidity and Alice Ashmore seemed to him at that moment the stupidest of creatures. He glanced over at her and thought, "Why the cow even looks stupid!"

Although Alice sensed that Jack was not pleased, unfortunately she kept her eyes down and hoped that it would pass. This meant that she did not see the look of pure malice on his face, a look that even Alice would have realized put her at risk. Then she might have demanded to be taken home, might—if Jack had refused—have made a scene and alerted the driver. But she didn't see, and the wheels were so firmly set in motion now that most likely Alice would have lacked the courage to act.

Jack Crestfield was, indeed, furious and had begun a familiar rehearsal of his sufferings when he suddenly realized what had happened. Although he had certainly been treated shabbily, kept waiting for an hour or more then subjected to nonsense by that man, Benjamin, he saw that the master plan with which he had begun the day had been unrealistic from the beginning. His idea of a long courtship, followed by marriage and a lifetime of access to a reliable source of money, wouldn't have withstood even the first examination of his background.

Jack Crestfield was not a happy man, not a man capable even of the most basic sense of contentment. His was a state of perpetual dissatisfaction on a large scale. Jack felt he was always at a disadvantage, always losing, always falling short, always disliked—and, most importantly, never due to any fault of his. Jack believed himself misunderstood and badly used by everyone he met.

—

So after the events at the Ashmore home, following on the heels of his near-brush with disaster every time he entered the card room, his chronic poverty, his many debts, and the impatience of a variety of creditors, it was an easy step back into the grip of the terrible despair that had preceded only by minutes his first encounter with Alice.

Caught in it again, Jack recalled the only options he could see—suicide or marriage to a wealthy woman. Having lost the remote possibility of such a marriage, and not yet ready to take his own life, he decided that for today at least, if he couldn't have what he wanted, he would take what he could get. Jack Crestfield was an unstable, mean-spirited, violent man, and what happened next was in many ways the inevitable end to an unusually bad day for the man Jack Crestfield was. Alice never had a chance.

He leaned forward and quietly gave the driver an address of which Alice's parents would certainly not have approved. Then he turned his attention to Alice.

"Miss Ashmore, I have packed a thermos of strong tea with milk and two rather lovely cups that a cousin brought back from a trip abroad. Could I invite you to join me?"

Relieved to find her companion again charming and attentive, she agreed readily and felt so restored that she drank a second cup. Poor, foolish Alice. She was too drowsy to object when

Jack walked her up the stairs of a once elegant old row house, into an entry that was just a little too lavishly decorated, and up another flight of stairs to a set of tastefully appointed rooms that were reserved for his exclusive use. In fact, this apartment in one of the city's finest brothels, was Jack's primary residence.

At about the same time, Clarke and Jessie were waking up from the entirely pleasant semi-conscious state into which they had both drifted, Jessie's head on Clarke's chest and his hand tangled in her hair. For her part, Jessie would have been content to stay just as they were for as long as the sun warmed her and just possibly to haverepeated the surprising and entirely delicious event of an hour earlier. But Clarke was restless and persuaded Jessie to straighten her garments and her hair and come with him on a walk to see the gardens.

"Jessie, dear, although it is understandable that we would find it unpleasant to rouse ourselves and go on as before, I think it would be beneficial if we could take a bit of exercise and just get our minds away from any worry. We will have much to consider soon enough, but would you feel able to join me for a walk?"

It didn't escape Jessie's notice that Clarke was speaking to her as if she were a patient who might not make it, and she found she was offended by what sounded like condescension. Why should he assume she had been traumatized by what had been a thoroughly enjoyable experience? However, she decided to ignore him and respond only to the idea of a walk.

She shook out her skirts, pinned up her hair, and replied,

"Of course I would love to walk off some of that lunch, and I would dearly love to see those trees and flowers. Let's be off."

They wandered for an hour among the most astounding tangle of trees and shrubs and flowering plants that Jessie had ever seen or even imagined. She was immediately engaged and full of questions, both about the gardens and about the odd history of this ninety acres that had been a much larger private estate, then a public park and garden, and for the past twenty years one of the city's two most prestigious cemeteries.

Clarke was able to answer most of her questions, but he couldn't match her enthusiasm. He was puzzled by what seemed her casual acceptance of what had happened between them.

He watched her with confusion, as her natural curiosity led her almost racing down the cleverly designed pathways, stopping at whatever caught her eye, then searching for the sign that would identify it. Had it not begun to grow uncomfortably cold, she really could have spent hours investigating this new place, and as it was Clarke had to remind her that they had promised to be back in time to have dinner with her parents and Alice.

"Oh, I do hope Alice has managed to stay at home at least one evening. Mother and Father worry so about the way she is running all over to parties of every kind, many of them with people who are complete strangers. I'm sure it's all perfectly fine, but Alice can be a bother when she is rushing headlong in this fashion."

Clarke, wise man that he was, refrained from drawing any obvious parallels between the two sisters. They arrived at Jessie's front door with time to spare before dinner. Jessie had thought to jump right out, but Clarke put a hand on her arm.

"Jessie, we will need to talk about what happened today. It marks a further step in our commitment to each other, and we will soon need to tell your parents, to announce our engagement, and to choose a day for our wedding."

As always, she felt terribly guilty, but Jessie found she was unable to respond and settled for planting a quick kiss on Clarke's cheek before she headed upstairs to dress for dinner. But she knew that Clarke was right; they would need to talk about the picnic.

As they gathered in the parlor, trying to relax before going in to dinner, everyone expressed some concern that Alice had not returned. Even by the most liberal rules of the house, it was beyond any reasonable hour at which they might expect her. Alice was, in fact, very late, and to add to their worries it had reached that time when the afternoon suddenly darkens and becomes evening. A young maid had come in to light the lamps.

Benjamin had related her departure, in the company of Mr. Jack Crestfield, approximately an hour after Jessie and Clarke had driven off.

"No, Mrs. Ashmore. I don't know where they were going. I admit I was caught off guard and I owe you all an apology for not being quick enough to extract that important information. I am to blame for your worry now."

"Nonsense, Benjamin." Gus was quick to reassure this faithful man who had done his best. As her anxiety increased, Gus was wishing she and Frank hadn't left Alice alone for so long. They did know she tended to get bored, and Gus at least was aware she had been more restless than usual lately.

"I am beginning to worry, but I can't think of a single thing to do other than pray and then sit down to dinner with the rest of the family and Dr. Stanbury. And wait. We are probably making a great deal out of nothing."

Having taken their seats around the informally laid table, the family joined hands comfortably and Gus had begun,

"Lord, for this food we are about to receive, give us grateful hearts," when they heard the sound of the carriage wheels on the driveway. Franklin stood, and held up his hand. "Let me go to the door and get Alice inside, then I will have some questions for the gentleman. Gus, I assume it is acceptable if I send Alice in to join you without asking her to change for dinner?"

"Good heavens, yes, Frank. Send her directly in to us. It's possible they weren't able to stop for dinner, in which case she will be hungry."

—

Chapter Ten
Changed Lives
(Summer and Fall 1863)

From Jessie's Journal
Thoughts on Love and Sex
If I am supposed to have any idea at all how to think about this day, I don't. What in the world is sex anyway if it can be the hour I spent with Clarke and can also be what happened to Alice? I have always believed sex is something a man and a woman do together. I am sure it isn't intended to be something a man does to a woman. It is also, I supposed and now know, a level of intimacy that leaves you, while you are in the middle of it, completely exposed and vulnerable. Based on that assumption, that you are without defenses during the act of sex, who in her right mind would choose it?

By the time Frank had the front door open, Jack Crestfield's carriage was turning onto the street and travelling at a good clip away from Society Hill. Alice was standing, bewildered and weeping, just a few feet beyond the door. Her father walked with her into the house, and Gus and Jessie helped her upstairs. Benjamin was sent to bring their doctor, a man who had known Alice since she was born and who was devoted to the family and a reliable keeper of secrets. He came in and, after very few words with Frank, walked up the stairs to tend to his patient.

Her mother and sister had cut away her torn clothes, brushed the worst tangles from her filthy hair, pinned it up, and washed her as best they could with warm water and large soft sponges. They knew it might be several days, or even longer, before they could fill the old iron tub with warm soapy water, give her a proper bath, wash the blond hair with castile soap, rinse it with vinegar, and brush it until it shone.

The doctor put cold compresses on the bruises that were now appearing on her face and arms, and he cleaned and applied cream to the places where the blows had been hard enough to break the skin. He looked closely enough at her vaginal area to see that she had been treated very badly and, with all the gentleness of a lifetime of doctoring, he spread an ointment that would bring some relief to the inflamed tissues, the ones he could see and those that lay deep and would almost certainly leave scars. He stood for no longer than a minute, looking at the familiar face and, shaking his head, he walked out with Frank, let Benjamin hand him into his carriage, and headed home to finish his own dinner. It was a sad night for him, as well.

After Franklin had closed the door behind the departing doctor, the family—as always, including Clarke—went to the parlor and sat down. They had no idea what to do, or even what to say to each other, but they instinctively kept together, not one of them wanting to be alone. Everyone had informally assigned seats in this favorite of all the sitting rooms in the house, and they went to them now. Jessie and Clarke settled comfortably on the large couch.

No one spoke, and at some time just before dawn they began to leave the parlor--first one of them, then another and another, their exits staggered by a few minutes. All the Ashmores except Jessie went upstairs to their rooms, and she stayed down just long enough to touch Clarke's arm gently before he left. They exchanged small reassuring smiles--two caring people, temporarily overwhelmed by the day.

The days passed, as they will in spite of the worst suffering. The doctor came and went—at first several times a day, then once a day, then once a week, and then, because his patient was healing and had the constant care of her family, he stopped coming altogether but would always inquire, when he saw Franklin coming out of his shop or Gus with a bag from the market, how young Alice was getting on.

The doctor and Frank shook hands,

"Good to see you, doctor, and thank you so much for asking and, of course, for everything you did. I am delighted to be able to say that Alice is doing very well."

And Gus always added, "She's coming down in the evenings now to join us for dinner and she occasionally stays to read or sew in the parlor. We are really quite pleased."

In fact, well before Alice started joining the family in the evenings, Gus had walked by the open kitchen door one morning and heard Alice's clear voice. She was laughing. After that, Gus paid closer attention and discovered that Alice spent a large part of every day at the old deal kitchen table with Cook, heads together, talking quietly, or chatting and laughing with whichever of the maids was there. Several times, when Gus looked in, Alice was shucking corn or shelling peas, then taking them to the sink and washing them. Once it was obvious that Cook was teaching her to make bread.

Fascinated, Gus lingered in the doorway to watch her daughter kneading the dough. Alice looked up and smiled.

"Good morning, Mother. Why don't you come in and sit with us for a while—not a long while, I think, since Cook and I are determined to finish this bread—but I know you look in most days to see how I am, and I'd like you to know that I am well, or I am getting well."

She seemed relaxed in a way Gus hadn't seen her since the attack. In fact, when Gus thought about it, she realized that Alice seemed happier than she had ever been—before or since what happened, and that forced Gus to admit that her youngest daughter, this beautiful, delicate, flighty, self-centered girl, had been unhappy for as many years as Gus could remember.

From Jessie's Journal
More Thoughts on Love and Sex
I haven't written about Clarke and me, not directly, but I certainly have thought about what happened, have remembered the picnic and the sun and sleeping for what couldn't have been more than a few minutes before I felt the weight, hesitant, gentle, of Clarke's hand on my breast. I tried to lie still but it wasn't possible. I pushed against his hand and again I was aware of the sun. I turned toward him. I saw the fear and the desire in those beautiful eyes, and I had just a moment's worry, not for myself because I was already floating in another place, but for Clarke who looked at me with such love and such concern.

He tried hard to explain why we couldn't go on, why we must stop, but I could only hold out my arms, I could only answer his words by moving my mouth against his, I could only protect him by lifting my skirts and pulling him into the secret country of my body. I don't know if it was enough to console him.

Was it enough to console me after we had come home? I close my eyes and I see Alice, stumbling, on Father's arm, into the hall. I remember she was crying but not making any sound. She was looking around as if she couldn't understand where she was. I still can feel the soft weight of her, and I remember the smell, as Mother and I half carried her up the stairs. We cut off her clothes and brushed the hair that was matted with unspeakable filth. We were ashamed to turn out heads away from that awful stench of sex and blood and dirt.

And as her clothes lay in a pile, like rags, on the floor, we poured out warm water and picked up the large soft sponges that Alice always preferred, and we began our sacred ritual of reclaiming the ruined body, cleaning it just enough to see the skin beneath the mud. We washed her hands and feet, then across the shoulders, down across the breasts and stomach, and up from her feet, moistening as well as we could the caked mud on her ankles and calves.

After that we both sat down because we had done everything we could do before we were forced to look at the trail of blood running down both her legs.

There was blood on my thighs that day in the park. Clarke took a linen napkin and wet it with water from his flask, water that was warm from the sun, and he washed away the blood. I watched as the water from the napkin grew pink and then clear.

—

Just as it seemed a terrible shame to me that Luke couldn't have run into Clarke out there on the battlefield, so I think it just as terrible that Alice could not have found a Clarke Stanbury to wash her wounds and keep her safe.

I am glad Alice has had the good sense to go to this kitchen and shell peas with Cook. She is a wise girl. I walked in once to steal a couple of peaches for Clarke and me and I surprised them with their heads together, Alice talking in a low, urgent voice and Cook had her arm behind Alice's back. And it came to me. Maybe Alice is talking to Cook, maybe she is telling the awful story to someone.

I will pray for that every day.

I have tried so many times, as has Mother, to knock on Alice's door, go in and pull a chair up to the bed, have tried to talk about what happened, but Alice shrinks back as if she's been burned and shouts for me to get out. It may be that we are too close; it may be that Cook is not connected, even indirectly, to the rape. It may be that Cook had enough sense to wait, to ask no questions, to let Alice come to her. Whatever the reason, we are all very grateful.

I overheard Father saying that man is gone, no sight of him, and no reports from the roads in any direction. I don't expect they will find him.

Although Gus had told the doctor that Alice was joining the family after dinner, those times were rare and, when they occurred, Alice was usually stopping by on her way from the kitchen back to her room. It was high summer before she was able to show up for those evenings regularly. It was fall before she showed any signs that she might come through. The family had managed at least a superficial return to normalcy. Gus started her day with a walk through the house, looking into rooms, talking with the staff, keeping an eye on her world. Frank left early for his shop and stopped to chat with every member of his staff and each apprentice, to encourage and inspire them to even more beautiful work than they were already producing. He never went more than an hour without thinking about Alice.

Nothing was the same and yet everything was the same. Jessie's days were full. She woke early for long walks, sometimes with Clarke, often alone. Periodically, she thought about the Arch Street Meeting House, and about Eleanor, but she wasn't ready to go back. She was sure that everything there was intensified and more urgent. She knew from Clarke that the war was getting worse and, at the same time, looked as if it might be over soon. The situation for the slaves in the southern states had grown bloody and dire, and everyone felt helpless. Arch Street, she felt sure, was at the very center of whatever was going on in the city. One day, besieged by doubts, she turned to Clarke.

"Do you think I should be going back to help out at Arch Street? Am I running away from a responsibility I should be meeting? What I did there wasn't that much but they counted on me, and I feel I'm letting them down." Clarke was quick with his response.

"No, Jess, absolutely not. Look at the dense cluster of events in your life. Some have been good, some terrible, but every one has had a profound impact. No one just gets over these things, Jess, not even you. And you are working down with the soldiers. For now I would say it's enough. Wait. Arch Street will be there and it will need you at just the time when you are ready and have something to give.

And so will Eleanor." Clarke often seemed able to read her mind.

She believed him, as she almost always did, but she missed Eleanor terribly and sometimes during these long months, as the year moved toward its end, she would panic at the thought that Eleanor would disappear, that she would never be able to find her. Jessie had thought she and Eleanor were the closest of friends, but she didn't know where Eleanor lived. Eleanor had never told her. Did that mean something? Had she imagined the friendship was more than it was? On her worst days, she worried.

The last time she had been with Eleanor, Jessie thought back, was about two weeks before her picnic with Clarke, and Jessie had talked, while Eleanor listened, about her fears, her excitement, her sexual longings. Eleanor had been silent until she finally said,

"Jessie, I believe you will find your way, and I believe you will have no doubt when it appears. You should go on your picnic and give yourself a glorious day, in whatever way that suits you. But I am not sure this is going to be your final stopping place. I just have a feeling there might be more."

Jessie, too, had a sense of something still to be discovered. And while the resolution of her relationship with Clarke was unclear, she began to explore what she could do in other parts of her life. Ignoring the echo of the oft-repeated disapproval of her wringing out bloody bandages-"There are other ways of helping with the war effort, dear. There is no need to act like that Florence Nightingale person"- every morning after her walk, Jessie met Warren out by the stables and helped to load the covered wagon that he now insisted they drive because he knew it was just a matter of time before they damaged the family's carriage. This wagon was just about the most wonderful thing Jessie had ever seen and she couldn't imagine where Warren had found it. He never told her, but in fact it was an old milk wagon. Jessie loved it.

Once they were sure the horses were settled, they climbed in for the ride to the medical stations that had been set up for the wounded soldiers. There were doctors there, the rare nurse, and more than a few volunteers—women and men—who had come to serve up food, to wash dirty uniforms and mend those that wouldn't have withstood a washing, and just to sit with the soldiers as they described the battles where they were wounded and the numbers of the Rebel forces. They seldom spoke directly of their own fear, but often,

"My best friend from home was fighting right beside me, Miss, and he was scared near to passing out."

"I'll bet it was hard for you to watch that. I expect you were some comfort to him, just being there. Sometimes it's easier to get through being afraid if you have a friend by you."

"Why, you do understand just how it is, and I expect having someone you know right there does help. Yep. I believe I might have done him some good." And Jessie knew they had safely navigated the terrible subject of this young soldier's fear as he had looked death in the face.

Jessie pitched in with the food and the washing and sewing and could sit patiently for a long time listening to the soldiers, but she found she was especially skillful at cleaning the men's wounds, terrible injuries that no one else wanted to touch. She would carefully cut away a caked and bloody uniform, then begin the process of cleaning the wound so that a doctor could apply ointment and a bandage.

These injuries were often crusted with dried blood and dirt, sometimes already infected and leaking yellow mucus, and Jessie would take up a sponge or a rag, whatever was there, soak it in warm water, and over and over, very carefully, she would squeeze the water onto the wound, let it sit for long enough to soften the hard surface, touch the moistened crust with the slightest movement, then stop and begin again.

In this way, she was frequently successful at removing most of the scabbed area and bathing the injured tissue underneath. Once this was done, she turned her attention to the soldier, not just his wounds, and inch-by-inch she would bathe the body of a man sometimes barely out of boyhood. Sometimes he would apologize to her for the smell—of blood and excrement—and she would smile and say,

" Oh, that doesn't bother me. It just smells like the terrible ordeal you've been through. And, besides, I've smelled worse."

Jessie always tried to get home so she and Clarke could have their afternoons on the chesterfield, though there was little of the sexual play of the days before the picnic. They talked desultorily, or read to each other. Often they sat,

—

side-by-side, in an agreeable silence. Gus always knocked softly before walking in on them, and once in a while when there was no answer she would open the door to find them both sound asleep and she would tiptoe in to retrieve whatever it was she needed and out again just as quietly.

There was such tranquility about the two of them, they seemed so entirely at ease with one another, and the whole family was so happy to have them around, that she had expected an engagement before now. Jessie and Clarke seemed to operate on their own time schedule, however, and Gus had no doubt it would come. They were approaching Christmas now; it had been a hard year. Perhaps Jessie and Clarke planned to celebrate 1864 with a January wedding.

The late November weather had turned cold and rainy at the beginning of the week in which Gus found Jessie's journal. By mid-week, the sky was clearing and there was a promise of sun. On the day it happened, Alice had been in the kitchen since breakfast helping Cook, a routine she had followed almost daily since she had been well enough to come downstairs. Jessie was up at dawn to take advantage of the day, and she got to the stable in time to get a ride to the largest of Philadelphia's military hospitals, where she volunteered when they needed an extra pair of hands.

It had taken a long time and a great deal of arguing, but she had finally convinced Warren to allow her to sit behind the horses and, if the day was at all pleasant, to drive the wagon—and even the carriage a few times. She arrived home that afternoon, as always, in plenty of time to dress for dinner and it was then, making her usual rounds to say a quick hello to everyone, that she found Gus waiting for her in the parlor, the journal in her lap.

Jessie sighed, closed the door behind her and sat down, crossing her hands and looking at Gus. "Do you want to talk to me now or would you rather we wait until after dinner?"

"I don't know, Jess. I have only just read this and, whatever else we say this evening or in the days to come, I feel I should apologize for reading it at all. I started and found I couldn't stop, but it is your private journal."

"It doesn't matter really. If I could have found the way, if I had known how to do it, I would have told you. And I hope the thoughts about Alice didn't cause you more pain than you already had."

"No, Jess, they didn't. I was glad to have read them. Somehow knowing you were as aware as I was of every bit of it makes it easier. I am glad we have each other in this terrible thing.

"I believe we can go up and dress—you look as if you and Warren had a hard day down with the soldiers. Oh, good heavens, Jess, of course

—

I know. I know that Warren drives you there andthat he often stays to help, that he sometimes lets you drive. I expect it will prove a more useful skill than needlepoint in the long run.

"So let's dress and come down to eat with your father and Clarke and Alice, then perhaps you and I can go up to my sitting room, close the door, and see what we need to say to one another. I expect I do have a few questions."

Dinner went remarkably well. Alice was describing the fancy dessert she and Cook were preparing for the following night, and the delight with which everyone greeted this outpouring of enthusiasm from Alice eclipsed any tension that might otherwise have plagued them. It was a pleasant meal that everyone was sorry to see come to an end. Jessie and Gus excused themselves, explaining the need to consult about the guest list for a dinner Gus had agreed to help Jessie plan for some visiting members of the Society of Friends. Clarke and Frank moved into the back parlor, both with books in hand, and Alice went up to bed.

In spite of the circumstances—or perhaps because of them—Gus had suggested that she and Jessie change out of their dinner clothes, including petticoats and corsets. And so it was that, about an hour later, more comfortable and somewhat restored by the extra time after dinner, mother and daughter sat down in the privacy of Gus's sitting room, in nightclothes and warm dressing gowns, to begin a conversation that was unknown territory for them both.

"Jessie, I do have to ask a practical question before we talk about anything else. May I assume that you took precautions against pregnancy?" She waited.

And with this first question Jessie realized she was at a disadvantage.

"Well, no. We didn't. It wasn't as if the whole thing was planned."

This sounded questionable, even to Jessie, because to a great extent she, at least, had gone to that picnic expecting exactly what happened and would have seen to it that it did happen if things hadn't just unfolded naturally.

"Jessie, if you are going to play games with me about this, I can't see much point in our taking the time to talk about it."

And with no need even to think it over, Jessie made her decision. She was going to be honest with her mother. She was not going to lie; she was not going to avoid anything or find words that made it all seem like an unfortunate accident; she was not going to leave anything out. And she was not going to make excuses. She somehow felt as if her life depended on this.

"Well, Mother, I just never even thought about getting pregnant. I know how that must sound; it sounds completely irresponsible to me now I hear myself saying it. But it really never entered my mind."

Gus waited, her silence more encouraging than anything she could have said. Jessie went on.

—

"The truth is that I was completely caught up in my plans for the day, and I think I should be feeling ashamed of this, but I don't think I am. What I mean is that I planned not to wear my corsets, which made sense just because they are so uncomfortable, but then I decided not to wear my petticoats or my chemise or any other undergarments and if I had let myself think about it I wouldn't have been able to come up with any reason for that except the real one. So I guess I chose not to think about it."

Jessie thought she was familiar with most of the subtle and not-so-subtle facial expressions that signaled what Gus was thinking, but the look on her face this time had Jessie completely puzzled. She could have sworn that her mother was smiling.

"Mother? Should I be worrying about this? Is there some way of, I don't know. I mean, what are the chances? Would most people get pregnant from just that once? Doesn't it seem as if the first time there's some obstacle or, you know, something in the way?"

For the first time, Jessie did seem genuinely embarrassed.

"It is obvious that I don't know one thing about it and I didn't even consider finding out anything."

Jessie was talking more and more slowly and finally just wound down. "I suppose I didn't handle any of this very well."

She glanced over at her mother, and Gus saw Jessie, five years old and frightened to tell her that she had broken a glass ornament in the parlor where she had been forbidden to go. And Gus saw herself, three years younger than Jessie was now, in love with the unacceptable stable boy and she remembered how she had schemed and plotted and planned and chosen the time, with all the risks involved, to take him to bed. And because she didn't trust that one time would do it, she kept on until she was sure she was pregnant, and then she married him.

"I think the answer to your question, Jessie, is that you shouldn't be worrying about it because in the unlikely event that you are pregnant, you and Clarke will just need to set your wedding date a few weeks earlier than you planned. I feel certain that Clarke wouldn't mind."

Jessie just stared. How could she not have anticipated her mother's assumption that after what happened in the park, marriage was understood. It had nothing to do with whether she was pregnant. Not even Gus—and Jessie knew how unusual her mother was--would have imagined that her daughter, having set out to make love to the man with whom she had been spending time for the better part of a year, would then be thinking of turning down that man's proposal of marriage. In fact, under those circumstances, a formal proposal seemed hardly even necessary.

"Jessie?"

Mother and daughter sat in mutual silence, trying to read each other's thoughts. Gus made one last attempt to fit this into some familiar framework.

"He hasn't refused to marry you, has he?" But she knew before the words were out that it wasn't the case, that Clarke Stanbury would have thought, as she did, that love—and certainly lovemaking—led automatically to marriage. She answered her own question,

"No, of course he hasn't."

Jessie sat perfectly still and couldn't think of a single word to say. She heard the big clock in the hall and knew it would soon be time for one of the maids to come out to wind it. She heard a door close somewhere in the house and thought Cook might be closing up her kitchen for the night. She anticipated the sound she heard every night from her own room—Alice whimpering in her sleep. All this, of course, took only minutes, although it felt to Jessie as if she had sat there, unable to move or speak, for an eternity.

"It's just that I am not sure that I want to get married right now."

This answer seemed not to satisfy Jessie, and she continued, working through her thoughts as she spoke,

"No. Yes, I am sure. I am sure that I don't want to get married right now. But I am also sure that, if I did want to get married, I would not want to marry Clarke."

Jessie's mother who, with this last statement found herself unprepared, summoned the presence of mind and discipline to reply, simply,

"Then if, as I suspect, Clarke is not aware of your feelings, I would suggest that you are obligated—for any number of reasons—to make him aware immediately.

"Nothing you have told me tonight, not even your decision not to marry, shocks or horrifies me. If you fail to do the decent thing, if you postpone for even one day the honesty and the consideration you owe this man, then, Jessie, I will be shocked and then I will be horrified that you have not learned in this house what is right."

The next morning, Jessie looked out her window just after the light broke and saw a completely cloudless sky. She knew Clarke had planned to go down to the medical stations today and she would have to hurry if she intended to catch him. She chose a dress she could put on quickly, and at the beginning of a beautiful day, Jessie Ashmore went, once again without corsets or petticoats, to meet her lover.

From Jessie's Journal

Clarke *I am certain that I will never know anyone as kind, as thoughtful, as intelligent, or as steady and sure of who he is, as Clarke Stanbury. I know that no one will ever love me as much as Clarke does. And, as odd as it might sound, I will never*

—

love anyone even half as much as I love Clarke. I am sure of those things. I am just as sure that I had to find him that morning, walk with him to the farthest point of our neighborhood, to the small secluded park with its untrimmed shrubbery and the old trees that throw a kaleidoscope of moving shadows over a day that is only sun, and tell him that I couldn't marry him.

I had to tell him and I had to tell him in that small hiding place that we had discovered on one of our walks sometime during the early months. We were like children who had come upon a hidden cave or a fairie wood. It was part of our history, something we had found together and had treasured. It was important. And it was from that place, after our long conversation was over, that we walked away—not from everything we had, because we got to keep every minute of that—but from everything we might have had. Clarke had not seemed surprised.

"Jessie, I expect you have something to tell me. I don't know what it is. In fact, I find I can't even make a guess. But before you begin, I am going to make one of my long-winded speeches, if you can bear with me"

I was familiar with Clarke's speeches, and I smiled in spite of myself.

"When have you ever known me not to bear with you, Doctor Stanbury?"

How very easy it always was to be with Clarke, easy for both of us. We fit together snugly and in every way.

"It is just this, Jess. No matter what you need to say, I want you to know right this minute that you do not need to be afraid of saying it. I want you to know that at no time ever in what I believe will be our long, long love for each other, should you ever be afraid with me. I really must know that you believe that.

"Can you promise me that you believe this? It is more important than whatever you say to me today. Do you understand, and do you promise?"

At first I didn't understand, but then suddenly I did. Clarke really did know what I was about to say, because he knew me, and he was telling me in no uncertain terms that he refused to be lost, refused to be absent from my life, refused— no matter what happened to either of us--to be less important to me than he had always been. And I understood, too, that he didn't intend to sacrifice himself, that he fully intended to have a life of his own, and he expected the same of me. He just wanted me to know that in some way it wouldn't matter.

What he needed me most to understand was that he believed in what we had and what we felt, believed that this love would not only survive but would sustain us. Clarke saw then what I only came to understand years later. The love in which he placed such faith had transformed us both, had made us people more capable of loving whoever came into our lives.

"I do understand, Clarke, and I do promise. I can't marry you, you know." And I started to cry.

—

The park is, I suppose, an ordinary neighborhood park, and yet for us it was always the sort of place you could imagine would disappear when you walked away. The day after Clarke and I talked, it had turned cold again and, wrapped in my warmest coat, I walked all the way back to satisfy myself that it was still there. I believe I was a little disappointed to find that it was. And in that place, saying words that also seemed fantastical, Clarke Stanbury and I said goodbye to our romance.

Chapter Eleven
Jessie and Eleanor; Meeting Sarah
(Christmas 1863-Spring 1864)

Christmas arrived and, even in this most heartbreaking of years, the Ashmores celebrated. Frank and Warren spent an afternoon cutting branches of fir and holly, pulling down mistletoe, and choosing and cutting the traditional tree that would fill one corner of the largest parlor. Gus and Jessie draped bannisters and mantels with the greens and the sparkling red berries; bunches of mistletoe, tied up with red ribbon, hung in every doorway. In the evening, the family gathered to decorate the tree. Alice and Cook hardly left the kitchen during the week before and the table, carefully laid on Christmas morning by two of the maids, was piled high with the finest dinner the household had ever seen. Alice was beaming.

Clarke did not join them, but not long after the New Year he simply showed up one afternoon, chose a comfortable chair in the familiar parlor, and settled in with a book. When Jessie knocked tentatively, he rose and embraced her, saying in his straightforward way,

"It's very good to see you, Jess. I have missed you." After that, it was easier and Clarke was welcomed into his old place in the family. As both family friend and physician, he paid particular attention to Alice and spent long hours discussing her progress with Gus and Frank. His early experience with his aunt, his study of mental illness, and his recent work with trauma on the battlefield made him the ideal person to try to understand what had happened to Alice and to monitor the impact it was continuing to have. Clarke was an unusually compassionate man in any circumstances; in this case he was devoted to the family and cared about Alice.

With her days suddenly empty in a way she hadn't anticipated, Jessie was spending nearly all her time with the soldiers, starting earlier than ever when she could convince Warren to be ready the minute dawn broke. There were even days when Jessie's sense of urgency was so great that they drove away in the dark with the lanterns lit.

On those mornings, when they couldn't see around the next turn in the road, Jessie was insistent on driving. Warren said nothing, but he watched her closely, alert to any sign of serious disturbance. He knew what had happened with Doctor Stanbury and, of course, there had been Luke's death and the terrible incident with Alice, so he worried. He was relieved when he finally could see a familiar Jessie. She was changed, had been profoundly altered by everything that had happened, but she was still Jessie. Eventually, he relaxed.

Warren couldn't now remember exactly when, during the terrible months after Alice was attacked, Jessie had looked at him one morning as they were laboring together to lift a badly injured and unconscious soldier up onto a cot, and laughed.

"You know, Warren, it does seem ridiculous, given what we're doing here, for you to still be calling me 'Miss Jessie.' How much of a hardship would it be for you to just say 'Jessie'?"

Warren looked at his hands and Jessie's as they settled the soldier, no more than a boy, unfolded a blanket, and covered him to stop the shivering that fever had induced. In a few minutes they would undress him and begin the long process of washing that Jessie had taught him. He grinned.

"No hardship at all, Jessie. Let's get this young soldier undressed and see what we're looking at."

It was also during this time that she began in earnest her work with the widows, many of whom had small children. Jessie had never been married, had no children, and yet all her instincts seemed tuned to the needs of women who had. She always had the right word, always knew the time to stand back, the time to reach out and touch, and the time when nothing would do except putting her arms around a crying woman and rocking her back and forth until she had cried as much as she needed to.

—

Jessie continued her work with the soldiers but, as the war continued into the next year, the death toll increased and the numbers they were hearing were borne out by the number of women who sat, bereft and helpless, watching every day for their husbands' bodies to arrive. It wasn't long before Jessie began to ask Clarke's advice, and slowly, with this common interest between them, they began the work of rebuilding. They sometimes spent hours at a time in the parlor's most comfortable chairs, talking about the soldiers, their widows, and Alice. They never again sat on the old chesterfield.

And, at last, in the spring of 1864, Jessie walked into the Arch Street Meeting House, and saw Eleanor. She didn't hesitate. It took no thought at all. Operating on the pure instinct she had felt the first time she saw Eleanor in that room, she walked with quiet deliberation across the expanse of floor. Eleanor was looking away from the door and hadn't seen her; in a steady, clear voice, Jessie found she couldn't say more than, "Eleanor." It was enough. Eleanor turned and held out her arms. Neither of them spoke, nor did they move from that embrace. Neither of them cried, but they could hear each other's deep sighs of relief. Finally, still without moving, Jessie started to whisper,

"Thank God. Thank God. Thank God."

The first week after their reunion was devoted entirely to Jessie's narration of every small detail of the developments in her relationship with Clarke since she had last seen Eleanor and told her what had happened on the chesterfield,

"Which," she assured her friend, "we have entirely vacated. I mean, I am absolutely certain of my decision about marriage to Clarke. I expect that an hour on the chesterfield would reveal to me that I am less sure about other sorts of—ah, interactions. And I do know how badly that would hurt Clarke."

Eleanor stopped her just long enough to suggest,

"Why don't we take a break and eat some lunch, maybe take a walk down Arch Street?"

Jess readily agreed and they set off from the Meeting House at as fast a pace as their dresses would allow. Jessie remembered fondly the day she spent without her corsets and petticoats, a detail she had shared with Eleanor.

"You just cannot imagine," she reiterated, "You absolutely have no idea what it feels like to be outside without all that."

Eleanor smiled,

"It sounds divine. Possibly I will try it one of these days."

Jessie continued to the end of her story about her decision not to marry Clarke,

"Can you believe that everyone—every single person—is making it clear that it is a struggle to condone or even understand my decision. Mother's friends arrive like a flock of underfed chickens and begin to peck away at me. Fortunately, Mother has been grand—both wonderfully and unexpectedly—and she listens for only a few minutes before chiming in with her lovely voice.

'Well, ladies, I believe Jess and I need to find some flowers to cut for the dinner table; Alice is preparing the meal again this evening and we like to do our part. And, incidentally, I entirely support Jessie in her decision about her relationship with Clarke Stanbury or, for that matter, in any other decisions she makes. My daughter is an exceptionally wise woman. Now if you will excuse us?'"

The relationship between mother and daughter had been changed in the crucible of Luke's death, Alice's rape, and the discovery of Jessie's journal. It was the two of them who had been best able to talk about Luke, about his troubled mind, and about how terribly they missed him. When Alice came home, Gus and Jessie had carried her together up the stairs and into the bedroom she would not leave for many weeks; Gus and Jessie had cut away the clothes, and bathed her, and together stood witness to the terrible wound between her thighs; Gus and Jessie had sat with her night after night, taking turns sleeping, when Alice woke screaming from nightmares and could not be consoled; Gus and Jessie had noticed her migration to the kitchen and had rejoiced together for Cook and for Alice's slow return. There was no longer any possibility that Gus would not stand up to the entire world for her daughter.

Eleanor had met Gus Ashmore the few times Jessie had taken her to Society Hill, and once Gus had attended a talk at the Meeting House. Eleanor had been intrigued and pleased that it was a talk about his days in battle by a very young soldier who had come home because he started crying one day and couldn't stop, and neither his superior officers nor the medics could figure out what to do with him.

She laughed at her image of Jessie's mother.

"You know, Jess, just from the little I have seen of Gus Ashmore, I am only surprised she let them go on at all about you and Clarke. Your mother has always seemed to me to be a pretty formidable lady."

The two friends walked around the city for hours, making a circle and ending up back at the Meeting House late in the afternoon. On the walk, Eleanor asked about Alice. She had heard only that

—

Alice had been "attacked." No details ever followed, which spoke well of the doctor who treated her. Jessie was grateful to finally talk her way through the attack, the long days of constant care, and Alice's odd retreat to the kitchen. She was also able for the first time to talk about her own confusing feelings that had fluctuated between compassion and what was for Jessie a shameful annoyance with Alice for the kind of flighty self-centered life where this could happen. All Eleanor said was,

"Yes. I know about those feelings; I have had them. Try not to worry about this." And Jessie continued, wanting suddenly to be finished with this story, wanting to listen to Eleanor's soothing voice talking about almost anything else.

"And now Clarke is working with Alice. For a long time he was just watching her carefully, then he would sit down with Mother and Father—and me, if I could find time away from the fallout from this war—and go over what he had observed, what he thought it meant, and what we might be able to do about it.

I sometimes feel as if those early days listening to Clarke go on about trauma and mental illness didn't do my own state of mind much good, but you were going to say something about Christmas and after—and Clarke."

"I was, Jessie, but I'm not sure if I should. I don't want to upset you."

But Jessie assured her that there wasn't much she couldn't hear.

"Well, then, I will say a couple of things. I think you are very smart to stay off that chesterfield because, in addition to your hormones having been recently awakened and the immediate risk that poses, Jessie—I think you are, in spite of what you're assuring me and yourself, still in love with Clarke, or at least still holding onto him, and jealous of the attention he's paying Alice."

She waited for the heated argument, but it didn't come.

"You might be right, Eleanor. I won't ever be sure that I'm not both of those things, but I am one hundred percent sure that my life lies in a forward direction, not looking back at what was. And I believe, as you suggested the last time we were together, there is something else, something more waiting for me.

"I can't even imagine what that 'something else' might be, but I know what I want now. I want Clarke to be my friend, I want to feel free to love him. I want to spend time with him without worrying about anything.

"Is all that completely selfish and unrealistic?"

"Yes, Jessie, yes it is."

Jessie set herself a regular schedule for coming to Arch Street to help out in whatever way she was needed. She was good at setting up for meetings and clearing up afterward. She could cook and sew. She could take inventories of supplies in the kitchen and the office. Jessie was a useful person to have around and the people at the Meeting House were happy to have her back.

The conversations about Clarke, about Alice and the awful Jack Crestfield, about Luke, and about Jessie's increased work with soldiers and their widows, continued for weeks, and woven seamlessly into them were Eleanor's stories about the Underground Railroad. She was fully engaged but still she doubted she was doing enough. She prepared food, found blankets to donate, and identified people who could be asked to hide a runaway slave for a few days. It wasn't as much as she would like to do, but it was all she could reasonably attempt as long as she was living with her parents.

And that brought them to the subject of Eleanor's plans for leaving home and moving into rooms with her friend, Sarah.

" I believe we are within a month of making the move. Sarah has her job at *Godey's Lady's Book* and that's secure, although she is still doing mostly clerical work. She spent the last year with a private tutor, working hard on her writing, so she is impatient with the filing, but we both believe there are possibilities there with Mrs. Hale moved down from New York to run the magazine personally. Meanwhile, I have at least a temporary clerical position at the Philadelphia Mint. I have consulted with the bank that holds my small trust fund, and they have made it very easy for me to use that money."

Several times during Eleanor's long recital of what sounded to Jessie like her trouble-free life—the jobs, the private tutors, the trust fund—Jessie had to interrupt. She struggled for excuses—a sudden thirst, a cramp in her leg that made it necessary to walk around—but she couldn't have sat still for the whole thing. The minute she returned from one of these small escapes, Eleanor would resume.

"And, most importantly, we have found the loveliest set of rooms you could imagine. We will have the entire second floor of a beautiful row house, tiny kitchen built in, and we will be sharing the building with the owner, an elderly lady who wants to avoid stairs, can't afford to move, and decided she thought it might be nice to have her own 'apartment' but to have neighbors who could help her if she needed help. I would guess she is probably about eighty years old, friendly and, it would seem, delighted to have us."

Jessie was ashamed of herself. Surely she was a bigger person than this, but she couldn't help thinking,

"Just marvelous. Wonderful. Even a little old lady downstairs, disabled enough to be grateful but not so much as to be a burden."

And it didn't help that Eleanor chose this moment to assure her that she was to be included in this magical world.

"The rooms are officially available on the first of next month, but we can really begin moving our things any time we like. There is furniture--a wonderful old bed, two chests, and a very large wardrobe in the bedroom and the requisite elegant but hideously uncomfortable sofa and, divinely, two fat, overstuffed armchairs in the sitting room. So you see you must visit soon and often as there is ample seating. We shall graciously offer you the horsehair sofa."

And with that, Eleanor was through, until suddenly she turned to Jessie, clapped her hands and said, "Good grief, Jessie. What am I thinking? It is nearly the time when Sarah will be finished with work for the day, and the magazine's offices are just around the corner. Let's hurry so we don't miss her and the three of us will go somewhere for coffee and a pastry. You have never met Sarah."

It was true. Jessie had never met Sarah and she realized with a start that she didn't *want* to meet Sarah. She supposed it was inevitable in the long run if she wanted to remain friends with Eleanor, but she didn't see why she had to deal with it today. She found she was, in fact, steaming at the casual mention that Sarah worked at *Godey's*, one of those jobs she had always considered an impossible dream. Nobody got a job with *Godey's Lady's Book*. Apparently, nobody but Sarah. Jessie just couldn't seem to stop thinking this way.

"Are you hesitating, Jess? You don't have to be nervous about meeting Sarah. She actually is the embodiment of the 'old shoe.' She doesn't dress well, her hair is usually a mess, and she doesn't care a fig about it. And yet, in spite of herself, she is devastatingly attractive. I've always thought it was her personality, which is disheveled and unvarnished and attractive like the rest of her, but you don't need my observations about Sarah.

"So, Miss Jessie Ashmore, do you want to tell me why you aren't keen on meeting my friend Sarah?"

It sometimes seemed to Jessie that her life consisted almost entirely of situations in which she was required to make some declaration about her feelings. This time it was Eleanor.

"Jess?"

"Alright, Eleanor. You asked this question. I am not ready to meet Sarah right now. In fact I very much do not want to meet Sarah right now. I am not, as you put it, 'keen' on meeting your friend Sarah right now because right now, I love you, and Sarah is sounding more and more like your best friend, and I want to be your best friend, and I am terribly, terribly jealous.

"You asked."

Eleanor took Jessie's hand and swung their arms back and forth as she said, in a voice full of caring, "When you are feeling better able to meet Sarah, come and tell me and I will arrange it. Perhaps you will be able to help us move. That way you would get to see the apartment."

—

It was late and Jessie did have to get home, so they left it at that. They were aware of something that had to be settled. It did not have to be settled today.

From Jessie's Journal
Meeting Sarah

But it did have to be settled, and I knew that it did, in spite of Eleanor's attempt to soothe my anxiety. Maybe I shouldn't have been that honest, but it felt important. It has been a brutal year and I feel as if I have had a whole layer of skin, a whole layer of "me" stripped away and I don't have enough time to be pretending. And that is why I went to meet Sarah. I asked Eleanor to arrange for us to meet Sarah after work and we went for coffee just as Eleanor suggested. Sarah is not important to me, and she might never be important to me, but I'm beginning to see how important she is to Eleanor— they have been friends for ten years. Ten years ago I was not yet fourteen years old. Yes. Sarah is important to Eleanor, and Eleanor is essential to me.

So Eleanor made the arrangements, and on a sunny afternoon, we stood across the street from Godey's offices, where Sarah would see us. No question about it, I was scared to death, but at one point Eleanor reached down and took my hand, and when she squeezed it, I looked up.

Sarah came striding out of her building, and I'll just say right here that she is an unbelievable looking person, and I mean that. I mean one doesn't at first quite believe she's real. The very first thing is that Eleanor's Sarah has a dark tan. Nobody has a tan; it is unthinkable. How does it even happen?

Where did she get it? I know she doesn't work outside, and anyway, once she was closer I could see perfectly well—because, let me just add this, her blouse was cut so low that her breasts, not small I also will observe, were nearly falling out—that her tan went down as far as you could see which was pretty far. I've never met anyone with that tanned skin. I'm going to be thinking for a long time trying to figure out how she did that. And somehow the rest of her looked like it just belonged with that tan.

So here comes this woman—and she's walking across the street just like someone tall would walk, in fact like Eleanor walks, except she's short. I think she can't be too much over five feet.

And she's a little plump, and the hair! It clearly started the day as a bun on top of her head but by the time I saw her it was sticking out all over the place and looking honestly like it wasn't going to make it home without just falling down altogether. And it's this very nice blond with a lot of gray streaked through it, actually quite pretty.

—

And on top of all this flurry of tan skin and tumbling breasts and crazy hair, she's wearing this extremely gray skirt and blouse that makes her look like our Quaker friends except, of course for the neckline. Oh, and the skirt just hangs because there are clearly no petticoats under it.

And the very strangest thing about this is that Sarah Portman is very attractive, really one of the most appealing women I've ever seen. And I'm thinking what I would look like with my hair falling down, with my skin cooked brown from the sun and age lines all around my eyes, with a simple gray dress and my breasts hanging out. I don't think I could pull it off.

And this person, who is like something out of a book except I can't think what book she would possibly be in, came to a halt right in front of me, looked me up and down, smiled this huge smile, wrapped her arms, practically her entire body, right around me, and said, "Jessie Ashmore. I am very happy to finally meet you. Eleanor thinks you are wonderful."

In the weeks before the move, the three women met often as Sarah was leaving work, walked around the city, inspected the rooms that would soon be home for two of them, and determined that the walk between there and Society Hill was manageable on a nice day.

On the day of the move, Jessie was with them. She carried boxes and unpacked them, hung clothes in the wardrobe, unwrapped dishes and found places for them in the small kitchen, and took out the bed linens and quilt. When she started to make the bed, Eleanor put a hand on her arm and just said,

"Jessie, you have really done more than your share today. Don't worry with that. Sarah and I will do it later."

So, all three stood back and looked around with satisfaction. The two new tenants were ecstatic, Jessie had to admit it was a lovely, welcoming place, and she collapsed gratefully on the dreadful horsehair sofa, while Sarah made cocoa.

—

Chapter Twelve
Eleanor and Sarah

Sarah Portman was six years older than Eleanor.

Her exuberance when she met Jessie was unusual and a response to a very specific set of circumstances. She was guarding her territory. Jessie was important to Eleanor; and Sarah knew she would never survive if Eleanor left her. Ordinarily, she was not unfriendly, but she was cautious. She responded when spoken to and engaged readily in any interesting discussion when invited, but she didn't initiate conversation and was perfectly content to sit or stand alone and silent. Her laugh was immediate, deep, and raucous, a delightful, infectious laugh, the kind of laugh not often heard from a woman. She was in some ways not unlike Gus Ashmore. The details of her early years were obscure and there were often several versions in circulation at any one time. Apparently everyone was interested in Sarah.

Even Eleanor didn't know the full story of Sarah's early life.

When they met, Eleanor was a fifteen-year-old schoolgirl and Sarah had just passed her twenty-second birthday. After nearly two years of working long hours as a seamstress in the kind of sweatshop where they gave you no breaks and a meal that consisted of water and a bowl of gruel, she had finally been offered a job sewing fine linens for a woman whose clients were the daughters of wealthy merchants on the occasions of their marriages and the births of their children. It had felt to Sarah like a break, like a small glimmer of hope when she had given up hoping quite a while ago. And although she knew she was still a laborer, still a sort of servant, she also knew that she now had access to a world where she might find a way to change that. So, she put her heart into those linens, spent long hours at the shop teaching herself new stitches, new ways of hemming a baby's blanket, refining her skill until she was sure she was the very best in the city.

On the face of it, the fact that she supported herself, and supported herself as a seamstress, would have automatically excluded her from any of the middle-class social life that surrounded her. She was welcomed into the homes of her clients to take orders or to deliver the delicate bridal linens or the sheets for a baby's first crib, but it should never have occurred to those women that she might be invited to the receptions and parties that celebrated these events. Those were the rules. No one spoke of them; no one needed to. But there seemed to be no rules in the case of Sarah Portman.

It was not possible to say exactly, but there was about Sarah something so enticing, so mysterious, so mesmerizing, that in the face of every tradition, every unwritten rule, and all expectations, she found herself with a steady stream of invitations, most of which she declined.

"Good afternoon. My name is Sarah Portman. I have an appointment with Miss Anita Harrison and her mother about the linens for Miss Harrison's wedding chest. I have brought samples."

"Yes, Miss Portman, you are expected. If you will follow me, I can show you to Miss Anita's sitting room and I believe I have chosen a table that will give you room to display what you have."

"Thank you. Let me just pick up my case--I left it leaning against the outside wall-- and I will be right behind you."

"Not at all, Miss Portman, I will carry that for you, and may I say, Miss, that the Harrisons have heard wonderful descriptions of your work. We are honored to have you."

Sarah actually blushed with pleasure. She had worked terribly hard. She knew the quality of her linens, but good merchandise, without the sort of advertising that only came from recommendations like this, was useless. Beautiful work didn't do you much good if people didn't buy it. Sarah was optimistic about today's appointment. She had built her reputation by the simple expedients of hard work and fine skill, but she hadn't yet built her clientele.

The Harrisons didn't keep her waiting. She had just arranged the last of the linens on the large marble-topped library table when the door opened and a lovely young woman, probably about her own age and wearing a simple navy day dress, walked in, followed by a woman who was clearly her mother. They had almost identical coloring—dark brown hair, pale skin, and brown eyes. They were certainly attractive, and they looked pleased with themselves and, as they wandered over to the table, equally pleased with the linens.

"Miss Portman, I am Marcia Harrison and this is my oldest daughter, Anita, who is about to be a bride. We very much appreciate your making time to meet with us, as we hear you are beginning to be in great demand."

Anita turned to Sarah, too excited to even say hello,

"Oh, Miss Portman, these are the most miraculous linens I have ever seen. I couldn't even have imagined anything that would look like this. I realize how soon this wedding is and how much we are asking of you.

"I want everything—the handkerchiefs, the pillowcases and sheets, the duvet cover, the nightgowns, the undergarments, every single thing—and, of course, at least two of the nightgowns and the undergarments.

"Mother, come here. Did you look at this chemise?

"Miss Portman, is there any possibility, any at all, that you can complete such an order in the time we've left you?

"Oh, Mother, how I wish we had known sooner!"

—

And Miss Anita Harrison, having run out of things to say, glanced back at the table with a sigh, sat down, and looked at Sarah with the desperate look of one whose very life depended on her answer.

It required all the self-control Sarah could muster not to laugh out loud, both with excitement at the order she was about to write, and with amusement at the youthful drama of Anita Harrison's self-absorbed enthusiasm. Not often, but every now and then, something would happen, some small thing would catch her attention or strike a nerve, and very briefly Sarah Portman would be overcome with sadness for everything she had missed. It didn't last; Sarah couldn't afford to let it last. She had learned many years ago that self-pity was for losers. Sarah planned to be a winner.

She walked back to the table, reached into her carryall and pulled out a pencil and a small notebook. She took a minute to glance over the linens, then turned to Anita and her mother, "If you two could come over to the table, you can show me exactly what you want and I will write up this order, take a minute to look it over, and then let you know what I can do."

Of course, the order was large but not too large and Miss Portman assured Miss and Mrs. Harrison that she could deliver the linens at least a week before the wedding which would give them enough time to correct any problems that should occur. She was about to arrange to deliver all the linens together, in one return visit, when the door to the sitting room opened again and Anita Harrison's younger sister, Eleanor, age fifteen, walked in, stopped, then in a throaty voice, addressed her sister, "Anita, I am sorry. I had forgotten you had this appointment, and I am interrupting. Should I come back later?"

"It is fine, Ellie. We have just finished. Come and look at these linens and, here, meet Miss Sarah Portman."

Sarah, in a typically inappropriate gesture, held out her hand to Eleanor, and Eleanor took it. "Miss Harrison, I am pleased to meet you."

Eleanor both did and did not resemble her mother and sister. Her hair was much darker, not brown but a shimmering black; her skin wasn't just pale, but something like porcelain; her eyes were a dark blue. She was tall.

Sarah looked at Mrs. Harrison and explained that, if it wouldn't be an inconvenience, she would like to deliver the linens, as they were finished, coming back to the house several times instead of just once. That way, she explained, they could be sure that each set—whether bed linens or nightgowns—was exactly as they wanted it.

The Harrisons agreed, Sarah said her goodbyes, packed the linen samples and her pad and pen, and headed out the door. She was confused and stunned into silence. She got back to her room, washed up, then lay down and went immediately to sleep. She didn't stir until the next morning.

She reported in to the shop where she worked and explained to her employer the size and nature of the order and the standing of the Harrison family, and she asked to be relieved of any other work until she could complete this job. She said she was sure that if she completed it on time and did her finest work the result would be to increase their client list. She was very convincing.

She worked steadily, coming to the shop every evening and sewing until she couldn't stay awake, then going home to pull down the shades in her room in the boarding house, undress down to her chemise, and lie down on top of the covers to get a few hours sleep before evening again and another trip to the shop. The work was coming along. In less than two weeks, Sarah had completed one set of bed linens, and sent a message to Mrs. Harrison with a boy she knew from the streets around her boarding house. He was a regular and she was almost certain his name was Barnabas. He took the note, and the coins she gave him, shoved the lot inside his pockets, and headed off. Within an hour, he had returned with a note from Mrs. Harrison asking Sarah to call at noon the next day.

This time it was Anita, and not the butler, who answered the door.

"Oh, Sarah, hello, come in, and welcome. I see you are carrying a very carefully wrapped package and I am wild with excitement to know what you've brought."

Sarah smiled. This young woman's enthusiasm really did amuse and interest her. What must it be like to have lived your first twenty-two years in a way that left you with this much enthusiasm for a parcel of bed linens? For a split second, Sarah was years back, in a bed whose sheets were gray with filth, hoping the man who had been there earlier wouldn't come back.

"Well, Miss Harrison, I will show you. I bring a complete set of your bed linens, and before I make a second set, I want you to take the time now to look at these very carefully, examine each stitch, look at the hems. And please can we ask your mother to do the same? When I walk out today I want to know very clearly what changes, if any, I need to make."

Getting Anita Harrison settled down and actually focused on the linens proved to be impossible. Mrs. Harrison arrived and didn't concentrate much better, and Sarah finally gave up the effort and was packing up when, once again, Eleanor came in quietly, apologized for interrupting, then appeared to be thinking about which chair she wanted, when Sarah asked her if she would look at the bed clothes.

Unlike her relations, Eleanor turned her full attention to the task at hand, praised Sarah's work, and did in fact find two small areas where the stitches were uneven. Sarah marked these with tiny pins, packed up, and was headed for the door when she realized that Eleanor was right behind her.

—

"Miss Portman, do you go in to your shop every morning and are you there all day? I would very much like to visit you there and see all the sewing machines and fabrics and watch how you sew the things you're making for Anita. If I can get permission from Mother, would that be convenient for you?"

All Sarah could think was, "This beautiful girl. This child." And, to Eleanor, she said, "Of course, Eleanor, but it won't be possible until after your sister's wedding. Until all my work for that is finished, I am only going to the shop in the evenings so that I can work undisturbed."

"I would like that ever so much, even better than going in the daytime. Mother likes you a great deal and I am sure would give her permission. Perhaps you could come here and we could take my parents' carriage, see the shop, and then I would buy you a coffee somewhere."

"I think that sounds lovely. But I believe we will still have to wait a few more weeks until I am nearly finished with your sister's linens."

Eleanor was quiet and stood there in the hallway, tall, slender, more elegant than one would expect of someone her age, looking directly at Sarah. For longer than was probably wise, Sarah returned her look, then she picked up the case she had brought with her and turned for the door.

"We will talk with your mother, then pick an evening a few weeks from now, and I will show you how to sew the finest linens anywhere."

Eleanor looked pleased.

Two more weeks passed and Sarah returned to the Harrisons' with a set of twelve white handkerchiefs, a few embroidered with small pink flowers, all bearing the initials that would be Anita's after her wedding, all sewn with such delicate perfection that Anita and her mother were even more enchanted than they had been with the bed linens, of which there were now two full sets, the small imperfections pointed out by Eleanor corrected.

On this visit, Eleanor didn't appear.

On the following Tuesday, after an especially long night of work on Anita Harrison's wedding night gowns and undergarments, Sarah had come in, thrown off as much as she could of her clothing, and was sleeping soundly in her linen chemise, which had pulled up high over one hip. She had been exhausted when she lay down and the soft touch of the linen, combined with a breeze coming in through her window, had dropped her into a much deeper sleep than usual. Undisturbed, Sarah might well have slept right through the day. In any event, she didn't hear the persistent knock on her door and Eleanor, discouraged but deciding just to see inside before she left, opened the door, looked at Sarah, and closed the door quietly behind her. Then she sat down on the room's only chair and watched Sarah sleeping. She sat without moving, into the afternoon and, when the room was growing dark, Sarah turned, stretched, yawned, and then she saw Eleanor. She just stared.

And in the half-dark room, looking at fifteen-year-old Eleanor curled in the cheap armchair her landlady had provided, Sarah began to cry, softly at first and then harder and finally in great wracking sobs. Eleanor was up out of the chair, knowing only that she did not want this woman to cry and that she must be the one to make it stop. And, awkwardly at first, Eleanor put her arms around Sarah, shushing, reassuring, saying over and over in that voice that was still a child's, however husky, "Don't cry, Sarah. Please don't cry."

Neither of them knew then, nor remembered afterward, exactly how it happened, although there was a point at which Eleanor became acutely aware of what she was doing and of the effect it was having on Sarah. Her hands, that had been around Sarah's back as she cradled and comforted her, moved to her hips. Sarah's breath caught in her throat. This wasn't something she did. After a childhood on the streets, there was no framework within which Sarah Portman could connect love, or even affection, with this kind of touching. She could feel a scream rising in her throat. But Eleanor's hands were barely moving, then they were slow and feather-light on her hips and belly and thighs and they were lifting the chemise over her head and after that everything in Sarah's world shifted.

Sarah Portman, child of a rough world, victim of every horror it is possible to imagine, felt a great tidal wave sweep over her body and she turned to find that Eleanor was smiling and saying her name. And, a little later,

"You know, Sarah, if they find out at home they will throw me out. When that happens, will you take me?"

Sarah just laughed. "I'll have to think that over, Miss Harrison. But I'll let you know." And they stayed in the bed in that small room through that night and the next day until Eleanor said it was time for her to go home and deal with whatever was waiting.

On the day that Jessie Ashmore walked into the Arch Street Meeting House for the first time, and saw Eleanor across the room, Sarah and Eleanor had been together for almost ten years.

Chapter Thirteen
Love and War

After Sarah and Eleanor's move, life slipped back quickly into its old grooves. Eleanor returned to her job at the Mint, and Sarah went back to filing at *Godey's Lady's Book*. For Sarah, it was a time of growing frustration. She had worked hard on her writing, had pushed and charmed her way into the rare job at *Godey's* and now it seemed to her she was once again starting over and waiting for a break. Eleanor was so pleased to have finally moved out of her parents' house and to be living in rooms and paying her share, that for her this was a time of near perfect contentment. With her small trust to back her up, she was in no hurry to begin looking for a better job. It was a time of adjustment for both of them.

Jessie was still spending as many hours as possible with soldiers and widows, and had carved out time to return to some of her duties at the Arch Street Meeting House.

In those rare moments when she wasn't managing to distract herself by staying busy, Jessie was in an emotional muddle. There were all those feelings about Clarke; there was the daily concern about Alice; and there were Eleanor and Sarah. To make matters worse, there was her father.

Since the night Alice came home and especially since it became clear that Jack Crestfield had gotten away, Jessie had watched as Frank Ashmore just stopped living. He had lost interest in everything. He came home early from work and fell asleep on the old chesterfield; he had told Gus he didn't want to have their parties anymore; and, except when Clarke insisted that both he and Gus be there to discuss something, Frank didn't even talk about Alice. He had not said one word to Jessie about Clarke, and she was sure Gus had told him what had happened.

"I have hesitated to say anything, because the terrible events of the past year have gotten us all down, but if you see this from his point of view, it must seem that he has lost every one of his children. And this kind of unhappiness and withdrawal has begun to affect his and Mother's relationship—which has always been so very fine. I am worried, Eleanor, and I don't know what I can say to him."

"*You* aren't lost, Jess. You are right here, you are working at something you love; you're content. You have to let your father know that."

"I don't think it's that simple, Eleanor. He was so pleased about my marrying Clarke because it would have meant I was settled and safe. After Luke and Alice, he must be terribly afraid for me, and I don't know how to convince him that I am not at risk. I don't think he is able to understand my decision the way Mother does. They are different."

—

Eleanor was quiet, then finally reached over and took Jessie's hand.

"You know, Jess, I think sometimes *you* don't believe that you made a good decision about Clarke. You should talk to your father, but you can't convince him you are doing well until you believe it yourself."

Jessie just shook her head and didn't respond. Eleanor was right. She didn't believe in her own choices and she didn't have any faith in what Eleanor had told her a long time ago—that she would find her independence and her happiness in the way that was right for her. She usually couldn't see it and, when she did, she believed it was because Eleanor had led her.

It was unfortunate that so much of Jessie's pondering still involved exaggerated examinations of her own weaknesses placed against idealized visions of someone else's supposed strengths and successes. Eleanor Harrison was a typical example of Jessie's skewed vision. Jessie had elevated her to a position of impossibly pure virtue and, by extension, she now imagined Eleanor's friendship with Sarah bathed in a romantic haze, through which Eleanor was completely contented with her life; Sarah, even though she was frustrated right now, would get the writing assignments she wanted soon; and, together they were the perfectly compatible pair.

She continued in the ultimately self-defeating belief that Eleanor would have the answers and could advise her. And, as with anyone else, Eleanor did often see Jessie's life more clearly than Jessie, who was in the midst of it. As so many times before, she walked over to where Eleanor had settled on one of the chairs and put her arms around her.

"As usual, Eleanor, you are right, annoyingly right about it all.

"I do not believe in my own decisions. I am still pining over Clarke—mostly because I enjoy pining. I don't believe for one minute that I'll ever do anything important, that I'll ever find someone I want to marry, that I'll ever have even one adventure."

Jessie too often could see herself as hopelessly lost, foolish, selfish, a complainer—the list really was endless. What she didn't understand was her wisdom and her strength and her caring. She was not able to grasp that she was just as important to her friends as they were to her.

She missed entirely the smiles on the faces, not just of the soldiers she helped, but of the doctors and nurses she worked beside. She saw herself as some kind of beggar or charity case. Her relationship with Eleanor was an extreme example: Jessie appeared with her latest crisis and Eleanor generously took the time to listen, to praise, and to advise. Eleanor happened to be perfectly willing to fill that position. It was an uneven friendship bound to hit a few rocks along the way.

Meanwhile, Jessie continued, in characteristic fashion, "That is all silly, selfish thinking, and the last thing you're right about is that I need to talk to Father. And I am going to do exactly that. Maybe if I reassure him, I'll feel better. In any case, it can't do a bit of harm."

"Jessie, my friend, you won't believe this, but you are sometimes a very wise woman."

"Well, just so you know I'm not too wise. I'm still holding out for that magic combination of marriage and a great adventure. And don't bother telling me there's no such thing.

"And, yes, yes. I will talk to Father tomorrow. I think I will go by his shop and surprise him with lunch."

And Jessie did exactly that. Right at noon, she opened the bright red door to Franklin's Clothiers, stepped inside, and was immediately reminded of how much she loved this place. When she was a little girl, her father brought her to the shop on the weekends when he had extra work to do, and even later, well into her adolescent years, she would often come by after school and watch the tailors and apprentices working at the huge sewing machines. She knew most of their names, and she always had questions. They appreciated her enthusiasm, and she knew her father was proud of her.

Today, she made her way slowly and spoke to everyone, especially to the older workers who had known her as a child, and she took the time to comment on the beautiful suits and shirts at every station. She finally knocked on the door of her father's office, looked in, and was delighted with his reaction.

"Jessie, my girl, you are a sight for these sore old eyes. Come right in here this minute. Did you see that tweed old Sam was working? Yes, of course you did. You always notice anything important. Come in, come in! What on earth brings you?"

"I thought I had come to cheer you up because you have seemed sad for too long, and to try to explain why I can't marry Clarke so you wouldn't worry about that. But now, Father, do you think we might be able to cheer each other up? And then I'll try to talk about Clarke because I'm not sure I know why I can't marry him. I just know I can't because I guess I'm waiting for an invitation to join the burlesque."

There was one short second when a frown crossed her father's face, and Jessie was certain she had gone too far and let her mouth get her into trouble again. And then, for the first time in a long while, for the first time since Luke had gone off to the war—maybe even earlier, since he first realized he had lost his chance with his only son-- Frankin Ashmore threw back his head and laughed a loud, long laugh of pure pleasure.

He stood up, pulled on his coat, and turned to Jessie,

"Jessie, let's buy the most beautiful bunch of flowers we can find, then we'll drive home as fast as we can, and take your mother out for lunch.

—

Are you with me?"

"Father, I promise you one thing. I will always be with you. Now let's hurry and get those flowers and get home because I think I might be starving!"

There are a few magical moments in the lives of those who love each other, when it isn't necessary to explain anything. Franklin and his daughter rode home in contented silence, walked with Gus to the indoor Farmer's Market for lunch, and in the evening when Clarke came by, they were all able to listen to what he had to say about Alice.

Like the rest of the day, it was encouraging. Clarke believed, as a doctor and as a friend, that Alice was improving, that she was going to come through all this. He did not think she would come through unscathed, but he was now confident she would survive. And he told them that it had been her own good instincts that had saved her.

She insisted on staying in bed longer than anyone had advised, and when she did come out, it was purest intuition that had sent her straight from the bedroom to the kitchen, bypassing the main floors of the house altogether. For once, the family was in agreement, with no defensiveness or need to take any of the credit for their unexpectedly resilient young daughter. They were just grateful. And by the time Clarke gave them this optimistic report about Alice's health, the day had been filled truly to overflowing with good news.

After Jessie and her parents got back to the house from lunch, Gus and Frank pleaded fatigue and went upstairs to rest. Smiling to herself, Jessie decided on a walk and, for some reason, headed toward the small park she hadn't visited since her brief return the day after she told Clarke she couldn't marry him. She was caught completely off guard, as she strolled though the gate, to see Clarke sitting on one of the iron benches, his head down, apparently in deep thought. She hesitated to approach him, but he looked up, smiled broadly, and gestured for her to join him. It was a strange reunion.

"Clarke, I have to thank you for everything you said today. You can't think how important it was. There has been so much unhappiness in this house for so long, and just today I saw a bit of hope—I'll bet you noticed that Mother and Father were happier together—and then you came along with that glowing report on Alice. Goodness, it really has been a lovely day.

"There I am, thinking only about the Ashmores. Clarke, how are you?"

She recognized the familiar furrow between Clarke's eyebrows. He had been puzzling over something serious on that park bench, and Jessie knew to wait.

"I suppose, Jess, that I, too, have been thinking about the Ashmores. I want to talk to Gus and Frank about Alice, but I would like to talk to you first."

—

He seemed subdued, but not concerned, so Jessie was content to say, "Of course, Clarke. Is it something I can help with?"

"Only to relieve my mind, Jess. Only that. You are aware I have spent a great deal of time with Alice since what happened to her and what happened with us the same day, and then after your decision. At first it was just a few hours here and there, checking in on her, at Gus's request, as a supporting doctor and a family friend. Then it was more hours, when Frank expressed his concerns about her isolating herself up in that bedroom. After that, my interest in the complexities of the trauma and its aftereffects increased our time together to several days a week as I observed, took notes, consulted some of the men at the University, and reported to you and your parents."

By this time, Jessie was having a complicated reaction. She had guessed the nature of what Clarke wanted to discuss with her and her parents, and she was growing impatient with Clarke's plodding, pedantic way of getting to the point. But overriding that impatience was a deep fondness for this man who she truly did love and who could have been sitting here as her intended husband. Jessie was torn between regret and relief. It was the moment at which she jumped over the last hurdle of doubt and knew she had made the right decision. Clarke Stanbury was going to be a wonderful husband, just not hers. And trading on their fondness for one another, and on her unique position, Jessie put a hand on Clarke's arm,

"Clarke! For heaven's sake, get to the point. You want to take Alice out, you most likely are ready to propose, and you feel you need my blessing. You don't, you know, but you shall have it anyway. What a splendid thing to have happen. It is the only possible ending I could have imagined that really would have made things even close to all right again. Thank you, Clarke." And Jessie, as she often did, shed a few tears.

"Thank you for loving me. Thank you for loving Alice, and Gus and Frank. Thank you for loving all of us."

After that, it got chilly in the park, but these two lovers still took a few minutes to reminisce, to declare again what Clarke had once called their long, long love, and to look ahead to a friendship that would sustain them both. After that, they hurried back to the house so Clarke could warm up before seeking permission from Alice's parents to ask their younger daughter for her hand in marriage.

A regular highlight of Jessie's weeks was the time she spent with Eleanor and Sarah. They had gotten into a routine, and Jessie normally showed up around four or five o'clock on Mondays and a bit later on Fridays. At the beginning of the week, and because she didn't have to be at a job at a certain time, Jessie would come early and have dinner ready. On Fridays, Eleanor and Sarah took turns cooking or they would all decide at the last minute to eat out somewhere. In this way, Jessie was gradually folded into the household and found she was not only getting to know Sarah but was beginning to like her.

It was a few months later when a friend at the Meeting House asked Jessie to come in to help on Friday night, and Jessie decided at the last minute to stop by the market, pick up something special to cook, and go for her visit with Eleanor and Sarah on Thursday. She and Warren had spent all morning finding extra supplies to take to the medical station on Saturday and had come home early so Jessie could wash up. Then Warren had taken her to the market and on to the apartment. Because she had nothing planned early on Friday morning, she decided—as she sometimes did—to sleep on the sofa and have Warren come for her after Eleanor and Sarah had left for their jobs.

Her arms full of parcels, Jessie knocked and when the door opened pushed her way in with her elbow and slid into the kitchen. That way, she didn't see Eleanor, who was just coming out of the bedroom. She was dressed in a man's suit, her hair was pulled up securely under a cap, she wore heavy work boots, and her face had been blackened.

"Jessie, what are you doing here? It's Thursday."

And finally Jessie turned around and took one step before she stopped.

"Eleanor, what on earth? What are you doing? Are you involved in some theatrical performance? You look like you belong in a minstrel show.

And you scared me half to death. Honestly."

When Eleanor didn't answer, Jessie began to feel a little afraid.

"Sarah? What's going on here?"

Eleanor still hadn't spoken. Sarah sat in silence in one of the armchairs. And suddenly, for no particular reason, Jessie understood.

She walked over to the other chair and sat down.

"It's the Railroad, isn't it, Eleanor? It's the damned Underground Railroad! And you just could not wait to leave home so you could dress up like a man and go out and play soldier. Right? Am I right, Eleanor? You *just could not wait*."

"Jessie, you have always known that I . . ."

"That you what, Eleanor? That you wanted to have a more dramatic role in this play? That you fancy yourself Joan of Arc? That you're a right idiot and you are going to get yourself killed out there and then, and then, Eleanor, what on earth do you expect that Sarah will do? And what do you expect that I will do?

"Damn you. Damn you. And damn that damned Railroad. I hate it." And, of course, Jessie started to cry. But she was angry and terrified, and when Eleanor walked over to put her arm around her, Jessie shrugged it off.

"I am going to regret for the rest of my life asking this question, because I know that the answer will break something forever, but I don't think I can help myself and I have no desire to spare you.

"So, my good friend and Sarah's good friend, will you—because you love us both and know how much we need you—will you change your mind and stay at home?

Will you, Eleanor?"

A great silence echoed behind Jessie's words. Eleanor, who had been sitting on the sofa, stood up, collected a small duffle bag from the floor inside the bedroom, and took out of the wardrobe what was obviously a large man's leather jacket. She pulled it on and slung the bag over one shoulder.

"Jessie, I can't make that kind of decision at the last minute like this. I am expected. Can we have dinner together tomorrow night and talk about it?"

Jessie had opened her mouth to scream and curse and rage, when she realized it would do no good at all. She turned to Sarah, who was staring down at her lap, then just leaned her head against the back of the sofa and closed her eyes. Eleanor pulled the door shut behind her. Jessie had no idea what time it was.

Nor did she have any sense of how much time had passed when she heard Sarah stand up, then the rattling of cups in the kitchen and what she recognized as the kettle being put on to boil. Yes, she could use a good strong cup of tea. She wondered if she had remembered to buy milk and, if she had, whether she'd remembered to put it on ice. Had she been expected to stop for ice on the way over? No need to worry about that; she hadn't been expected at all. She could feel hysterical laughter bubbling up.

"Jessie? Jess?" It could only have been a few minutes. Sarah was arranging two steaming cups with a pitcher of milk between them. Jessie wanted to weep, but she had the presence of mind to know that she couldn't impose that on Sarah.

"Oh, Sarah, what a blessing. This looks wonderful, and please tell me I put the milk away."

"You did, you did indeed, now drink up and let that work its magic. It is a very strong Irish black, and I have laced it liberally with milk and honey and one shot of the brandy I keep for emergencies. I believe this qualifies." And Sarah grinned comfortingly at Jessie.

Jessie took a huge mouthful, choked because it hadn't cooled, then sat back and sighed. It was excellent tea and Jessie could feel the effects of the sweet caffeine and the brandy.

"Well, Sarah, you obviously knew this was going on. How long has she been going out like this, and what exactly is she doing out there?" Jessie's voice sounded angry and accusing.

Sarah didn't answer at first. She picked up her mug but didn't drink it. It looked to Jessie as if she were just wrapping her hands around the warm cup for comfort.

—

"Yes, Jessie, obviously I have known. It would have been impossible not to know. And Eleanor and I had very much the same conversation the two of you just had. Like you, I asked her not to go. I asked her to give it up because I loved her and I needed her. I asked her not to go out because she loved me.

"And, just as she did tonight, she pulled on a jacket, picked up her bag, and went. Because she had to, because it isn't in her not to go, just as it isn't in me—or you—not to love her and need her. But she loves the going out more than she loves either of us, Jessie. What she gets, what she can give, who she is out there, Jess, is the kind of love she is good at. Do you understand that?" Jessie did not understand. In fact, she barely heard the last thing Sarah said.

"That just doesn't make sense, Sarah. Surely you could have stopped her. She loves you. She is risking her life. What she's doing is very dangerous. Couldn't you have told her you would leave if she went? Couldn't you have done that, Sarah? She would have stopped then.

"Aren't you partly responsible that she still does this? Aren't you, Sarah?"

"I expect I am, Jess. When Eleanor came home that night, or really the next morning—and you understand she did not start doing this until after we moved here—I asked her again to stop, and I did just what you suggest. I told her I would leave her."

"I guess it didn't work then; I guess there's no way to get her to stop. I apologize, Sarah. I thought you just hadn't tried."

"Oh, I tried, and I succeeded. Eleanor agreed that night to stop going out to help the slaves if only I wouldn't leave."

"Sarah, you just said she loves what's out there more than she loves you, so what are you talking about now?"

"Loves, Jess. Loves, not needs. Eleanor needs me and, in a different way, she needs you, because she is hollow inside and you and I are not. She believes that if I leave her she will blow away. And don't you understand what you do for Eleanor? You see her the way she would like to be. It's actually fairly simple, Jess. It's about survival. Eleanor cannot survive without us.

"Anyway, I was thrilled when she promised to stop the Railroad. And, of course, I stayed.

"And you do not ever want to be responsible for making someone you love that unhappy. It was as if Eleanor died that night. She went through all the motions. I know she still loved me. But she had given up something that was more important to her than you or I or anyone could ever be. She had turned her back on The Mission. She had abdicated her position as Missionary. She hated herself for it.

"In the end, I begged her to go back. Eventually, she did."

—

After a while Sarah got up and made each of them a second cup of the strong sweet tea, then for a while she wandered, cup in hand, looking out the big windows, opening the door and listening for the lightest step on the stairs, straightening pictures. None of it seemed to help her restlessness. Eventually she came back to the chair and sat down again next to Jessie. And she began to talk, so low at first that Jessie could barely catch all the words, but it wasn't long before she understood that Sarah was talking about her life many years before Eleanor.

What Jessie couldn't have known was that she was telling some of it for the first time, that there were a few details even Eleanor had not heard. Maybe it was the late hour, maybe it was finally sharing the burden of the fear every time Eleanor went out. The reasons weren't clear and don't matter. Maybe Sarah just needed to talk.

"I don't actually know what happened to my parents, but I heard much later, from some friends on the street, that my father left us when I was a baby and that my mother had died five years later of the croup.

"I don't remember much from those early years except always being hungry and awfully cold in the winter.

"The earliest real memories are from when I was probably eight—I might have been younger— and the man who had rescued me from the street and fed me and bought me clothes for school came into my room and, well, I don't want to go on about it, but he did just about everything you can imagine a man doing to an eight-year-old girl. But that wasn't the worst part. The worst part was that he gave me as a sort of present to some of his friends and they gave me to their friends and that was my life for a long time."

"Sarah, stop for a minute. You don't have to tell me all this. I don't want you to think I blame you that Eleanor does these things. I am just afraid and need to be angry to keep the fear away. I will listen as long as you want me to, but you don't have to tell me."

But Sarah had started now, and nothing could break her rhythm. She described the terrible work rolling cigars all night and how at first the jobs as a seamstress in sweatshops, sewing in rooms with twenty or thirty other girls, had seemed like a blessing but had made her so ill that she was close to death when the woman from the linens shop had come right by that sweatshop one day, taken her by the hand, walked her out, and put her to work learning how to sew the finest linens in Philadelphia.

"When I got my first contract to sew fancy-work, it was with the Harrisons, Eleanor's family; her sister was getting married and I was hired to sew all her bridal and bed linens. The first day I was there, Eleanor walked in. She was fifteen years old; I was twenty-one."

Jessie stopped her again. She didn't want Sarah to talk like this if it was hurting her and, to be honest, Jessie was afraid to hear more. But again Sarah went on as if Jessie hadn't spoken. It was possible that she didn't even hear Jessie, that by now she was just telling the story to herself.

"And then, a few weeks later, I was asleep in the single room I rented in a boardinghouse; I was going into the shop at night to work in the quiet, then sleeping most of the day. That day I was especially tired and slept very soundly and for a long time. It was almost dark when I woke up and saw Eleanor sitting in my one chair, staring at me. I believe she had been there most of the day. We tried to talk but found that we could not, then I started to cry. I have no idea what I was crying about, but Eleanor, this young girl, came over to comfort me."

Jessie reached over and put a hand on Sarah's arm to stop her.

"Please, Sarah. It's really all right to stop there. I can look at you and Eleanor and see that comforting each other is something you still do all these years later. It's a wonderful part of your friendship that anyone can see."

"You need to hear this to the end, Jess. I know you are terribly afraid to hear it. I know it is going to force you to think about a lot of things in a different way. But if you are going to leave here, whenever you do, and get on about the business of your life, then you have to sit still and listen now. You are going to have to know at least everything I can tell you about who she is before Eleanor walks back in that door."

What Jessie didn't understand until later was that Sarah intended something more than even the story of her long love affair with Eleanor. That last piece of the puzzle that was Eleanor was one that Sarah couldn't have given her, that no one could have helped her fit into the whole. It was the final piece and Jessie had to come to it herself, alone, and without help. Before she left for home, driving the carriage because Warren saw without being told that she needed to do it, she would have seen.

In that short period of grace just before Eleanor returned, though, Jessie believed she had it all, and she was pleased that she was able to absorb it. Sarah was trying so hard to warn her, but it wasn't quite enough.

From Jessie's Journal
About Sarah and Eleanor
I just couldn't stop Sarah. She had started and there was no way to stop her. I think, in a way, it was the greatest compliment she could have paid me. She trusted me and I will be better able to talk

to Eleanor when she gets home. Then, after that, I will, as Sarah warned me, have to think about everything in a different way, so different in fact that it's as if I have just been born. But that is not tonight.

You see, it is late now, or rather it is early, very early in the morning, the sky still dark, and Sarah has gone to rest for a while. I have made another cup of tea and am sitting in Eleanor's chair—the one she always chooses when we are all here together—and I am waiting. And knowing I am not waiting alone is a help, but I am still terribly afraid, as if what happens here, what we all say here, is going to change just about everything.

I have to believe that all this—Sarah and Eleanor and the Railroad—will turn out just fine. But I have to admit I have no idea how that might happen.

I have known since the day I met her that Eleanor Harrison is an unusual, an exceptional person. There has never been any question about that. She is beautiful in a way that isn't anything like anyone else who is beautiful. She is smart, I mean smart from reading, smart in the ways that only men are supposed to be. She knows every single fact about the history of Philadelphia and the Quakers and the Abolitionist movement and the slave system and all the reasons for the current fighting.

But now all at once there are these new things about her, and one is the fact that she loves danger, she courts it. She actually likes going out there at night, dressed like a man, knowing that she might not live to come home.

What can I possibly think or feel or even try to understand about Sarah and Eleanor? I already knew they were good friends, that the strength of that friendship had held them together for ten years, that they had met when Sarah came to sew wedding linens for Eleanor's sister. Eleanor told me all that soon after we met.

But I didn't consider that they might be lovers. I wouldn't have known even how to imagine it. Or would I have known? Did I know? You see, I have to rethink everything because what I just wrote isn't true. It is a lie. I never actually thought about it, had ideas in my head about it, but I could feel it. I could close my eyes and feel Eleanor's touch, or Sarah's. And I just wiggled that around in my brain until it wasn't what it was, was something different or wasn't there at all.

I will write down here what is true. I know what it felt like when Clarke touched me on my breasts and between my legs. I know, I loved it, I wanted more. And yes yes all right yes I can imagine Eleanor or Sarah or both of them touching me in just that same way. And I think I would love it and would want more.

And what on God's earth am I supposed to do with that?

—

And Eleanor did, indeed, walk back in the door. It was later than either Sarah or Jessie had expected. Sarah had gotten up before dawn, during the hour when the light is still gray and hasn't yet made any difference, before any of it has spilled onto the floor or the corners of furniture, the hour that often appears to be darker than the middle of the night. She had come out in a frayed wool dressing gown, in her bare feet, filled another pot, handed a cup to Jessie, and without a word sat down on the awful sofa. Jessie almost jumped up to offer her chair, but realized that Sarah's chair, next to Eleanor's, was empty had she chosen to take it. She had not.

"Sarah, are you going to talk to her when she comes in?"

"I think you should talk to her first, Jessie, because tonight was your night to beg and be rejected. Remember, I already had my turn." The sharp edge of sarcasm and pain in Sarah's voice was truly terrible.

"And then I think that you and Eleanor and I will sit down together and will find that we have a great many things to say to one another. And at some point, I don't know when, we will send word to Warren to come to take you home.

"I believe that will turn out to be exactly how it goes. But, I have been surprised before, especially where Eleanor is concerned, so we will have to see."

They heard the sound of the key in the lock

and a look of apprehension passed between them just before the door opened slowly and Eleanor, alarmingly pale, stood and smiled at them. It was obvious she had expected them to be there.

"I appreciate the welcoming committee, ladies, and I will impose on your good will further by asking for the time to walk down the hall and spend just a very few minutes in a tub full of hot water."

Without waiting for an answer, Eleanor took a towel and her dressing gown from the top shelf of the wardrobe and walked back out the door. Sarah and Jessie waited for nearly an hour before she returned, her wet hair wrapped in the thick towel, wearing a dressing gown so simple that Jessie couldn't afterwards remember anything about it. It was, in some way, the Eleanor she had always known, nearly invisible in her cloak of elegance.

"I suppose I am in some trouble with you two."

And, all of a sudden, Jessie understood how wrong she had been about almost everything.

From Jessie's Journal
Eleanor: An Insight

"I suppose I am in some trouble with you two."

I heard the words but it was the voice that cut right through me. Having denied or ignored or failed to see for well over two years, this time I wasn't able to turn away quickly enough to avoid the clean blow. I thought I had heard a monster.

The voice was devoid of emotion. It was flat. It was without expression except for the slightest touch of amusement. It was a voice that mocked. It wounded, and could kill, because every inflection said one thing, "I do not care. I do not even see you/"

I don't suppose I will ever be sure whether I knew right from that first evening on Arch Street or was so blinded that I missed the signals altogether. Whichever might be the truth of the thing, it was Eleanor's apparently innocuous words, and the tone in which she delivered them that morning two years later, that made everything clear, "I suppose I am in some trouble with you two."

Not, of course, quite a monster. I am given to drama and exaggeration. Still, close enough. Whatever searching of my own soul lies ahead for me, it is nonetheless true that Eleanor Harrison is something not quite human, at least not by the standards of humanness the people I respect and love use to conduct their lives.

I do feel a fool. Sarah, at least, was never that. She saw the truth all along but she could not get away. Because of every experience of her life right up to the moment that she woke up to find Eleanor in her room, and because of Eleanor's perverse need to exploit that, Sarah was helpless from the first touch of Eleanor's fifteen-year-old hands.

When I walked into the Meeting House that first night what did I see? I saw an unusually striking woman, slightly foreign in appearance, taller than average, dressed with such simple elegance that I didn't notice what she was wearing. I did notice the casual confidence with which she held herself, the familiarity with which she addressed anyone who approached her. And, yes, I saw but did not linger on the fact that her smile never reached her eyes, which were beautiful but almost without expression. For a young woman discontent with her life and confused about who she was and who she wanted to be, Eleanor was the answer—that, I said to myself, that right there, is what I want to do and who I want to be. For someone perhaps less naïve, with even just a little more exposure to the world outside her neighborhood, Eleanor would not have seemed so thrilling.

Child of privilege, Eleanor was the charismatic, intelligent, younger sister who, according to Sarah's story of her first visit to the Harrison household, held sway over her older sibling by the same tactics of condescension and dismissal that she had practiced and polished for the day when they would serve her best, the day she met Sarah Portman. And I have no right, even if I had the insight, to dissect that long relationship. I can only say that, from the minute Eleanor said those ordinary words in that dead voice, I knew that Sarah was wrong, that there was nothing the three of us had to say to each other.

Finally, I believe I have to consider Clarke and what happened between us. I do not, I want to say, regret one single minute of my time with him. He is a good man. Again, I try to take myself back, this time to the evening I came late to help Eleanor, the night I met Clarke, the night I saw Eleanor and Clarke talking and laughing with such familiarity.

They didn't know each other and Clarke even commented to me later that he had been uncomfortable with her assumption of intimacy. At the time, I put it down to what I considered Clarke's prudishness. Today I wonder at what would certainly have been, if it were the case, odd at the best--Eleanor almost flirting with Clarke while, at the same time, she was praising me and encouraging a relationship between the two of us. Eleanor and Jessie and Sarah. Yes, I can see it. I only wish I had been able to see what was happening a little sooner.

I suppose I can stop here. There is a great deal more to be said about Eleanor and about all of us who came under her sway, but for today I am tired and, after what seemed weeks but was less than forty-eight hours, I feel the need to sleep for a long time.

Jessie found that, after all, she had very little to say to Eleanor, because she saw there really was no point. Eleanor, who appeared so sure and so strong, was the one who was, of them all, lost completely. She had left behind the girl she might still have had a chance of holding onto before that day in Sarah's room. And when she started to speak, Jessie's voice softened, not into weakness but into compassion.

"I won't talk for long, Eleanor, so you needn't be worried that I am going to either accuse you or beg you. It has been a long night, and the morning is already half gone, and I have had a great deal of time to think—to listen to Sarah, and to think.

"I have loved you, you know. Most likely I will always love you. I want to feel angry—angry on Sarah's behalf, angry because just by being who you are you deceived me—or, at least, didn't stop me from deceiving myself.

"But it really was my job to separate what I wanted from what there was. And I didn't want to do that. I believe I have learned something in all this. I hope that from now on I will pay closer attention to my life. So I guess I ought to thank you."

A look of confusion crossed Eleanor's face. She did not like the unexpected; she had no way to prepare for it. Anger and pleading were responses for which she had long ago written a script; she was ready for those. The caring, close to pity, with which Jessie addressed her, drew her fire.

"Well, Jess, it does indeed sound as if you and my friend Sarah have had quite a night of it. I assume you have satisfied your mutual need for sympathy? It's no wonder you're tired. I know for certain that Sarah can be long-winded in her reliving of her very sad story."

"Not at all, Eleanor. I was really the one guilty of long-windedness. But, I expect we are all tired. "

Jessie moved to the sofa to sit next to Sarah, to be clearly on her side while Sarah said whatever it was she needed to say to her lover of ten years. But Jessie's night of shattered illusions wasn't quite over. She had faced the hard reality of Eleanor and even understood she had learned something in the process, but one final illusion stood waiting to be exposed. Jessie was preparing to be Sarah's support as Sarah, freed—just as Jessie had been--from the shackles that bound her to Eleanor, described just what she had felt, told Eleanor just how much pain she had inflicted over the years.

Jessie was about to march into battle one more time, saw herself walking right out of there with the newly liberated Sarah. But Sarah simply and quietly looked up at Eleanor and smiled.

"Ellie, I think we could all use a cup of coffee. Jessie was thoughtful enough to bring milk, and I believe we have a bit of sugar. Then we will send for Warren to come to take Jessie home, and you and I will go to bed. We all need some rest."

Warren appeared so quickly one might have thought he had been waiting nearby all night. Jessie drove the carriage slowly on the way home, letting the horses amble, chatting with Warren about the medical supplies they had delivered in the wagon just the morning before, making their plans for the hours they would spend with the soldiers on the weekend. Warren sensed a difference in Jessie who was, for someone who knew her as well as he did, obviously not the same woman he had left here twenty-four hours ago. But he never asked, and it was a long time before Jessie was able to talk about what had happened.

She and Warren were up before dawn on the Saturday. The cart was loaded with all the supplies they had been unable to find room for on Thursday, the horses were comfortably harnessed, and they were on their way to the medical station just as the sun rose on another clear day.

Chapter Fourteen
Mother and Daughter
(Late Spring 1864)

The old row house in Society Hill, where Jessie had grown up, the house that was the only home she had ever known, looked especially lovely on the morning she woke early and knew she was ready to talk about Eleanor and Sarah and that the person she would talk to was her mother. She pulled on her most comfortable dress and, her feet bare, went as quietly as she could down to the kitchen to make a cup of coffee. Gus was sitting at the deal table, hands around her usual large mug of tea, and she looked up and smiled when Jessie walked in.

"Good morning, daughter."

"An excellent good morning, Mother. You are looking either very peaceful or very thoughtful. Or is it possible to be both?" Jessie and Gus, veterans of many domestic crises over the last few years, had developed an easy banter that often started with this kind of rhetorical question. On this occasion, Gus actually had an answer.

"I can testify from my current state of mind that it is," and Gus's smile lit up her face. "I am feeling more peaceful than I have felt in a long time, Jess, and I believe it is because I was thinking about you."

Jessie shook her head slightly, as if to dismiss what her mother had said, and she walked all the way into the room and poured herself a mug of coffee from the pot that someone had already brewed, most likely Alice who recently had been going out for a walk at first light. She pulled out a chair and sat down across from Gus.

"I'm having so many thoughts right now I can barely manage them all but, honestly Mother, the first one is 'How in the world can you have deluded yourself or forgotten the last few years to such an extent that thinking about me gives you peace of mind?' And I mean that as an entirely serious question."

Gus was prepared to take it seriously and she turned her mug around in her hands a few times before she spoke, "I think, Jess, that it is precisely those years, and their effect on you, that bring me what I can only call contentment about you—who you are, what you are doing, who you are becoming, and whatever unknown life waits in the future."

It was Jessie's turn to look into her mug as she considered her response,

"It makes me awfully glad that you can think about me without worrying, but don't give me credit for too much change for the better. I still feel capable of running right off the tracks with the slightest provocation. Sometimes I scare myself with what feels like an endless capacity for rocking the boat."

"But, Jessie, don't you see that's part of it? I have already seen you 'run right off the tracks,' only it turned out not to be that at all. What horrified everybody at the time was exactly the right thing to do, for you and for everyone. I'm talking about Clarke, of course, but also your work with the Friends and then with the soldiers, your relationship with Warren, driving that carriage— every one rocked some boats, and every one was just the right thing."

Jessie got up, set her mug in the sink, straightened a pot that was about to fall off its hook over the stove, stretched her back, then turned around and looked at her mother. "I came downstairs early today, Mother, because I have had an experience that has disturbed me and confused me—and, I have to admit, frightened me--and it has caused me to ask a lot of questions about who I really am and what I really want. And when I woke up I knew that today was the day when I had to talk to someone about it and I also knew there was only one person that could be.

"I must admit I didn't expect you to be sitting here already waiting for me. Is that what being a mother is all about?"

Gus was trying to stop herself from imagining all the terrible experiences that could be described as disturbing and frightening, so it took her a minute to respond with a genuine grin, "I have a feeling you'll know one of these days exactly what being a mother is all about.

"Now, do we need to clear out of the kitchen and find somewhere to talk before Cook shows up?"

"Yes. Yes, we do."

Gus Ashmore had also changed, and one of the most significant shifts was in her feelings about her older daughter. Gus had always loved and respected Jessie, even when they were arguing over appointments with the dressmaker, but what she felt now was a different thing altogether. She often brought to mind images from recent events; she could almost see them: Jessie's calm face when she walked in and found Gus with her journal; Jessie's honesty in answering Gus's questions and her courage in going the very next morning to tell Clarke she couldn't marry him; the compassion and stamina that kept her by Alice's bedside week after week, sitting in one of the hideously uncomfortable chairs Alice had chosen for her rooms, then sleeping on a cot next to the bed, until Alice finally got exasperated.

"For God's sake, Jessie, go to your own room to sleep. You snore!"

And there was Jessie, right at this kitchen table, holding Gus's hand after they had buried Luke, "I miss him." She said it just that way, knowing it was enough. "I miss him, too, Jessie." Gus had become more conscious and more tolerant of just about everyone, but most especially Jessie, who had somewhere during these past two years become a partner in pain. As she prepared herself for another one of Jessie's declarations, she realized that Jessie could tell her anything and it would have no effect except to make her love this child more. "It would be helpful to me, Jess, if you could give me just a hint, some idea about this disturbing event."

"Well, Gus—and when did I start calling you Gus?"

"I believe about thirty seconds ago. Go on, please."

"I suppose it's easiest just to say it is about men and women and sex."

"Now that is my girl. Let's wash up, put on some walking shoes, and—if it suits you—go down to the little park at the end of the neighborhood."

"I sometimes think that little park is at the end of the world, Gus, which makes it just about perfect for the telling of this tale. Shall we meet at the front door in an hour?"

"I can be ready in half an hour if you can, Miss Jessie Ashmore, unless you're determined to tie up corsets and wear five petticoats."

"Half an hour, Mrs. Augusta Ashmore. Half an hour. And without corsets."

The lovely thing about this morning encounter in the quiet kitchen was that, regardless of the ordeal ahead of them, these two Ashmore women had received the great gift of enjoying each other. They were more fortunate, and more unusual, than they knew.

Jessie didn't change the heavy cotton dress she had put on earlier, so she only needed to find the pair of old boots she had always worn on the long walks she and Clarke had taken and a reasonably warm jacket, and she was ready. She found herself actually a few minutes ahead of Gus this time. She took a deep breath, closed her eyes, and whispered, "I'm going to need a little help with this."

Gus came down, already laced into boots and wearing her jacket, and they walked out the door and into a perfect Pennsylvania day. They walked slowly, looking at the familiar houses as they passed them, hearing in the distance the rumble of noise from the Market as vendors arrived and unloaded their produce. Once they arrived at the gate to the park, Jessie led the way and chose the bench that was certain to be in full sun in a few minutes. And they sat. Jessie looked at a sundial that had been cracked and was nearly overtaken with ivy, turned to Gus, and said,

"Eleanor and Sarah are lovers. Eleanor has turned out to be a sort of horrible person who treats Sarah badly. Sarah had an awful childhood and is too weak to leave. And I don't know whether I want to have sex with men or with women."

Gus burst out laughing.

"Jessie, if there were no other reason, I would still keep you around because you can always surprise me. Good Lord in Heaven, what a way to start. Have you been rehearsing that?"

—

"I hope if I had been rehearsing I would have come up with something a little better." And Jessie, too, laughed. "Oh, Gus, where would I be without you?"

And they sat, mother and daughter, through the morning and well into the afternoon, on the bench they had made more comfortable for a while by folding their jackets underneath them. When the sun moved away, they retrieved them and, close together on their bench, they managed to stay warm enough that they didn't leave for home until near dark. The fact was that they weren't eager to leave this place where everything that could be said was said.

Jessie told Gus the whole long story, not just of the one night but of her friendship with Eleanor from the beginning, of her blindness about Eleanor's real nature, especially as she remembered small things that might have told her something if only she had been paying attention. She had clearly relived every minute since she first met Eleanor, and it was at this point that Gus interrupted,

"I suppose it was necessary for you to go back over every detail looking for the clues you missed. But you have done that now, and it's time to stop it. First of all, it is easy to recognize something once we know about it, but much more important, Jess, is that you are looking at Eleanor's relationship with Sarah as all of who Eleanor is, and you know from your friendship with her that just isn't true."

"But how is it possible that I could have seen someone who is capable of that kind of cruelty as not just kind, but as some model of compassion and generosity. I believed everything about Eleanor was good, I watched how she talked to people and you could tell how wonderful she made them feel, and she was always at the Meeting House, volunteering."

Jessie ran out of energy. "I just can't see how I could have been so wrong, and I can't see how anyone could act the way Eleanor acts with Sarah and still act like some saint out in the world."

They were both quiet for a while before Gus spoke again,

"Jess, you can learn something very important now. You have told me you believed Eleanor was entirely, spectacularly good and now you have seen a terribly dark side of her and so you believe she is just as spectacularly bad. And you may trust me entirely about this. There is not one person who is entirely anything. And none of us is exactly the way we appear. That just isn't how we are made. Eleanor might well be an extreme example of those ingredients, but we are all rather messy combinations of the lovely and the really awful.

"I don't think I'm telling you anything you don't already know. You have had the unfortunate experience of seeing the demons in an especially angelic friend and it has hurt you and it has frightened you. But it honestly is just life, writ larger than usual.

—

"You might not believe this today, but I would not be surprised if you were able sometime later, to rebuild that friendship. Only this time you will be making a friendship with a real person.

"I don't know about you but I could use a break and I am so stiff I'm not sure I can stand up. Assuming I can, would you be interested in taking a walk around to one of the other sections of Society Hill? I know you explored just about everywhere when you were younger—yes, I knew your father let you wander around on your own—but there's a corner not too far away that I would like to show you."

"Yes! to an adventure. My brain and my legs could use an airing out." And off they went, arriving not more than fifteen minutes later at a steep incline and a path leading down to what looked to Jessie like abandoned buildings.

"The people who live in those houses, Jess, are of mixed race, the children of white plantation owners and the black women they often raped. In the dreadful and punishing slave system in the South, which itself created the conditions in which this could happen, nonetheless these people—perhaps out of guilt--are folded into the community, sometimes even given special attention by their white fathers. But every once in a while, the mother of one of them will believe that life will be better for her child in the North, that we are somehow different or better people, and so they appear here where, it turns out, that for all our shouting about abolition, we are just like people everywhere. We have no place at all for these children with two strains of blood running in their veins. And when slavery finally ends, and it will, I can guarantee you these beautiful people will be cast out there as well. We human beings do not like what we cannot name or control.

"At some point a few families settled here in Society Hill. I believe it was in the very early days, many years ago. They don't often leave their houses; they grow most of their own food. Over my whole lifetime, I have gotten to know only one old woman down there; they don't trust many people, but she has told me some of her history. One day I will find out if she would let me bring you along."

"Oh, Gus, I would love that. Please try."

Jessie stood, looking down at the cabins, then she turned toward Gus and nodded. She knew why they had come. These people of mixed race were as far as it was possible to be from Eleanor Harrison's reality, and yet they were unfathomable for the same reasons. They couldn't be identified, they were confusing, they disturbed people with unanswerable questions—are they black, are they white? Is she good or is she bad? And Jessie also understood the larger lesson her mother had been determined she learn today: never look at anything—person, relationship, life in general— through only one pair of glasses, and never ever assume that a person is just one way or another.

—

And Gus wasn't just offering a lesson, she was throwing down a challenge to her daughter: have the courage to dive in, to give life a try, even if you can't define it.

"I'm not sure I've grasped it all, Gus, but I think I understand the basics. I think it will take a long time and a great deal of practice to make that shift in how I see things, but I have all the time in the world and I will practice faithfully because what I do see today is how important it is. Thank you."

"You're welcome, Jessie. Now let's be walking. There is a lot more to be said." They turned and headed back to the park.

"If you don't mind, Jess, I would like to talk about your journal. I'm sure you think we've said all we can say on that subject, and I know you have more that you need to say about the relationship between Eleanor and Sarah and the questions it has raised, but I would appreciate your giving me a few minutes before you begin."

Jessie was puzzled but, of course, agreed. They surveyed the park as they came through the gate and chose the only bench that was catching the afternoon sun. Again they rolled their jackets into cushions, and sat.

"I am going to try very hard to keep this short, Jessie, but there is something you should know about your mother. It was reading your journal that made me realize that and especially your description of how it happened, how it started.

I hope you don't mind—I suppose it's too late to worry about it now—but I copied this down so I could read it again to be sure I wasn't just imagining things. I would like to read you what I copied before I tell you a story. I believe I left out a few words, but I wrote what I needed."

And Gus pulled out a crumpled piece of paper and started reading.

"I turned toward him. I saw the fear and the desire in those beautiful eyes, and I could only hold out my arms, I could only answer by moving my mouth against his, I could only protect him by lifting my skirts and pulling him into the secret country of my body."

Jess was watching Gus closely now, nothing more than curiosity in her eyes, a bit of confusion but mostly just real interest in what her mother could have to say about the entry. She remembered their conversation about the journal. Gus didn't seem in the least shocked, so why was she bringing it up again? And on a day already too full of things they needed to discuss.

"That is very much the story of how your brother was conceived. It was in the last stall in the large barn where your father was working as a stable boy. We had met, as you already know, when I was looking for help with a broken wagon wheel. And you know that I was quite taken with Frank and started coming around the barn, helping out, flirting I suppose.

—

"I had really made up my mind almost from that first meeting, but I waited, I was there as much as possible so Frank could get used to me, then I made a plan. I showed up early in the morning on a day I knew almost no one was around, I got your father—who might have expected a kiss and a tickle--into that stall, I took off all my clothes and there we were. I didn't have much faith that I would get pregnant the first time, so I kept right on coming to the barn once a week until I was sure. Then we got married." She stopped, shrugged, and was silent.

"You knew before I was even born about not wearing corsets or undergarments when you're setting out to seduce someone? Did you really, Gus? Oh gracious, do you think that sort of behavior is inherited? Could that have been passed down from mother to daughter, and do you suppose my own daughters will be at risk?"

Jessie laughed until her sides ached. Then she stood up and pulled her mother with her.

"Mrs. Ashmore, could I have the pleasure of this dance?" And the two disgraceful women danced their way to the broken sundial and back. Unfortunately, the park was empty and there was no one to witness the performance.

Jessie understood that her mother had told her the story of the barn for many reasons, but one of them must surely have been that Gus's confession made it easier for Jessie to talk about

Eleanor and Sarah in the most straightforward way. And so she described the first flush of desire when she saw Eleanor standing there in those men's clothes.

"Gus, I confess to you honestly, I wanted to take her to bed right that minute." But Eleanor had been cold and had walked out the door, leaving Jessie with the silent, unhelpful Sarah.

She told Gus about how Sarah had made tea, had listened, and how, finally, she had begun to tell the story of her childhood on the streets and the terrible, unexpected story of her seduction by the fifteen-year-old Eleanor.

But mostly Jessie talked to Gus about her unbearable confusion about her own sexual desires, confessed to Gus that her fantasies about sex with Eleanor or Sarah were just as exciting as her fantasies had been about Clarke. And she was certain, and was honest about that, too, that if she ever did have sex with either of those women, her pleasure would also be the same.

"I can't tell any difference, Gus. As far as I know from what I've felt and experienced, I don't think there would be any difference. What am I supposed to think about that? What am I supposed to do about that?"

There was much that needed saying between Jessie and Gus, and they stayed until nearly dark. When Jess asked these questions, time was already running out and Gus decided there wasn't enough of it for her to stall on addressing her daughter's most pressing question.

"The answer to 'What am I supposed to think?' is to get rid of those words 'supposed to' and get back to what you've learned today, that we are all about half black and half white and that can be a struggle, but looking away from it doesn't change it.

"As to what you are supposed to do, I would like to say do what is in your heart. But it isn't that simple. You also have to answer that question in a practical way. For no better reason than its existence, the life that Eleanor and Sarah have is a hidden life. Life is hard, Jessie, and a hidden life is twice as hard. So when you are thinking, don't think so much about who you are but about what you will decide to do.

"And I hope that makes at least a grain of sense."

"It makes a great deal of sense, Gus, all the sense in the world. For a while, I am going to try hard to just *be* who I am instead of thinking about it, and as for what I will do, I don't have time to 'do' anything other than to get up before dawn, ride in that crazy milk wagon with Warren, and help out with the soldiers.

"So, I expect I'm safe for now from the temptation to take up the hidden life just to prove a point."

They smiled and headed home. It had been a most satisfactory day.

Chapter Fifteen
The Captain
(Summer 1864)

Not too long after she and Gus talked all day in the park, Jessie and Warren got their usual early start and spent another morning unloading supplies. There was always a need and many items, like syringes, were hard to find, but Warren seemed to have an unlimited number of sources who could get them. They worked together comfortably, their routine developed over time. With little need to talk, Warren started wrestling the heaviest containers out of the cart, and into stacks that would be moved later when he could find another man to help him. Jessie, pleased to have learned to drive just about anything pulled by horses, waved back at Warren and walked across the large field to the area most crowded with soldiers who were waiting, alone or in groups, for whatever treatment was available for their particular injuries. She often ran into Clarke, who spent more hours there than she did.

"Clarke, you can't be here again? Surely, with everything you are managing right now—a thorough analysis and an article for the journals about Alice, in addition to the fact that you are about to marry her—you have earned a few days off. And what about the planning for the Big Event? I realize that most of that falls to the bride, but I'm hoping you will jump in. I know that

Mother gets overwhelmed easily and panics early, and it's chaos."

Jessie didn't know when she and Clarke had finally shed the last bit of awkwardness between them. It was might have started after Alice was getting better and Clarke was coming to the house every day, or when Clarke finally proposed and Alice accepted, or even when they had discovered this common cause in caring for the soldiers. Whenever it was, now when they met they were always genuinely pleased to see each other and usually took the time for some conversation.

But Jessie was mindful of Warren and soon headed back to help with the unloading of the smaller boxes, most of which she could handle easily. After nearly a year of hard physical work, there wasn't much that she couldn't do, and she was proud of having muscles in places where proper young ladies didn't. She also didn't miss the irony of the golden brown skin on her face, neck, and forearms. She remembered how shocked she had been by Sarah's tan the first time she saw her. Thinking about Sarah and Eleanor, Jessie still found it hard to imagine that cauldron of conflicting emotions and needs in which these two women loved and hated and tortured and comforted each other year after year. She had no response other than the response she had always had when she saw what she considered unacceptable lives,

"There has to be something else, or different, something better. I am going to wait it out and, if it doesn't come along, then I think I can make a good life on my own."

"Warren, do you think you could ever find a young man who would be a better driver or a stronger worker than I am? Be honest now; don't humor me. I want to know where my weaknesses lie, so I can correct them."

"I know you are only half serious, Jess, but you'll forgive me for being completely serious for a minute. First of all, you have asked the wrong question. I can find muscles anywhere, but there is never going to be anyone who is a better partner for me than you have been.

"Are you applying for a job, young lady?"

"You know, Warren, I might be. I might very well be."

Jessie and Warren, as they did at least three days a week, worked side-by-side until late in the afternoon, doing what they could for the wounded soldiers and sitting down to talk to the widows who seemed on some days to be haunting the place. On this particular Saturday, there was an overflow of wounded men from the time they arrived, and just when they were ready to pack up and head back to Society Hill, a large open wagon carrying no fewer than twenty men, pulled up next to them, almost too close. They could see that these soldiers had just come from a battle and, from the looks of them, a pretty bad one. Jessie saw arms hanging loose from the elbow or missing altogether; blood-soaked bandages wrapped tightly around bulging eyes; deep neck wounds that looked as if they should have severed the heads above them.

"I don't think we can leave now, Warren, do you?"

"No, and I don't think we should plan on getting home any time tonight. Let's introduce ourselves to the gentleman whose uniform, under all that dirt, suggests he's the captain, then get started. It's one wound, and one soldier at a time, and we'll get through them all."

"Yes. Let's get started."

Jessie was eager to begin her work, and she didn't notice Captain Patrick Hastings at all, other than as the person they had to speak to in order to begin examining, bathing, and treating the soldiers in the large wagon. She saw a good many soldiers, of all ranks, in the course of a typical week, and they had all begun to look alike. Her attention was on their injuries, physical and emotional, and on what she could do to help them. There just wasn't time for anything beyond that.

What did get her attention was the relationship this officer seemed to have with his men—just the right balance of an easy informality--they called him "Cap'n Paddy,"--and the formality and respect demanded any time he issued a command or even made a suggestion. It was clear, in fact, that the soldiers liked their captain and that he liked them just as much. Jessie didn't think that kind of attachment was common in the army. She did notice that, and she liked it, but she couldn't have described Hastings even minutes after they met, and by evening she had forgotten him altogether.

From Jessie's Journal
First Impressions of the Captain
I suppose I didn't altogether forget him, the captain whose name I did in fact forget if I was even paying enough attention to hear it in the first place. I do remember looking over to where he was standing by that wagon full of his men, talking to them steadily, but not just talking. He was touching them, touching without hesitation the bloody legs, the arms dangling from their sockets, reaching up to wipe a trail of blood or mucus or maybe tears from the face of a soldier who had lost an eye. And I have the image behind my eyes now of the faces of those soldiers looking at him. I saw what I would have expected to see in the eyes of wounded men-- confidence, certainly, and trust, but I also saw something else. I saw affection. Oh, for goodness sake! When did I get so hesitant? What I saw was love. And love where I least expected it—at this outpost on the way back from the killing fields.

They were at it all night, as Warren had predicted. Some of the men had superficial wounds and those they washed, examined quickly, bandaged, and sent along to someone who could find them a place to sleep for a few hours. Others, those whose injuries were severe and would require professional attention, possibly surgery, were stripped, bathed thoroughly, their wounds dressed, and referred to whatever doctor was available.

On this particular night one of those doctors was Clarke who, like Jessie, had taken in the situation when the wagon arrived, and had decided he couldn't leave.

As the sun came up, Jessie looked around and saw that they had taken the best care they could of most of the soldiers who had been waiting and had, in fact, dealt with every injured man on the wagon that she noticed still sat too close. It had been a good day's work, and Jessie was pleased. She saw Clarke, pulling on a light jacket against the morning chill, walking toward her deep in conversation with the captain from the wagon.

It would be difficult to imagine a more inauspicious meeting than the one between Jessie Ashmore and Captain Patrick Hastings. Clarke and the captain, still talking, nearly ran into Jessie who had turned back to the wagon and was rolling up the last of the unused gauze to put away for tomorrow's wounds. Hastings stopped just short of Jessie's back, close enough to get her attention, and he gave her a wink and his best grin.

"I don't know about Doctor Stanbury here, whose acquaintance I have just made, but I owe you an apology, miss. It's hard to know what two men could find to talk about that would explain almost walking right into a beautiful woman. I am very sorry. And sorry again for the lack of manners—my name is Patrick Hastings and I am in charge of that wagon full of wounded men that drove up practically on top of you last night."

Jessie was temporarily stunned by the non-stop flow of words, but when she listened to the quaint formality of the little speech, she was suddenly sure that the Captain was giving a performance, mostly for his own benefit, and was enjoying it immensely. And behind that unconvincing wink, she sensed he was laughing at himself. She didn't yet know that this complex dance was something he had developed early in life to remain sane and reasonably cheerful through hard times, and that it was currently serving him well after a long day of tending the men in his care and watching three of them die. Captain Hastings didn't much like this war.

Jessie had some practice at this kind of banter and had developed her own skills. "Captain Hastings, I also owe an apology for standing just on the spot where you and Doctor Stanbury were walking and for not introducing myself the minute I realized what a roadblock I presented. I am Jessie Ashmore, Captain, and I am honored to make the acquaintance of a man who looks very much like a hero." That last was spoken more seriously than Jessie had intended.

—

Very few people surprised or caught Patrick Hastings off guard, but Miss Jessie Ashmore had succeeded in doing both, and on the basis of a ten-minute acquaintance. He gave her a long, hard look, but he couldn't quite make up his mind about what she was doing. It didn't seem possible that this young woman had watched him walk across a field, heard him say a few nonsensical words, and seen right though him. In Patrick Hastings' world, that wasn't possible.

Chapter Sixteen
Alice and Clarke

From Jessie's Journal
About Alice and Clarke

It was no surprise to me that Clarke was very interested in Alice. Anyone who was paying any attention at all would have known; in fact, I believe even Gus and Frank had guessed long before Clarke came to ask their permission to propose. Incidentally, since our long day in the park, I have called Mother nothing but Gus and we both seem as comfortable with it as if I had never called her anything else. I am currently practicing to see how Frank sounds before I try it out on Father. I can sense the day is coming, though. The oddest things seem to be changing all around me.

Alice Morris Ashmore, my sister, younger by four years, has always been a bit of a puzzle. On the surface, and especially to anyone who didn't know her well, Alice never appeared to be much of a mystery. She was typically pretty, vain, flighty and flirtatious, crazy for clothes and men, not someone in whom you would expect melancholy. But there didn't seem to be anything I could do. I did try to talk to her a few times but it just made her angry and so I stopped. I wish to goodness I hadn't stopped, no matter what, because I watched things get worse with her, watched her little fidgets in the chair, her little trips to the dressmaker, escalate and become night after night of parties, mostly with people she hardly knew, and I heard the talk about

—

her, about how she was pushing herself in where she wasn't wanted and was being laughed at and talked about. People thought she was looking for a man.

And then on that terrible night, she found one—and just the wrong one. And she was raped and beaten and left bleeding and nearly mad at our door, and I for one didn't think she was ever going to come out of her room. She allowed me to sit with her for many weeks before she just threw me out, and she always was happy when Clarke came, but she was hidden up there for a long time. I remember the day Gus heard her laughing with Cook in the kitchen. We didn't even know she had come downstairs. But there she was. And everything has gotten better every day since then. Alice has survived. Alice is getting well. Alice is going to marry Clarke.

And that is all splendid news. The only problem for me is that this Alice is a stranger. She is not just changed; she is an entirely different person. The foolishness is gone, and that was to be expected. But the sadness, the melancholy is gone, too. I hardly know how to describe it. It's as if several layers have been stripped away and the person left underneath is calm, quiet—and, yes, I do know those sound like grand things, but somehow they aren't all that grand. Anyway, I am writing myself around in a circle and getting nowhere. Alice is better in important ways.

She is still pretty but her prettiness is deeper, and she is a much kinder, less selfish, more focused Alice—she can stand in that kitchen kneading bread for an hour. She is still Alice, or I think that she is. She just isn't my Alice anymore. And so, she is going to marry Clarke, and that is another thing. Because although Clarke will no longer be mine, he is still Clarke, and that is more understandable. I realize I am being entirely selfish, as I always have been about Clarke; I just didn't know I would feel the loss of Alice so keenly.

I am happy for them both, and especially grateful and pleased that Clarke seems completely devoted to this Alice. Because I see that this new Alice is really the only Alice Clarke has ever known well. I suppose he noticed Alice all those times he came to see me, but I don't believe they ever even had a conversation.

So they only actually met each other in any serious way after the terrible night, and Clarke was the only person Alice could stand to have in her room—Clarke, who was almost a stranger, Clarke who hadn't known that other Alice at all, Clarke who didn't think she was foolish or selfish or hunting a man, who didn't even think she was sad. He just thought she was Alice.

I believe they will be happy, these two. I believe Clarke will take very good care of Alice wh,o no matter how much better she is, will always be wounded, and funnily enough, I believe Alice will also take very good care of Clarke, who is also much better and who is also wounded.

—

On the morning after Clarke spoke with Jessie in the park and with Gus and Frank, securing to his satisfaction the blessing of the whole family, he reappeared at the row house in Society Hill, a house that was more familiar to him than anywhere had ever been in his wandering life, entered without knocking, and walked down to the kitchen to talk to Cook. It was early and Cook had just lit the fire from last night's embers and started the coffee, when Clarke tapped lightly—on Cook's door he did knock—and walked in. Cook looked up, gave him her biggest smile, and scolded.

"Doctor Stanbury, I was beginning to think I was going to have to hear about this marriage from the neighbors. You have arrived just in time to avoid making me mad."

"Well, I can tell you one thing, Cook. I would do a great deal to avoid making you mad. I am glad I got here in time. Now tell me. How is it you know about a marriage when I have not yet asked the young lady in question for her hand?"

"I expect, Doctor, although I can't be sure, that this is the sort of information that just floats around in the air when the young lady in question has been waiting for her suitor to get around to the asking."

"Do you think, then, that I should just skip the asking and go upstairs, tell her to get dressed, and drive her right over to the church? If we took our time—say as much time as I have taken to ask—then I expect you and Gus and Frank would have time to invite the neighbors in for the post-wedding feast. In fact, that sounds like a much more practical plan, don't you think?"

"What I think, Doctor Stanbury, is that you should probably stop talking to me and turn around and do some fast proposing." Cook laughed loudly as Clarke whipped around to find Alice standing in the doorway with a lovely smile on her face.

"Well, Alice, even though I am late and slow and everyone in the world seems to already know about this, will you consider marrying me anyway?"

Alice stood looking at Clarke almost long enough to make him nervous. Her face was serious and her eyes never wavered from his. He had never seen her quite like this. He was just about to ask if she was feeling alright, when she answered in a clear voice, "Yes, Clarke. Yes, I will marry you. Yes, of course I will."

Now that she was out of her bed, down every day, dressed, still spending most days with Cook but little by little starting to go out—to Market Street to buy vegetables or to walk with Clarke or even to call on neighbors—now that she was pronounced "getting better every day," now that she was about to be a wife, Alice wondered what everyone had thought all those months she lay in her bed, hardly talking at all, eating very little, refusing all efforts to comfort, to help, to cheer her up. Did they think she would die? Did they believe she had been driven mad by what that man had done to her?

She recalled hearing that somewhere years ago—that women who were raped went crazy and were never the same again, if they survived at all. She had also heard, unfortunately, that a proper lady would have been so ashamed of what had happened that she would simply turn her face to the wall and perish. Well, Alice Morris Ashmore made up her mind very early that she would do no such thing. She might have been a foolish girl with too many dresses and not enough sense, but she was also a great deal tougher than anyone suspected, and she intended to rise right up from this dreadfulness, and surprise them all by being neither ashamed nor mad.

Clarke and Alice didn't leave the kitchen that day until late in the morning. They sat at the old table and talked to Cook. Clarke told Cook how he had first known he was caring about Alice in a way that didn't have anything to do with his concerns as a doctor or even as a friend of the family, but as a man. He wasn't blind, he said, so of course he was aware of how pretty Alice was, but it was one day when she wasn't even looking her best, when she had started getting out of bed and sitting in her big chair by the window, and he had knocked and come in on a day he wasn't expected. It was not one of the regularly scheduled days for him to check on her health.

Anyway, in he walked and there sat Alice in the worst-looking dressing gown he had ever seen.

He thought it must have come from the rubbish heap. And her hair was dirty and tangled and her skin was blotched, and she was clearly not in a good mood and very annoyed to see him, and Clarke knew he was in love with her. It was love, and he had felt that for Jessie as he might never for anyone else. This was so very different because he knew, as he hadn't with Jessie, that this was not only love, it was exactly the right love for him.

Then Cook turned to Alice who shrugged and smiled and said,

"Oh for goodness' sake. I knew the first time he came to my room after I was attacked. Then it was only a matter of getting well, and waiting."

Suddenly Cook screamed, "You two have done it now! It is one hour until lunch has to be on the table, and I believe Mrs. Ashmore has invited two of her friends from the neighborhood to join us. I have not put one thing on to cook, and I've gotten so distracted thinking about this marriage I don't even have any ideas.

"Doctor Stanbury, I want you out of my kitchen.

"Alice, you get an apron on and then look in the pantry and anywhere else you can think of and let's see if we can get a meal together.

"Doctor, out! Oh, and congratulations

From Alice's Diary
My Life

I know that Jessie has kept a journal for years. I even once looked at it, when we were younger, but it hasn't ever really been something I wanted to do. I mean, how could you just write about what you do every day? All I ever did anyway was have dresses made and go to little parties in the neighborhood and flirt with boys and then I tried to do the parties and boys thing when I got a little older and that turned out badly. I think I did it all the wrong way.

Well, really, I'm pretty sure I did it all the wrong way. I know Jessie sometimes couldn't keep herself from commenting about my going out to all those parties and I always got furious with her when she tried to talk to me about it, and finally she just gave up on me. Or maybe she didn't give up. Maybe she just couldn't think of anything else to do.

I'll bet Jessie wishes the same thing I do— that we could go back and say or do things differently so that Jack Crestfield. Yes, I can write that name now and it doesn't kill me, and I think that just writing it occasionally for practice will get me so used to it that one day it won't bother me at all. I know that if I could go back, I would listen to Jess, take her advice—even if I didn't agree—and then it wouldn't have happened. And I imagine I'm right when I think that Jessie wishes she hadn't stopped telling me, warning me, saying how foolish I was being. And I can't speak for Jess, but when I think about it and want it to have been different I realize that it couldn't have been because I was the girl I was and that girl could only have done what I did, regardless.

For as long as I could remember I was what Mother calls "fidgety." I just could not sit still. She finally almost gave up taking me out anywhere when I was about eleven or twelve; she even mostly quit taking me to church. I bounced my legs and twiddled my fingers and squirmed around in my chair. I'm sure it was enough to drive anyone sitting near me to get up and leave. But sometime before I turned seventeen something started changing. I got what seems to me a lot worse crazy than I have been since "it" happened—why can't we all just say what it was instead of calling it "the terrible thing" or "Alice's horrible experience"? It was rape. I didn't have a "terrible thing" happen to me. I was raped, repeatedly, and I was beaten— before the rape, during the rape, and after the rape.

So before I was raped, something started changing and the fidgets got worse and I wanted out of this house and out I went. And I just could not stop myself from any single thing I did. And now suddenly I'm in the "after the rape" stage, and it's as if a scarf has been thrown over my head and muffles all sound and blurs my vision so everyone looks a little hazy, like there's this halo around them.

—

Clarke came into my life just when that scarf was dropping down over my head and he couldn't stop it but he watched it drop and when he was with me he had a way of lifting it right up high enough to uncover my eyes and my ears. So Clarke was never blurry or muffled. He was the one part of my world that was crystal clear. And that is why I must love him and that is why I must marry him because if I don't I believe the world will drift away and I will stop breathing.

I am about to spend more time with Mother and Jessie than I have ever in my life, except when I was a little girl and Jessie stayed in my room a lot and she made up stories to tell me and sometimes she would stay until I went to sleep. I remember I liked that. But now I will be with her and with Mother to plan a huge lovely wedding. And I get to climb into our carriage, accompanied by these two women I love, and be driven to the dressmaker's to look at wonderful fabrics and decide on a pattern and order my wedding dress. I have to admit I am very excited about the dress.

Chapter Seventeen
Patrick Wyndham Hastings, Captain
Army of the United States of America

In any other kind of war, Patrick Wyndham Hastings most likely would never have made the rank of Captain. He had showed up late, wasn't good at following directions, and had an attitude that made most situations worse. Physically, he was too short and too slight to have been promoted. But Patrick Hastings was fearless, an excellent marksman, and there was about him something that drew men to him and kept them loyal. Everyone knew that Hastings was difficult, and everyone knew that Hastings would be a great Captain.

On the day that Jessie met him at the medical station, Patrick Hastings—called Paddy, not just by the men in his troop but also by the owner of the general store where he apprenticed as a young boy and by a few of the customers who especially liked him—was twenty-nine years old. Jessie was twenty-four. Jessie was born and grew up in a prosperous family with a father who had worked his way up from an apprenticeship in a sweat shop to the ownership of one the finest and most well-respected tailoring shops in the city. Her mother ran the household, did volunteer work around the city, and was devoted to her family; she and Jessie had grown close. Jessie had grown up with many dresses as she needed or even wanted, a Cook who adored the family, a sister and a brother, both of whom—although they were certainly not without their problems—loved and respected her.

****

Almost ready for the trip home, Jessie turned to Warren.

"I'll tell you one thing, Warren, I am beginning to believe you when you keep insisting you're not old. You surely have got more stamina than I can even imagine. How in the world do you stay up all night, tending to those men, one after another, with no breaks, and then come strolling back across the field in casual conversation with some officer you hardly know? And now you've done most of the work loading the wagon while I sit here trying to stay awake. I hope you're not planning to drive us home."

"I hadn't given it a lot of thought, but if you're having trouble staying awake, who exactly do you think *is* going to drive us?

"Because I can say one thing for certain. However I get there, I intend to get home, take off these terrible clothes, wash as fast as I can, and get into my bed. I intend to do that today. So you let me know when you've figured this out. But don't take long, because in about another two minutes you'll see me climbing up and getting ready to leave."

"Oh, honestly, Warren. I am going to drive us home. I drive faster than you do, and I want to get started soaking this dirt off before I collapse. Let's get going."

Just as Jessie was pulling on her gloves and gathering up the reins, Patrick Hastings walked around the side of the carriage.

"Miss Ashmore? Jessie, is it? I was wondering if you and Warren were planning to be here working any other days this week."

Jessie looked at Warren, who said, "I expect we'll need about twenty-four hours of rest, Paddy, but then I'd guess Jessie here won't be able to stay away so I'd say we'll be back. Hope to see you if you're still around. It couldn't hurt for you to take a couple of days before going back to the fighting."

"Thanks, Warren. I hope to be able to do that.

"Jessie. Drive safely and get this old man home. You two take care, now." And after that peculiar exchange, the Captain turned and walked off across the field. Jessie flicked the reins, spoke softly to the horses, and they were out on the road and on their way. Neither Jessie nor Warren had a word to say until they had been driving a while.

When Paddy Hastings was not yet a year old, his father, James Wyndham Hastings, was killed in an accident at one of the rough jobs he took for a week or two, just to keep bread on the table. Patrick's mother, Clementine, who had some skill as a seamstress, was left the sole provider for three children: Patrick, the baby; a sister who was three; and an older boy who was around ten. Her husband, a man of great charm but little ambition, didn't have much money when he was alive and certainly left none for his family when he died.

At first Clementine must have believed she could manage. For weeks after her husband died, friends and neighbors, men who had worked with him, perfect strangers from a local church, all came by bringing food and bags full of hand-me-down clothes for the children. They stayed and warmed the casseroles, washed up after meals, even cleaned the house when they saw that Clementine wasn't able to do it while she was trying to get the word out that she would take in sewing in her home. The word did get out, but Mifflin County was a rural area, with a large population of Amish and Mennonites, and the number of women who could afford to use a seamstress was small and, even when nearly all of them were bringing baskets of sewing to Clementine, the money was nowhere near what was needed to take care of those children.

Patrick Hastings almost worshipped his mother. In his mind she was the shining example of pure womanhood, thrown upon hard times, working her fingers to the bone for the sake of her children, always sacrificing, always loving. It was possible that the older children, especially Patrick's brother, would tell a different tale, but the siblings were no longer in contact with each other. Patrick didn't know where his brother was, and his sister was married to a millworker in Philadelphia, a city big enough that they never needed to see each other unless one or the other pursued it. Neither did.

Finally, after they had been driving for several miles, Jessie concentrating on handling the horses at a slightly faster speed than they were accustomed to, Warren couldn't hold his tongue. He was trying not to sound too amused.

"Jessie, I do understand this is none of my business, but I could not avoid noticing that the Captain seemed to be expressing an interest in seeing you again.

"Would you agree?"

"In the first place, it's as much your business as anyone's since it was you who made friends with the man and came strolling back to the wagon with him. And to answer your question, *Warren*, I frankly have no idea what the Captain was expressing. You know very well that I am not one to insist on the niceties. But correct me if I'm wrong. Did your Captain just come right out and call me Jessie?"

"I believe he did, Jess, and I am beginning to detect that my Captain has gotten under your skin just a bit. I haven't seen you this agitated in a while. Good sign, I'd say, if anyone were to ask. Excellent indication.

"And I think a long hot soak is probably a good plan. What day are you thinking about going back with more supplies? I think I can put my hands on bandages and some syringes."

"I have no idea what day. Oh, well, I don't know, Warren. Let's say the day after tomorrow. Unless you can get those supplies later today." Jessie's look suggested that it would be wise for Warren not to reply.

Patrick's older brother, ten at the time of his father's death, was the first to go. By the time he was twelve, Clementine had realized the futility of her efforts to support herself and her children, and she apprenticed him to a local shoemaker for a period of fifteen years. He would have been twenty-seven when his apprenticeship ended, but he ran away at the age of eighteen. Clementine never heard from him again. Patrick's sister, only three when James Hastings died, wasn't apprenticed until she was eight. Clementine let her daughter pack a small suitcase full of her favorite things, and together they made the long trip into Philadelphia. She found an advertisement for an apprentice to a seamstress, and when they got there she saw it was a clean and successful business. The seamstress herself spoke kindly to the little girl and gave her a ball of thread to hold. Clementine left her daughter there, having signed an agreement for a twenty-year term of service.

When his brother left for his apprenticeship, Patrick was two. When his sister went to Philadelphia, Patrick was five. He was only eight when his brother disappeared altogether. Patrick had Clementine all to himself until, when he was twelve, he was sent as an apprentice to the owner of the general store where he stayed, working at every job in the place, until he left for California at the age of twenty-one in search of wealth in the goldmines. The year was 1856. He didn't return to Pennsylvania until 1861, the first year of the Civil War. When he joined the army and headed south, he was concerned that he might be killed and he wanted to be sure his mother would be taken care of, so he left his earnings from the goldmines—and from selling California timber when the weather didn't encourage mining—with the man with whom he had spent nine years, the owner of the general store. The money amounted, at that time, to about a thousand dollars.

Warren wasn't sure how he felt about the war, the Friends' tradition of peace in all circumstances, any of the big questions, but he had no doubt about doing everything he possibly could for those boys coming home bleeding, missing arms or legs, some of them half mad. No doubts about that, and no doubts about this unlikely friendship with Jessie. For her, as for those soldiers, there was no limit to what he was willing to do. Right now, it seemed possible that what he could do for Jessie was to get her back to the medical station to spend a little more time with Captain Patrick Hastings. Warren had a feeling about this. On his way out, he stopped by the house.

"Alright, Miss Ashmore. I'm on my way to hunt up more supplies, should be back by late afternoon. I'm thinking tomorrow morning early we can head back. Will that suit you?"

"It will suit me admirably well, Mr. Griggs. I will see you at the stable before dawn." The two friends were smiling with pleasure at the prospect of another day together, and they both were thinking about the possibilities of seeing Hastings again.

The morning was overcast and chilly, and the dark sky threatened rain. Jessie arrived at the barn before six o'clock, wearing a heavy cable-knit sweater over her oldest dress and a rain cape of her father's that she had grabbed on impulse on her way out the door. She could only pray that it wasn't one of those wardrobe items of Father's about which he was protective. This one would never be the same after a day in the mud and rain. She shivered.

"Good morning, Warren. I suppose we should be grateful that the gardens are getting watered or the tiny birds are finding flowers filled with water for drinking or some nonsense like that?"

"I have found on occasion that a bit of hard labor takes that chill right away. I would be more than willing to share a bit of this loading with you."

"I get the point. Let's get it finished up and head out. We can be unloading by seven o'clock if we step it up.

"Besides, I did promise Captain Hastings I would look after a certain old man and I know you are much happier when you're on the way."

"That's grand, Jess, and I appreciate your concern. I will point out, however, and I do intend to be keeping track, that you were the first person to mention Hastings' name, and before sunrise— should there be such a thing today."

"Climb up, Warren. Would you mind driving?"

"No. No, of course not. Let's head out." Warren immediately detected the change in tone. It was unusual for Jessie to ask him to drive and now he thought about it her asking was almost always after something upsetting had happened. And besides the request, there was also a change in her voice. She had suddenly become serious and thoughtful. They were familiar enough with each other by now that Warren knew to just leave her alone.

They pulled into the end of the field where most people parked their vehicles and, as they were about to begin the unloading, Warren put his hand on Jessie's arm. "I am going to assume, Jess, that if something is wrong you will tell me."

"Nothing is wrong at all. I am just all of a sudden finding I need to think over some things. It's my usual, Warren. I'm thinking about what I can do to change my life. Why I want to change my life is the real question. I'm happy. I am, in fact, happier, more content than I think I have ever been. Why am I walking around thinking of all the possible options I have for changing that?"

"I expect it has something to do with turning over apple carts, Jess. Some people do that, and I'm afraid you're one of those people.

"And take a look behind you. I believe we have a coffee delivery."

Sure enough, Patrick Hastings was walking toward them, carefully balancing three steaming cups of coffee. When he got closer, Jessie could see milk had been added. She was plunged into the night at Eleanor and Sarah's, an evening that had started with her arrival with milk for their tea. With some effort, she shook it off.

"Goodness, Captain Hastings. This is what I consider service of the finest order. I am both impressed and truly grateful. A cup of hot coffee has seldom looked or smelled so delicious. May I relieve you of a part of your burden?"

Jessie reached for one of the large, cracked, stoneware mugs, and she found herself looking up and directly into a pair of eyes that were fixed intently on her face. There was just that flicker of seriousness during which Jessie took the mug, unable to look away, and Hastings said,

"Jessie, it would mean a great deal to me if you were willing to call me Patrick, or Paddy—whichever suits you. It would mean a great deal."

The moment passed, Jessie looked away, then with a face defined by a smile that reached all the way to her eyes and wrinkled the skin around them, she said, simply,

"Patrick, I would be honored, and I do thank you again for the coffee."

For the rest of the morning, until early afternoon, Jessie and Patrick and Warren worked together taking care of the steady stream of soldiers who straggled in through the increasingly bad weather. Not more than an hour past mid-day, the rain started, slow at first, then turning into a steady downpour with heavy winds. The three volunteers looked at each other and reached a mutual agreement, without a word spoken, to stop for the day. They raced toward their two wagons, holding anything they could find over their heads, arriving in spite of it, drenched nearly to the skin.

Jessie turned to look at Hastings and without a breath of hesitation, said,

"Patrick, there is no question about this. We have plenty of room and you must come right back with us. Warren, I am going to insist on something that is going to make you uncomfortable, that you are not going to like, that might disturb you, and to which you will say an absolute 'no.' Before you expend the energy, I'll warn you that I won't accept any answer other than 'yes,' and that any time you spend arguing will be time wasted.

"That said, gentlemen, here is the afternoon's plan. We are all going back to Society Hill. We will take care of the horses and get them settled. From there you two will get dry clothes from Warren's extensive wardrobe, and, finally, we all—all of us, Warren—are going to my house where we will take full advantage of the several baths. Each of us will have a tub of hot water and unlimited time for soaking, refills provided as needed. We will then dry off, come downstairs, relax in one of the sitting rooms, light a fire, drink something hot and strong, and have a rest and a visit. If we are not in the mood for chatting, I can provide newspapers and books. Cook will find us something for dinner, then you two can go back to Warren's and climb into bed or stay up all night gossiping.

Get into the wagon. I am driving."

Both Warren and Hastings climbed aboard without a word and Jessie drove them home.

The rest of the day went according to Jessie's impromptu plan, and the three exhausted workers actually allowed Cook to bring them an early dinner on trays so they never left their chairs in the parlor. About halfway through the meal, Gus walked in, greeted Warren as if he had his dinner in her parlor every evening, then held out her hand and introduced herself to Hastings. In a strange way, it all seemed perfectly natural.

"Are you here for long, Captain, or are you rushing back south?"

"I'm afraid I have word that I am expected back the day after tomorrow, so I am especially indebted to you and your daughter for providing me with the rest and nourishment that will make my journey easier. I will get a few hours' sleep with Warren, then venture out in the morning to find a horse and head south as fast as I can."

Gus didn't hesitate, "Captain Hastings, we would all consider it a great honor if you would allow us to do this small thing for the Union cause and provide you with a horse from our stable. I believe Jessie and Warren have their favorites, and Warren can show you those. I'm afraid if you took my daughter's horse, she would be tearing after you."

Hastings smiled. "I don't believe I would mind having Jessie tearing after me, though I do get your point. Those probably wouldn't be ideal circumstances."

"I expect I won't see you again, Captain. Have a good ride and do what you can to see this war to an end."

"My every effort is toward that, Mrs. Ashmore. I am not by nature a warrior, and I will be very glad to be done with fighting."

Soon after they had eaten, and Warren and Patrick had insisted on taking the trays back to the kitchen, Warren stood up, stretched, and announced that he was heading home, that Patrick knew where he was and was free to come in any time as long as he did it quietly. In a peculiar day, among the most peculiar details was the fact that they all seemed to have taken this for granted and Jessie and Patrick never uttered a word to object. Patrick stood up, shook Warren's hand, and thanked him. Jessie walked over and gave him a hug.

Patrick and Jessie settled back into the two armchairs that faced each other in front of the fireplace. The room was warm and, when the young maid came in to add logs to the fire, Jessie asked her just to stack them to the side in case they needed them later.

"I am most grateful to you for inviting me into your home in this way."

"And you are most welcome, Patrick. It has been a pleasure and I know Warren has enjoyed it, too. I sometimes worry that he spends all his time with me or working and seems to have no time for a life outside our family."

"My impression of Warren, and of your family—none of whom I know well enough to remark as I'm about to—is that all of you are very satisfied with things as they are. I know Warren is quiet, but don't you believe he would have spoken up or just moved on years ago if that weren't the case?"

"I hadn't thought of it that way at all, but yes, yes I think he would have. So you have put my mind to rest."

Patrick sat without speaking and when he looked up at Jessie his tone had changed. "I would like to speak about something that will most likely rob you of your peace of mind, Jessie, and I wonder if I may have your permission to begin."

The pauses were getting longer, but finally Jessie answered. "I believe I would like to hear at least the beginning of what you want to say."

"You don't know me at all, Jess, and I would like to tell you a little about my life."

Patrick spoke quietly but without hesitation as he told Jessie about his childhood, the apprenticeship, the years of living rough in California. He didn't know quite why, but he had known it was time to come home. When he got there, he found the war going strong. He spoke of his great love and concern for his mother should he be killed down south. He told her about the money from the goldmines that he had left with a friend for safekeeping.

"But here's the thing, Jessie. Here's what happens on the day this war is over. When I was in California, there was weather that made mining for gold unproductive and during those seasons we would cut down certain trees, strip them, and sell them to lumber yards. We made a lot of money with that very disorganized effort. And in the process, I learned quite a bit about timber.

"In the area down south where I have been stationed for the whole time I've served there are rich groves of trees of a remarkable variety, and they are just there for the picking. I would need to start with one really fine sawmill and some canals dug to get the trees—I guess I didn't mention that many of them are in the middle of a deep swamp—anyway, to float those trees out of the swamp, headed toward the big water.

"I'm hoping to come back to Pennsylvania, collect my money from the mines, and return to the Tidewater region of Virginia to start building that first sawmill and cutting trees. I aim to build an empire, Jessie, a lumber empire. I intend to have sons to take it over after I'm gone."

Jessie was excited just thinking about the adventure Patrick Hastings had ahead of him. She was genuinely pleased for him,

"I am thrilled just listening, Patrick. What a splendid dream, or-it really does sound more like a splendid plan-and I wish you well and more than well. Although I will admit to just the smallest amount of envy."

"Not much need for that, Jessie. If you could see your way clear to it, I would like very much for you to come with me."

And it was out. Right in front of them. "I might as well get the rest of it out, Jessie, then you can ask me to leave, if you like, and I couldn't blame you." And without allowing Jessie time for any response, he continued.

"I am going to be an unwelcome guest in the city that my troops and I occupied for four years. And not only an unwelcome guest, but a guest who doesn't intend to leave because he is there to cut down and sell all the timber he can get his hands on, and to get rich doing it. I am going to make people angry. So I will need a wife who can smooth out a few of my rougher edges, apologize for me when necessary, and generally charm the very people I am offending."

Jessie started to interrupt but he held up his hand, "In addition to getting rich and building that lumber empire, I have plans for a different kind of empire, I think it's called a dynasty. I want children, Jessie, lots of children, a half dozen at least. So I'm going to need a wife who is physically up to the job but also one who will be sure they are raised with good values and that they have reasonably clean clothes for school."

"Are you willing to take a short breath to let me respond just to your main points?" Patrick nodded his consent.

"I want to be perfectly clear as to what you are saying, Patrick. As I understand it, you plan to return to Virginia, make a great many people angry while you get rich off their timber groves and build both a lumber empire and a family dynasty. And you need a hostess and a breeder cow to accompany you. Correct me anywhere I've misheard."

Jessie was steaming. Unfortunately, she looked her best when she was outraged.

With the good grace to be at least a bit chagrined, Patrick nodded,

"I don't suppose that's too far off. But I haven't talked about the other side of the deal. I would, for obvious reasons, have to ask you to discontinue any activities on behalf of the slaves. Making everyone angry would be my job.

"I happen to know that you are passionate about your work with women and children—those born in lawful marriage and those not so born—and for that work, Jessie, I would support you in every way. I would speak for you in public and I would provide the money for whatever you wanted to do, on however large a scale. No conditions and no limits.

"I guess I've finished, and you have been very good to listen."

Jessie clearly had something to say, but Patrick interrupted. "I guess I haven't quite finished because I left out what I wanted to say in the first place and was afraid I would say it wrong or look a fool—and there's nothing much worse for a man like me. What I want to say, Jessie, is that I find you very attractive—physically, certainly, especially the glow of your tanned skin and the movement, when you are lifting something heavy, of those inappropriate muscles in your forearms. I admire your wit, your unfiltered honesty, and the way you work with Warren.

"I guess what I'm trying to say, and I did warn you that I might say it badly, is that when I look at you, I see everything I have wanted and everything I need. It is entirely possible that I have already fallen in love with you, and it is a sure thing that, if I haven't already, I will soon. And now, I think I really have finished."

Jessie was surprised that she felt actually calm, when she turned to Patrick and said, "It has gotten late, and I expect we are both tired. I wonder if you could stop by here for a cup of coffee on your way out tomorrow morning?"

"I'll be happy to do that, Jessie, and the coffee will be welcome on the road."

The next morning, as agreed, Patrick Hastings knocked on the door of the Ashmore house. It was Jessie who answered and led him down to the kitchen for the promised cup of coffee. They sat companionably, until Jessie stood up.

"Let me walk you to the door, Patrick. I know you need to be going." She pulled back the heavy door and stepped with him outside into a morning still shrouded in fog. As he was about to thank her again for the hospitality, she smiled.

"When the fighting is over, Captain, and you return to collect your money, I would be pleased to join you on the trip back to Virginia."

—

Chapter Eighteen
After Appomattox
Eleanor and Sarah

News of the war increased during those final months before Appomattox and Jessie, after such a long period of calm, began to be agitated. She had, of course, talked to Cook, to Gus and Frank, to Alice and Clarke and Warren, and probably to several of the horses, within minutes after the Captain's departure. Her usual, and often infuriating, insistence on "time to consider all the options" before discussing her personal life seemed, even to Jessie, a bit foolish in light of the nature of the proposal and its acceptance, both of which—in addition to their general oddity—had occurred within a week of her meeting Hastings for the first time. And here was a fine glimpse of Jessie Ashmore making a leap into the unknown.

But as the reports from the fighting poured in, Jessie had trouble getting to sleep at night and often startled awake in the hours before dawn. On these occasions, unable to fall asleep, she would go, as quietly as possible, down to the kitchen to make coffee or cocoa, build up the fire and, leaving the stove door open, sit and watch the burning embers. As a young girl, Jessie had learned the skill of watching the fire from Cook. On just such early mornings, long before the household was awake, she had crept down to the kitchen where Cook, carefully supervising the open stove, taught her how to watch the coals until she could see in their shifting shapes and colors the outlines of whole cities—cities that Cook, and later the two of them together, would people with brave ladies and horrid villains.

On one of these mornings, again unable to get back to sleep after waking not long after midnight, Jessie pulled on her dressing gown and slippers and headed for her usual retreat in the kitchen. Cook was there before her, just pouring a cup of coffee from a fresh pot. Without asking, she poured one for Jessie, then sat across from her at the table, and said,

"Do you remember when I taught you how to find houses and cities in the burning coals?"

"In fact, I have been thinking about it every morning I retreat to this kitchen to escape tossing and turning in my bed. Of course I remember. It was very important to me. It still is. Because I haven't just been thinking about it. Every morning I am here, I build up the fire then leave the door open so I can see the city taking shape."

"I'm glad, Jessie. I always found that old ritual comforting myself. Hard to know why. If you recall, some of the villains and monsters we conjured up were pretty scary. And I did always feel we called them up from wherever they lived rather than just making them up out of our own heads."

"Did I ever tell you the story that I made up once, when I was a little older—maybe ten—about the family that lived somewhere in the fireplace

—

city, the family that was just like mine?" Cook just looked puzzled and shook her head no.

"Well, it became my favorite story and, too late to be angry with me now, I used to sneak down here late at night, when even you weren't around, and build the fire, leave the door open, and wait for my duplicate family, and especially my other self, who was called Elaine, to show up. And they always did." They were content for a while to sit together, each of them recalling her own version of those days. Finally, Cook asked, "Was the family just like yours, or were there any differences?"

"They were not identical. They were identical but exactly opposite, if that makes sense, like everything on them was reversed from what it was on us. If I had a freckle on my left arm, Elaine would have the exact freckle, but on her right arm. Like when you look in a mirror.

"But the biggest difference was one that always made me afraid for some reason. Elaine, and I think the rest of her family, were trapped in the city in the fireplace. They could never leave. Elaine could see me just as clearly as I could—well, as I imagined I could—see her. But when the fire started burning down and the city was crumbling, she couldn't leave, she couldn't get out. Ever."

Cook shook her head to clear it of Jessie's story, then reached out to take her hand.

"You don't ever have to worry about that story, Jessie, because you are about to do exactly that. You are about to get out. I don't believe for one instant that this city is crumbling behind you, but I will be happy thinking about you down there in Virginia. I have never been to the South. I would very much like to visit you there one of these days."

"Oh, Cook, I would like that more than anything I can think of."

And as when anything serious had happened, on the morning of May 10, the day after the battle at Appomattox, Jessie and Gus and Cook sat in the kitchen together. Gus looked at her daughter and smiled. "I'm sure you are aware, that after almost a year of waiting, you suddenly don't have much time left. Patrick will be home the minute this war is over and, although I'm sure he will be spending time over in Mifflin County with his mother and settling up his affairs there, he will not be lingering a day more than necessary. You will be a bride very soon, and you will be setting out on your grand adventure. I believe you have been looking for it for an awfully long time, Jessie, and now, as you always said it would have to, it has come and found you.

"So, you are going to find yourself in a mad rush. We have used the time since Patrick went back to assemble every bit of marriage linen and clothing that is practical for a journey as far as Norfolk, Virginia; so that part is done. I have made a list of everything else we must see to, and we'll have all the help we could want from Cook here and Warren and your sister and Clarke and Benjamin and, of course, your father. He is very afraid he won't be able to do without you, Jess, so one of the things you must do even more than you have been is to spend every minute you can with him."

"I'm not concerned about any of that; we'll get it done. As for Father, don't worry. I feel nearly the same about being without him, and I will be with him every second I can before I go. Now, Gus, I believe I know what you're going to talk about next and, as you once did, I want to read you a few of your own words that I wrote down so I wouldn't forget them." And Jessie pulled from the pocket of her dressing gown a wrinkled piece of paper, on which she had written:

"I don't think I'm telling you anything you don't already know. You have had the unfortunate experience of seeing the demons in an especially angelic friend and it has hurt you and it has frightened you. But it honestly is just life, writ larger than usual.

"You might not believe this today, but I would not be surprised if you were able sometime later, to rebuild that friendship. Only this time you will be making friends with a real person."

The three women sat in silence, which Jessie finally broke. "It is time for me to see Eleanor."

And so it happened that on a fogbound and chilly Saturday morning near the middle of May, Jessie wrapped herself in an old jacket of her father's, pulled on her most comfortable boots and a warm hat and set out to walk to the rooms that Eleanor Harrison and Sarah Portman shared. It was a long walk, but Jessie was in no hurry, and she found herself stopping at every corner to look at the trees of her city in spring: the gigantic flowering magnolias, and what looked like great bouquets of all the more delicate trees—the cherry, the plum, and the pink and white dogwoods, the nearly purple redbud and the crepe myrtle that she loved as much for its bark as for its flowers--most already in bloom. The walk did her good.

Because their rooms took up the entire second floor, she knocked on the front door and hoped that the elderly widow who owned the house would hear her. The door was solid oak, so Jessie couldn't tell she was approaching and was startled when the door opened. It couldn't possibly have been this long; the old woman had aged terribly. Still, she embraced Jessie, called her by name, and said,

"Of course I remember you, dear. And where in the world have you been all these months? Your friends speak of you often; I hear them chatting as they come and go. It is lovely that you have come back. Here, let me take all your outdoor things, then you just go straight up. Oh, they will be so pleased."

Jessie walked slowly and quietly up the stairs to the second floor, tried and failed to slow her heartbeat, took a deep breath, and knocked firmly on the door to the rooms that she had last seen on one of the most distressing nights of her life. She didn't have to wait long before the door was pulled open sharply and Eleanor stood looking at her with an expression Jessie couldn't read.

"Hello, Jessie. Come in. You have arrived just as Sarah is brewing our second pot of tea. And we have milk. Will you join us?"

"Hello, Eleanor. Yes. I would love a cup, a mug actually if you have it." And in the direction of the kitchen, "Sarah, hello."

"Hi, Jessie, I will be out of here and out of this apron in about one minute and I intend to have a hug."

Sarah emerged, effusive as she always was with Jessie, and held out her arms in her characteristic gesture. There was no way Jessie could do anything other than walk right into them and, in fact, Jessie had no desire to do anything else. Until she had felt the familiar comfort of another woman's arms around her, their bodies next to each other, she had forgotten how much she had missed it. She remembered what her mother had said about not trying so hard to figure her feelings out. She could hear Gus's voice.

"The answer to 'What am I supposed to think?' is to get rid of those words 'supposed to.'

We are all about half black and half white and that can be a struggle, but looking away from it doesn't change it."

Eleanor's voice broke the spell, "Ladies, it is time to return to polite chit-chat and drink our tea. We have a great deal of catching-up to do, and I would assume that Jessie doesn't have days to spend doing it.

"Jess, come and sit. You take my chair as our guest of honor. I believe it's where you sat the last time you were here."

"You know, Eleanor, I think I want to take my old spot on the horrid sofa, just for the sake of sentiment.

"And oh my it is still horrid."

"Have it your way. But the offer is not likely to come round again. Now, Jessie Ashmore, why have you come on this particular day of the year? What can we do for you? What have you come to do for us?"

There was no mistaking the sarcasm in Eleanor's voice, any more than the slightly excessive warmth in Sarah's greeting. It was an awkward situation which provoked predictable responses: Eleanor was becoming cold and mocking, with a tone that threatened worse to come; Sarah, as she had learned from the cradle, had offered her body at the kitchen door, and now she was hovering over Eleanor to be sure she wasn't angry; Jessie could feel herself floating right up to the ceiling to watch from a safe distance.

—

"I hate to be unable to meet expectations, Eleanor, but would you be terribly disappointed if I had come neither to do something for you nor to ask you to do something for me?

"What if, for instance, I had come to visit for a while, to see what might be possible among us since the terrible last time I was here. What if I had come to identify my mistakes and to work toward some reconciliation. Would that be a believable thing? A hopeful thing?"

"Jessie, you sound like your Doctor Stanbury, student of the new science of the mind. You know you are the only one in this room who remembers anything like a "terrible last time" you were here. Sarah and I have talked at length about that evening and really agree that the serious melodrama was in your mind."

And Jessie understood that Eleanor and Sarah believed that, they absolutely believed it, and she realized they would be unable to hear anything else she said. She decided not to try.

"I don't intend to argue with you, Eleanor. It is not what I recall, and I suppose we will have to leave it there."

Jessie looked at the two women, at her two friends in their unmatched armchairs, with their great, flawed love that had lasted more than a decade, and she had only her news to tell before she headed home.

"I have accepted a proposal of marriage from a captain in the United States Army. He will be coming back to Philadelphia soon to see his mother and to collect some money that he left here before he went to fight. We will be settling in the coastal southern city where he was stationed and where he plans to start a lumber business. He wants a houseful of children and he intends to finance my work with women to whatever extent I want. I expect to be gone within a month.

"I came today to tell you both goodbye, although I have the unlikely idea that we may see each other again. Who knows? Anything is possible."

Neither Sarah nor Eleanor had any response. They both put their arms around her and hugged her—real hugs, even from Eleanor. And when she stopped halfway down the stairs and turned to look back, Jessie saw them standing in the doorway, Sarah's head on Eleanor's shoulder, Eleanor stroking Sarah's thick hair. They looked happy.

Chapter Nineteen
Warren and Frank

It was June and, although there was no way to predict when the war would really be over, all the news suggested it would be soon. Jessie had begun to say her goodbyes in earnest. Talking to Eleanor and Sarah had been the challenging one, because the emotions were not only intense, they were a tangled mess of contradictions. But she felt good about what had happened there, even though it didn't match her fantasies about what it should be. It wasn't the grand outpouring of love she had wanted, but it was something. She was satisfied.

She had sat down with Benjamin for a long time. He had been overseeing the Ashmore household since well before she was born, and he had opened that heavy front door to a great many people, most but not all of whom had been welcome guests, had opened it really to the world and to all the experiences of the twenty-four years of her life.

So she and Benjamin had reminisced, had told stories they both knew by heart but loved to hear again. Jessie was surprised to discover just how much she was going to miss this old man. Not so long ago, she would have said that she and Benjamin had never talked about anything of substance, anything other than the details of housekeeping. But housekeeping, of course, *is* something of substance, and it was Benjamin with whom she had consulted about sponges and warm water, about extra pillows and bed linens and extra logs for the small fireplace the night that Alice came home. It was Benjamin who, except for the doctor, was the only person who saw Alice that night when he brought in the sponges. It was Benjamin with whom they were so comfortable that it never occurred to them that he should be anywhere but with them.

Jessie was beginning to understand, as she walked around the house and said goodbye to the young women who dusted the furniture and polished the silver and laid the fires, that there are all sorts of relationships and all kinds of love. It is possible to be bound to someone just by living together in the same place, with the same people, year after year. Jessie felt she was back in school. She couldn't know that each of these goodbyes and every small insight she gained from them, would be what she would draw on to survive the strange new life that was ahead of her.

The day came when Jessie had talked to everyone in the house, had visited the neighbors she knew well, had even gone down to the market and to the medical station and the hospitals to tell the merchants who sold her fruit and vegetables, and the doctors and nurses who had worked beside her, that she was going south, to Virginia, with a new husband, to start a new life. She wanted to say goodbye to every single one of them, and she did.

She had even talked to Clarke and Alice, separately and together, those goodbyes made surprisingly easy by the very fact of their being so entirely together. So many complications, so many memories, were smoothed away or had just vanished in the light of their unlikely relationship. When Jessie was with them, it seemed to her that they were growing into each other, twining around each other like two beautiful plants, and were becoming some new thing, some flower no one could have imagined. Yes, leaving Clarke and Alice, together as they were, had not been as bitter as she had feared.

But the day did finally come when all those goodbyes had been said. The day arrived when Jessie knew that the only people left were Frank and Warren.

Sitting down with her father for the last time would be terrible, but it would be less terrible, perhaps not terrible at all, because—all their other commitments set aside--they had marked off the time to begin. Every day they met in Frank's sitting room and closed the door behind them. It gave them both great pleasure that, during that hour or more, not one person in the house knew where they were and even more pleasure when they discovered that they were often searched for. But Jessie and her father were busy saying everything they wanted to say, in an almost desultory manner, parceling it out into small segments, one memory at a time, one declaration of love at a time, one worrisome question at a time.

The unspoken rule, in this long drawn-out goodbye that they refused to acknowledge as such, was no more than one of each in a day—one memory, one declaration, one question--so that the whole endeavor lost the feeling of a goodbye and turned itself into nothing more onerous than a father and daughter spending a little extra time together. That final conversation would wound them both, no doubt about it, but they had been taking very good care of each other, and she knew it would go well.

But when she thought about Warren, her knees buckled. This was the one she had avoided, because this was the one she didn't think was possible.

"I can't do this. I cannot manage it. I cannot say goodbye to Warren because life without him will be insupportable. I do not believe for one minute that I can make it without him. And I don't know what to do."

She found Gus and Cook at the kitchen table, where they now spent most mornings. Everyone in the house knew that if they needed Mrs. Ashmore anytime before noon the kitchen was the place to look. Funny that it had been so natural to talk long into the night with Cook, to say that goodbye. Maybe it was because they were both women and just understood things differently, maybe women carry each other around inside and so there aren't ever really any goodbyes. She didn't know, and the reasons didn't matter. That was just the way it was.

"I want the two of you to stop whatever you're doing here, and tell me what in the world I'm going to say to Warren."

Warren, who had always seemed old to the young Jessie, was only twenty years her senior. He had started driving for the Ashmores when he was just a boy, seventeen years old. The elderly man who had driven for them for as long as anyone could remember had suffered some kind of seizure or stroke that left his right arm paralyzed. He was gruff and hard to talk to, but he took Warren in and, day after day, for many weeks, he taught him how to drive for Franklin and Augusta Ashmore and their young son, Frank Junior. When the baby was not quite two, and Mrs. Ashmore was expecting again, Warren Griggs became the official driver for the family. He was driving the carriage the day Jessie had announced her early appearance and Mrs. Ashmore had to be rushed home where the midwife was waiting. Jessie hadn't needed any help.

At the end of the second week in June 1865, although the news was filled with reports of one surrender after another, there still was no final declaration that the war was over and won. There was no word from Hastings. In retrospect it seems uncanny that not one person in the Ashmore household doubted that this soldier, this man who had rushed into their lives, claimed Jessie in less than a week, and ridden out the same day his proposal was accepted, would fail to return. And without any specific plans, Jessie went to her father's room at their regular time, sat in her usual chair, tucked her feet up under her—this unlikely position made possible by the fact that Jessie had finally just abandoned petticoats altogether—and looked at her father for a long time before she spoke.

"I think, Father, that you and I have done a fine job. I can't think of anything we have left out, not one feeling we haven't declared, not a question we haven't asked. I can't think of one embarrassing detail of all the things I thought only Gus knew that you haven't told me you knew all along. Can you come up with anything else?"

"You're probably right, Jess, but—in a pinch-- if it would give us a little more time, I'll bet I could think of something," Frank's smile was full of love and an awful sadness.

"Oh, God, girl. I am afraid of not having you here. I'm afraid I will wake up on the day after you go and just not want to get out of my bed. And I am afraid, if I do get up, if I do go to my shop, if I talk to the good people who work there, if I chat with Alice and Clarke at the dinner table, and compliment Cook on her roast, and make love to your mother, I am very afraid, Jessie, that after I have gotten up and done all those things, I will find that I am just no longer interested.

"You are my heart, Jessie. You always have been. And that is a piss-poor excuse for a goodbye."

Jessie was not stunned or shocked or caught by surprise by what her father said. It was what she knew he felt and so she knew it would be what he said. "No pretense between them." That had been the rule. "All walls down." And the thing they didn't say. "Last chance." Jessie uncurled herself from her chair and walked over to where her father sat, head bowed, and she lowered herself to the floor, put her arms around him and her head in his lap.

It is possible that they both went to sleep, sitting just so, and it is even possible that they slept for quite some time. However it was, when Jessie lifted her head, the right side of her face bearing the marks of sleep and the buttons on her father's jacket, and looked around, it was nearly dark and the shadows were stretching across the floor in the last light from the window. Someone was knocking on the door.

"Mr. Ashmore. Miss Jessie. Are you in there?" Jessie recognized the high voice of one of the girls who helped Cook in the kitchen—Marie, that was her name.

"Marie, yes here we are. If you can wait just a second I will open the door. Did you bring makings for a fire?"

"Yes. Yes, I did."

"Then, Marie, why don't you just come in and let's get a fire going and this room warmed up a bit."

Frank was a little slower waking up, but Marie told them that dinner was about to be served so they loosened the tendrils of everything that had happened in that room and turned to join the rest of the family. As they were closing the door behind them, Frank turned to his daughter and said, "How would you feel about calling me Frank?"

And Jessie Augusta Brynley Ashmore was left, all goodbyes said, all accounts settled, most of the inevitable tears shed, with nothing that stood between her and the conversation she had to have with Warren. She knew he was waiting. She knew he must have been trying to prepare himself, just as she had been. She guessed he had gone over in his mind a thousand times the words he could say that would help them over this impossible thing, this leave-taking. She did know that she wasn't alone in this, that she did not carry this stone's weight of sorrow by herself, that Warren had picked up his half and would help her. And despite every bit of that, she did not think she could do this.

"Dear God, wherever you are, I have— believe it or not—not one idea about this. I don't see how I can do it. I don't have any words that are the right words. Do you think you could maybe just give me a few notes on where to start? A couple of sentences to get me going would be enough."

Jessie's prayer life was sketchy, some would say irreverent. She never felt confident about who she was supposed to be talking to when she prayed or where that someone or something might live. Mostly she skipped the praying, but today she needed all possible resources.

"Warren."

"Hello, Warren. Do you have a couple of minutes?"

"Warren, I think it is time for us to talk."

Jessie was standing by the open door to the stables, trying to find some courage and rehearsing possible opening lines, when Warren cleared his throat behind her. She was horrified. "Oh, Warren. You startled me."

"Well, Jessie, I got a little jolt myself, hearing you down here saying my name over and over.

"But, you're right. It is time for us to talk, and I expect we have both put it off for about as long as we can. Why don't you go on up to my place—I don't think you've ever been there—I have to check one horse, then I'll be right behind you."

Jessie walked up the narrow stairs, whose risers she could see had been painted in bright colors, and opened the door to Warren's home— which she had thought of for years as a small, cramped, dusty space, that had been Warren's only option. She had known nothing about his personal life then and didn't know much more now. But her imagination had put him in this horrid apartment, dark, windows grimy with years of accumulated dust from the stable, floors un-swept because Warren's interest lay below with the horses, a miserable little prison which, for mysterious reasons, he could not escape.

She pushed the scrubbed and bleached pine door open all the way and her eyes travelled immediately upward through the broad unfinished beams to a peak so high that she couldn't quite understand why she hadn't noticed it from outside. As she looked, trying to concentrate on one thing at a time, she was repeatedly distracted by the light, coming in through large windows that had been cut into the walls, light that blinked and shimmered and danced along the floors, filtered through the many prisms that had been hung from the beams. The floors that absorbed this light in motion were, like the door, bleached pine.

She turned as Warren came in, "Warren, how could you not have warned me? I suppose that's a ridiculous question. Opening that door was like walking right into some other world. I assume you know this is not what one would expect to find in the apartment over the stable. I expect it to turn back into its real self when I leave--if I can ever bring myself to leave.

"Oh, Lord. I am in fine form. I hope you heard that: Jessie Ashmore opens her mouth and brings the conversation directly to the point of greatest pain. No side trips for this girl. Nope. Because that's just it, isn't it. *That is just it*; if I can ever bring myself to leave; if you can ever bring yourself to let me leave; if we can ever figure out a way to make this a thing that, while terrible, is possible.

I have discovered that I can't. So it's up to you."

Warren began with a story. It was a fairly long story. Although Warren could usually address any question in a sentence or two, given the right topic he was capable of elaborate pronouncements. His relationship with Jessie was one of those "right" topics, and he wanted very much to tell her everything he remembered about this particular story. So he began.

"Did I ever tell you that I was driving the carriage when your mother went into labor, when you apparently decided that nine months had become burdensome and much too long to wait? I had been driving her out alone, as she liked me to do during those last couple of months, when I heard what I thought at first was just her coughing but soon realized wasn't coughing but grunting and the kind of panting an animal does when it's hurt or frightened. She was calling my name, and I heard the panic in her voice.

"I found somewhere to pull that carriage over and out of the road, and I went back and climbed in next to her and held her hand, and we just sat there together, not saying a word, until her breathing slowed down and then we went on to the house. Aunt Morris and the midwife were waiting right at the door and they got Gus as far as the parlor and that chesterfield of Frank's. She was able to lie back for about thirty seconds, then they helped her back up into a sitting position and there you were."

"No. I have never heard that story. I wonder why Gus has never told it; it's a terrific story. I think it's fitting that you drove me into the world, Warren.

"Do you know that the earliest memories I have are about you, driving the big carriage, bent over brushing the horses, and then when you finally let me touch their soft noses, the first time I got to hold the brush, the first time you pulled me up behind you, told me to hold on, and rode me around the neighborhood, the first time you let me sit on a horse by myself. I had most of my first times with you. Or that's how I remember it."

"Oh, I think that's about right, Jess. But what you don't know is that I had one of my firsts with you." He looked at her with that Warren grin. "I expected as much. You didn't know. Well. The first time some smart-mouthed twelve-year-old girl told me I didn't know what I was talking about because I was old. You. And a life-changing first it was."

They were both making an admirable effort to keep the conversation light, to tell only the stories that didn't break the skin, the ones that didn't bleed, the ones that only occasionally brushed up against a tender place. They tried hard to make each other smile. It wasn't long before they both knew it wasn't working and that it wasn't going to work. It wasn't long before Warren held up his hand and shook his head. Before he could say anything, Jessie nodded.

"Yes. Let's stop. I have an idea. Let's take a walk. You know the little park down the road? It seems as if every important conversation I've had in the last year has happened in that park. Maybe if we go there we'll be able to do this. Sometimes I can think better outside walking than inside sitting. But whatever we say in the park, no matter how sad we get, I'd like to come back here after. Just for a little while.

Jessie was finding it hard to sit still in this small world that belonged entirely to Warren; it was making it even harder to think about leaving. She wanted to say that it surprised her, that it wasn't like Warren at all, that it revealed a side of him she hadn't known, but the minute she walked in she had seen that here was just exactly the Warren she had known for all these years, every day of all the twenty-four years since Warren drove her mother home to deliver her on her father's sofa.

Every day, never a day missed. Twenty-four years. There really was nothing they needed to say that they hadn't said already--nothing except just the one thing that they couldn't say. Just the one word. Only that.

And then the absolutely most unlikely thing came right into her mind, and she whipped around.

"Warren, why couldn't you just?"

At the exact same moment Warren, who had walked to the other end of the apartment to take some cuttings from one of his plants that he had oddly, and for no particular reason, suddenly decided he wanted to plant in the park, turned and walked thoughtfully toward Jessie, cuttings in hand.

"Jessie, how would you feel if I?

Then she did sit down, and Warren sat facing her across the room. She looked at him steadily before she asked, "Can you think of a reason, a really good reason, why it wouldn't be possible? A reason we couldn't at least talk about it?"

"Why talk about it, Jess? I can't think of a really good reason why we can't just do it. You don't think the Captain would object?"

"Oh, Warren, how on earth am I to know what the Captain would do. I've never spoken to the man but twice—once a few sentences down on the field, the other the hour we spent trying to introduce ourselves before he proposed and I accepted. The Captain, Lord help me, is a complete unknown. So, since you and I are sure about what we think, and can't even guess what he thinks, I say we decide. He did give me a list of things I must do, and things I may not do, and then a perfectly lovely list of all the things I may do to my heart's content and for which he will pay. I believe, with a bit of wiggling, you will fit nicely into that last category."

Jessie could no longer sit still or hold her tongue. She jumped up from the chair, grabbed the straggling leaves out of Warren's hand, threw them as high in the air as she could, and let out a whoop so loud that it must have been heard by the angels in heaven or, at the very least, by the horses down below and maybe even a neighbor or two who happened to be out walking.

"I have to tell Gus, and everyone will be furious with me but then they will see that it's the only thing that makes sense." She stopped, walked up to Warren and took both his hands in hers. "Oh, Warren, I am so very glad. I am really just so very glad. Thank you."

"Well, be on about it, young lady. Look around you. I have to decide who's to inherit my kingdom."

It required barely a day for the answer to present itself. Alice was reluctant to leave her parents and the security of the home where she had lived her whole life, and unfortunately the usually agreeable Clarke would not even discuss living with his in-laws, no matter how much he cared for them.

Alice walked up Warren's painted stairs with Jessie that very Monday and when she opened the door she literally shrieked and clapped her hands with delight. And the decision was made. No amount of stubbornness on Clarke's part stood a chance against Alice's enthusiasm. She hijacked Warren, who was already nearly defeated by the number and variety of tasks involved in a move like this. He had lived in the same place, with the same people, had done the same job for the nearly twenty-seven years since Luke was born. He had no idea where to even begin. Alice, when she set her sights on something, wasn't easily avoided, and for a while, Warren welcomed the chance both to get away from packing and to show off his place which—it can be said again—was truly marvelous.

Chapter Twenty
The packing of Linens

At no time on that Monday, the beginning of the second week in June, was there any announcement about the war, nothing more than the same reports of straggling Confederate troops approaching the first Union officers they met and asking to surrender their weapons. It seemed endless. There was still no word from Hastings.

Meanwhile, in the kitchen, the *Final Strategy for The Packing* was being laid out in detail by the Officer in Charge. Gus and Jessie sat at the table; Cook stood across the room, clipboard and pencil in hand, and cleared her throat. Jessie tried, but could not dispel the thought that Cook's entire demeanor had been influenced by the appearance of an officer of the United States Army in their midst. And Cook began.

"We will begin by setting aside most of a day and see what we can get done. I have no doubt we will want at least one more day. Sorting is the first job, and the biggest. We need to go through all Jessie's clothes: recent items hanging in the wardrobe; older ones in that wardrobe in the spare bedroom; even older ones packed away in the attic. We will pull out any she is considering taking to Virginia. Gus, I think we should lay out every single piece of clothing, every item of underclothes, every pair of shoes, where you and Jessie can walk around and look at all of them, discuss them, and she can decide what she wants to pack. Then I'll get all my girls together and give them a week to get everything cleaned and pressed and set aside for packing.

"And, yes, I know that I haven't included Alice, but she is so caught up in her wedding plans that I thought looking at the evidence that Jessie is leaving might not do her much good. We can just wait and see."

Gus had drunk three large mugs of tea while she was listening to Cook.

"Looking at the evidence that Jessie is leaving might not do any of us much good."

For one of the few times in her life, Gus had no desire to be in charge. She could see how all of them were doing whatever they had to do to survive this greatest loss of any she could imagine. Alice was looking at her linens, trying on clothes, and monopolizing Warren to hang more prisms in his loft; Cook was building a structure of time and place that would ensure that everything that needed to be done, would be done. Gus was also sure that Cook knew that when she and Gus and Jessie and all the maids, and probably Alice, got together to look through Jessie's clothes and talk about her romantic marriage proposal and the adventure to Virginia, it would be a lovely time and a real celebration for Jessie.

There is something strong and funny and altogether encouraging about what happens when women gather in groups. Gus was pleased for Jessie's sake; the whole thing had been uncanny, difficult to grasp, and clearly the right thing. But, in the meantime, her daughter, her best friend, this child she had carried not quite eight months, this impulsive girl who had rushed headlong into the world and hadn't slowed down since, was going very far away. Gus couldn't see how they were to find a lifeline that would reach from Pennsylvania to Virginia.

"Well, naturally, I want to be included, Cook," said an exasperated Alice.

"I appreciate your understanding how much I have to do, but I am not going to miss all this preparation for Jessie's big trip. I can hardly believe it. I mean, don't you wonder at all whether she's doing the right thing? One minute I am thinking she is the bravest, smartest person in the world to just pick up and move to Virginia; the next minute, Cook, I swear to you I wonder if she is entirely in her right mind. She said yes to a proposal of marriage from a man she had known two days. Two days, Cook! I can't be the only one around here who finds that a little alarming.

"But, to get back to your question, yes, I will be there. You just tell me what day and what time and where we're spreading out all the clothes and you can count on me. Besides, I might get a few dresses that Jessie doesn't want, and Madame Prous can make them over so they look new. Don't forget to let me know. Now I'm off to find Warren because I have this enormous prism that is the perfect thing to hang from the center beam."

And that was Alice.

While the women flocked around Jessie and helped both Jessie and themselves to prepare for this entirely unfamiliar event, Frank was spending a great deal of time with Warren. When Alice wasn't monopolizing what she seemed to forget was still Warren's home, he and Frank would lock the door, refuse to answer when there was knocking, and sit for hours with coffee or ale or shots of the whiskey that Warren kept on hand, "in case of snakebite," he explained to Frank with a twinkle in his eye. They talked, as men do, about the practical things, the most pressing of which was finding someone to replace Warren.

They couldn't come up with even an idea, not one name. They thought about the young men in the neighborhood, the apprentices at Frank's shop, even men on Market Street who appeared to be ambitious but at loose ends. Nothing. Frank even asked Jessie if she knew of anyone at the Friends' Meeting House who might be interested in training for a good job that, if he performed well and liked it, was almost guaranteed for as long as he wanted to stay. Jessie asked. Nothing at all.

But one day Jessie and Gus were in the kitchen, discussing the problem with Cook, when Gus's eyes lit up.

"Alright, you two. You have to be my thinkers on this, because it is—on two counts—a radical idea, and it may be too crazy to even mention outside this kitchen." Gus cleared her throat and took a big gulp of tea.

"Jessie, you remember that I have been building a very tenuous relationship with the old woman I told you about down in the Bottoms, which is the name the residents call their neighborhood."

She turned to Cook to explain, but Cook surprised her.

"You must be talking about Mrs. Elkwood. She and I go way back, and usually on the few mornings when I'm not sitting at this table with you two, I walk down for a cup of her strong coffee and a visit. I don't want to steal your thunder, Gus, but I will put this money from my pocket on the table and I'll bet you that I know just exactly what you are going to suggest." And she did, in fact, put that small stack of money in the middle of the table.

No one remembered exactly when Cook had started calling her employer by her first name. Their recollections were different but they agree that it had been during one of the many Ashmore Family Emergencies over the years. It didn't matter and neither of them even noticed. They both enjoyed telling about an event they did both remember. Gus had once suggested to Cook that it would be nice if she were called Elmira instead of Cook, but Cook had insisted on continuing to be called "Cook." Her reasons were unclear, but then one day Gus had actually said, "Good morning, Elmira," Cook had come as close to losing her temper as she ever had, and she had raised her voice loud enough it was heard outside the kitchen,

"Cook, Gus. It is Cook. I have asked you. It's Cook!"

So Cook it was. Cook and Gus.

Jessie was lost but she was content to watch these two old friends, known to each other for decades as simply "Cook" and "Gus," vying for the chance to say something that must be pretty outrageous if they both thought it was. Gus gave Cook a steady look, then just said,

"You go ahead, Cook, because you know the family much better than I do. I expect you might make the strongest case. I warn you, though, if you're thinking about what I'm thinking about, you are the one who is going out to talk to Warren. Jess and I will take care of Frank."

The idea that both Cook and Gus had come up with was, indeed, radical. First, there was no guarantee that the person they had in mind would even talk to them, let alone entertain a proposal like the one they were bringing. They discussed it and decided that the best way to go about it was for Cook to go first, and alone, to the cabins at the low corner of Society Hill, for her usual visit with Mrs. Elkwood, and that sometime during their visit she would bring up the subject. Beyond that, they could do no planning since everything would depend on Mrs. Elkwood's response.

Time was passing, and Warren wanted to be ready, when Jessie and Hastings headed to Virginia, to come whenever and however they needed him. The women were aware of all this, so two days later, Cook packed a basket full of her best pie, a large pot roast, and a mixed dish of new potatoes, thin-sliced onions, and apples, and headed out to see Mrs. Elkwood. She was gone most of the day, and Gus and Jessie really were just about to come looking for her when she strolled in the kitchen door, looking tired.

"Who in this kitchen is going to make me a cup of tea with loads of milk and even more sugar?" Jessie was up and moving. "Can you tell us just a little, Cook?"

"I can tell you the whole thing. Just as soon as I have two swallows of that tea."

Jessie had never made a pot of tea so quickly in her life. She even blew on Cook's cup so she could take her two swallows immediately.

"There is a good side and there is a bad side to my story. The good side is that Ethel Elkwood, Mrs. Elkwood's granddaughter, age twenty, will be available to talk to Gus and me tomorrow morning, here in the kitchen, at precisely 10:00. She can spare us an hour."

Jessie was about to complain about not being included, when she thought better of it. And Cook continued.

"The not-so-good side is that Mrs. Elkwood is entirely opposed to the idea, has already made that clear to her granddaughter, and—in the event that her granddaughter is interested in our offer—will do everything in her power to talk her out of it."

There was a good deal of unladylike slurping of tea, before Gus shrugged and turned to Cook.

"Any ideas about what I should wear tomorrow?"

At the same time that the *Kitchen Cabal* was meeting, those in charge of *Clothing for Virginia* were not idle upstairs. Cook, being an active member, if not the head of both groups, had a bit of a struggle. Of course she managed. And, as predicted, every day that the ladies of the household gathered to sort Jessie's clothes was indeed just like a party. First they went through the older dresses, Jessie picked a few for the trip. It was always referred to as a trip. At no time was anyone ever heard to say the word "move." Alice was thrilled to walk away with four new dresses including one of her favorites of Jessie's, the dark blue silk day dress.

After that, half a day was given entirely to all the new clothes. Jessie modeled one beautiful dress after another. She had objected at first to Gus's insistence on what Jessie still called "fancy" dresses, but her mother pointed out that she was going to be hostess for a man who planned to be a wealthy and respected member of the community and who, until he reached that goal, would as Patrick had confessed, need a wife who could charm the people he was insulting. The "fancy" dresses would work well for that. Jessie agreed.

Still, she was better pleased with the rather ordinary-looking cotton dresses that she could, if necessary, tie up onto the belt to make working easier. Gus didn't bother to tell her that she doubted she would be called on to do quite that kind of work.

But after lunch, when everyone returned to Jessie's room, even Jessie, who deplored unnecessary "glamor," was enchanted by the all the white linen and silk and voile: bed linens—sheets, a duvet and cover, pillow shams, handkerchiefs, undergarments of every sort—petticoats, chemises, bloomers. Jessie wanted to bury her face in them. At the end of the day, when everyone on the staff had suddenly to rush out to get dinner together, Jessie stood.

"I mean it when I say that I have no idea how it might be possible to thank you all for everything you have done for me, in the past week, and in my whole life. I can't do anything that would compare, but I would like each of you to choose something from all this beautiful collection in white—yes, Marie, anything at all, pick your favorite. And thank you all again."

Since the trip south wasn't to begin for nearly a month, Jessie's clothes, her linens, her best shoes (and her old boots), were packed in boxes until the trunks were brought down from the attic. The dresses were folded carefully in butcher's paper, the best thing in the world to prevent wrinkling, and the white things in all their delicate beauty were wrapped in layers and layers of tissue and packed on top of the dresses. They were ready for the day when all the preparation was over and Jessie had to go.

Gus and Cook spent over two hours talking with Ethel Elkwood, who then went home for was sure to be a thorny conversation with her grandmother who was a woman of few words and an iron will. Cook headed immediately to the stable, climbed the familiar stairs, knocked and entered without waiting for an answer. Warren had recognized her step and handed her a shot glass of whiskey.

"Well, Cook, what brings you up those stairs? I am going to hope that whatever you women have been up to is going to solve my problem."

"Yes, I believe I can say that it is all but taken care of. There is a bit of a family consultation going on between the young candidate and an elderly grandmother, but I have little doubt about a favorable outcome for that."

"Cook, you and I are old friends and I have to say there is something in your voice that's making me nervous."

"Here's what I can tell you. The person we have in mind for you to train to drive the family carriage and other vehicles, to tend those horses, take care of the stable, and generally learn over time to do what you do so well, is young, physically strong and agile, willing to try just about anything, learns quickly, and although I cannot say you won't get any backtalk at all, is generally willing to be trained. I am convinced this is the ideal person to succeed you."

"Alright. I am pouring two more shots of whiskey and then you are going to tell me the truth."

Cook looked at Warren for just the minute it took her to decide that he wasn't going to put up with any more evasion. "Well, Warren, her name is Ethel Elkwood and she is a person of mixed race."

Warren snorted, he guffawed, he held his sides, he laughed until the tears ran down his face. When he finally was able to stop, he poured himself a glass of water, drank the whole thing, and looked at Cook.

"Go home, do whatever is necessary with the grandmother, and engage Miss Ethel Elkwood on the spot. I would like her to report to me day after tomorrow, with a bag packed to spend at least a week getting started. If she does well, and still wants the job, she'll have to move up here permanently. It's just as well that Clarke and Alice are taking my place, because Ethel is far too young to live over the stable alone. Can you find her a room in the house?"

"I believe I can manage that."

Ethel Elkwood turned up right on time. Her first week's training went well, and Warren started making plans for his departure from Philadelphia.

The household was still waiting for some communication from Hastings.

Chapter Twenty-One
The Captain Returns

The war had dragged on for nearly a year after Jessie accepted Patrick Hastings' proposal of marriage and watched him ride away. On the ninth of April 1865, at the Battle of Appomattox, Robert E. Lee had surrendered to Ulysses S. Grant, and five days later, at Ford's Theater, President Abraham Lincoln had been shot by a southern sympathizer named John Wilkes Booth. After Appomattox, surrender followed surrender, as the army of the Confederate States of America slowly collapsed. It wasn't an especially tidy end, but then it had been a bloody mess of a conflict. On the twenty-third of June, Stand Watie, leader of the Cherokee Nation and a general in the Confederate army, surrendered the last of the Confederate forces. The American Civil War was over and Patrick Hastings headed home.

The morning of June 30 was blanketed in a thick fog, so damp that water dripped from the large trees and from the eaves of the houses in Society Hill. Jessie couldn't see more than a few feet beyond the parlor window. Still not sleeping well, and almost never through the night, Jessie had come downstairs well before sunrise, lit the fire that had been laid the night before, and added a few logs. She wrapped herself more tightly in her dressing gown and the heavy shawl that was her favorite and that she had kept for years in spite of Gus's determination to replace it. It might well be a "moth-eaten old rag," as Cook called it, but Jessie loved it. Her father had given it to her the Christmas she turned twelve.

In spite of war and uncertainty, it had been a good year, a solid year. The waiting had opened a pocket of time in which she could pay attention to her life. She had done what she could to safeguard every important relationship; she had conspired with Warren in two marvelously outlandish decisions; she had spent entire mornings in the kitchen with her mother and Cook; and she had surrendered entirely the preparations for her move, letting herself enjoy the role of pampered child. She had discovered the unexpected pleasures of whole days in the company of women, doing the foolish things that men think don't matter but that are, in fact, the life blood of a home. She learned the vital lesson of laughter and the pleasure of beds covered with dresses and camisoles.

From Jessie's Journal
Nearing the End
It will happen very soon now. If Patrick is going to come at all, it will not be long. Funny how we all have behaved as if there is no question that he will come. Not one single word to the contrary has been

uttered. There is this unspoken conspiracy to act as if all is well. No one is able to acknowledge the abject terror that this situation could inspire. There is, on the face of it, not one detail about the circumstances or the man or the proposal that should not be cause for alarm. No one even dares to mention the obvious danger, that Patrick could be killed in the fighting. But the specter of death has always been less dreadful than the specter of betrayal. Bad as it would be, if Patrick were killed, at least he wouldn't have humiliated me. Goodness, what a world we live in.

The waiting has actually been rather nice. I am here, and yet I am not here. The part of me that is here is more sharply here than ever. I suppose what I mean is that I am looking at every single thing, every person, every minute, every picture on the wall as if for the first time and as if for the last time. And the thing that no one says, that in fact I don't believe anyone has ever even whispered, is that there is a strong possibility that everything is for the last time. That's a little idea that sounds innocuous until it becomes more than an idea. It is possible, maybe it is even probable, that I will never be back in this house, that I will never see my parents or Alice or Clarke or Cook or anyone in this place ever again. It is likely that I will go and not come again. So, you see why we have this understanding that no one is to mention it. Should that be the case, should I embark on this adventure, this life for which I have longed and waited, and find there is no road back, what do I know about where I am going? Not what do I know about Norfolk, Virginia—although I have found every bit of information I can about this city that is going to be my home—but what do I know about the whole circumstance and what do I know about Patrick Hastings? The short answer is: almost nothing.

And that is a fact that should have me paralyzed with fear or just backing out of the whole deal completely. Who, in her right mind (and I understand that Alice, of all people, has expressed concern about my sanity), would meet a man one day, invite him into her home that evening, allow him to speak to her, in the most familiar terms, of his whole life and of his plans to leave the state and start fresh, and then not stop him or ask Benjamin to show him out, when he suggests that she might consider going with him. Who, with even a shred of sanity remaining, would think about it for one night and say yes. And, in point of fact, I didn't really have to think about it for even one minute. I knew when I met him that Patrick was the right one, and I knew when he asked me what my answer would be. I, who think and think and think too much about everything, never gave one thought to Patrick's question. 'Yes' was part of the conversation from the beginning.

Obviously, the big question here is why? Why was the answer yes from the minute the question was asked? Why did I respond with that uncharacteristic impulsiveness? What is it about Patrick Hastings that so swept me off my feet?

The answer to all those questions is: "I have no idea."

When she looked up from her musings, Jessie discovered that the sun had scattered most of the fog; the filmy tendrils that were so treacherous to sailors floated harmlessly out on the slight breeze. The fire had burned all the way down, and she turned her head at the sound of Cook's voice.

"Jessie Ashmore, how long have you been down here? I don't suppose there's any hope that you got something from the kitchen to eat? No I didn't imagine so. Well, come join your mother and me, and let's get you fed. Then, why don't you get some clothes on—yes, I know you're not going to put on those corsets--because I think Gus would like to stroll around the neighborhood a bit if that sun keeps shining. She's restless, and you two haven't had much time together with everything that's been going on."

An hour later, Gus and Jessie, both looking just fine--although neither mother nor daughter was laced into any corsets—walked out into a beautiful day, turned left so they would pass the stables, and started their walk. Both women wore their favorite old boots—Jessie was keeping a close watch on hers to be sure they were packed for Virginia and not sent to the rubbish heap where Cook thought they belonged--and they were prepared for a long walk.

During the rest of the morning and well into the afternoon, Jessie and her mother walked, sometimes in silence, sometimes talking quietly about nothing in particular, sometimes one or the other just saying, "I love you." Often they held hands for a while. They stopped at the stable to see how Ethel was coming along and spent at least half an hour listening to her enthusiastic report on every detail of just how splendidly she *was* doing; she was so obviously happy, and Cook had told them she was getting on well with the young maids who slept in the house.

When they came around the last corner, not too long before dinnertime, they could see Patrick, stretched out and sleeping soundly on the old bench that had sat next to the front door for as long as Gus could remember. They stopped and watched him, this stranger who had come to marry Jessie.

They both felt they should say something, have some words to say to one another in this final moment before Patrick opened his eyes, before nothing would ever be the same again, but neither of them could think of anything, and so they stood, and before very long, Patrick Hastings sat up and smiled.

"Seeing you two beautiful women makes me glad to be on this earth. Now if you'll allow me inside in this condition, I would be grateful for a bath and a bit of food. I have walked from northern Virginia, up around Washington, and I don't expect I'm fit for human company. Jessie, once I'm a bit more presentable, I'd like to find out if you're still willing to marry me."

She smiled at Patrick, took his hand and walked him up the stairs, stopping when she saw Marie.

"Marie, I don't think you met Captain Hastings when he was here last year. Patrick, this is Marie Thomason." Patrick tipped his hat.

"I am not quite sure I believe what I'm seeing. Can it be true that every woman in this house is beautiful?"

And when he saw that she was embarrassed, he stopped, "Marie, pay no attention to my nonsense. I am very glad to meet you."

"Marie, Patrick is going to need the biggest and the longest bath anyone has ever had in this house, so can you help me get started?"

"Oh, absolutely, Miss Jessie, what do I need to do first?"

"It's going to take several of you to handle this, so see who you can find. Fill the large bath with steaming hot water and find several of the new sponges—I'm sure I saw some unusually big ones-- and two bars of soap—look for one that Warren brought to clean up after working with the horses; I believe he left a brand new bar in the linen cupboard on this floor. Then we need the soft perfumed square that Alice bought from one of the vendors on Market Street. If she asks, tell her I promise to replace it."

After showing Patrick the bath, Jessie left him in the capable hands of Marie and her crew and wandered down to the kitchen where she sat with Gus, drinking strong, sweet, milky tea, and occasionally chatting about things like tomorrow's lunch menu or whether Gus remembered exactly where Alice had found the lavender soap.

"Shouldn't we send someone over to let Warren know Patrick is here?"

They agreed that they should, but never got around to doing anything about it. They had been so busy planning and preparing and interviewing Ethel and trying to keep Alice out of Warren's way, and sorting and folding and packing, that the pause that had happened the minute they had seen Patrick on that bench, had left both of them pleasantly lethargic. It was odd, but no odder than anything else in this strange story.

Perhaps the very oddest was that Jessie's reunion with Patrick, after nearly a year apart and on the basis of a week's acquaintance, was natural as seeing her father on a Tuesday after she had somehow missed him on the Monday. Jessie felt happy, but not ecstatic; she felt content, and completely at home in this man's company. When

—

she gave it any thought, it seemed so unlikely, so peculiar, that she was grateful she seldom felt any need to think of it. She did wonder sometimes, in those early days, if she loved him. She decided it didn't matter and that it wasn't even a word she understood.

Patrick was in the bath for two hours. Washing off the dirt from days on the road, washing off the filth of war and killing and the blood of boys who wouldn't be coming home, required that the tub be emptied and refilled twice, required new sponges and a second bar of Warren's soap, required that a fire be lit and built up when Patrick began to shake and couldn't stop.

Marie handled herself well, but she finally sent for Cook who arrived, greeted the captain, sent Marie and the other girls out for a break, and picked up the soap and the sponges.

"Captain Hastings, can you dunk yourself right down in that clean water, get your hair wet, too, then sit up as straight as possible?

"If you will excuse my taking the liberty, I am about to give you the most thorough scrubbing of your life."

Patrick, distracted by the commanding nature of Cook's voice, did exactly as she asked. Cook sat down on a stool at the head of the tub and she didn't get up until she had made good on that promise. She then called for Marie to bring at least four of their thickest bath towels, ordered the captain to step out of the tub, rubbed him dry, then kept rubbing until his skin shone red. She left him with a set of Frank's clothes.

"Captain Hastings, we will expect you to join us for dinner just as soon as you're ready.

"And, Patrick, we are very happy to have you home."

Epilogue

"On the twelfth of August 1865, at the Colonial Avenue Methodist Church in Philadelphia, Pennsylvania, Miss Jessie Augusta Brynley Ashmore and Captain Patrick Wyndham Hastings, of the Army of the United States of America, exchanged the vows of Holy Matrimony. In attendance were Miss Ashmore's parents, Augusta and Franklin Ashmore; her sister and brother-in-law, Alice and Clarke Stanbury, who were married in their own small ceremony just two weeks earlier; and close family friends, Warren Griggs and Elmira Winship. Captain Hastings' mother, Mrs. Clementine Hastings, of Mifflin County, Pennsylvania, was unable to attend due to illness. Captain and Mrs. Hastings will spend the rest of August with the Ashmores at their home in Society Hill, and will set out, in early September, on the way to their new home in Norfolk, Virginia. Accompanying them to Virginia will be Warren Griggs, who plans to make his home there."

Patrick went home to see Clementine and to collect the thousand dollars he had left with his old employer at the general store. They were together for an hour while Sam Bryant showed Patrick the United States bonds that he had purchased at the beginning of the war and tried to explain to him how his one thousand dollars had become nearly ten thousand in the four years he had been away. Patrick folded the bonds and slid them into his jacket pocket, and when he got back to his mother's house he sewed them into the hem of that same jacket until he could buy himself a fine leather wallet. He told Clementine not to worry. He would find a way to bring her to Virginia.

On the third of September 1865, Jessie and Patrick Hastings and Warren Griggs boarded a train in Philadelphia for the journey to Norfolk. Although by this time travel by rail was fast becoming the dominant mode of passenger transportation, the effects of the Civil War were devastating. In Virginia, Richmond had been burned, and the extent of the damage along the tracks from Richmond south was unknown.

Still, Patrick and Warren were confident that by some combination of railway, stagecoach, and possibly even steamboat, they could count on arriving in Norfolk within the month. Meanwhile, the trip would allow all three to concentrate on what lay ahead.

On the train, Warren made up elaborate lists, with sketches and measurements, of the various kinds of carriages, buggies, and wagons that might be needed immediately. He would not realize until they arrived that resources in Norfolk were limited as the result of the war. For a while, a great deal simply wouldn't be possible, but Norfolk was a busy port city and the arrival of ambitious men from the North, men just like Patrick Hastings, would speed up the rebuilding of the city.

Jessie, Cook and Marie had organized and packed most of what Jessie would need, and Jessie had spent hours at the kitchen table with a pad and a pencil taking notes as Cook and Gus, and occasionally Marie, told her everything they knew about setting up a new house. As a result of all this preparation, Jessie spent her time watching the changing countryside through the train's sooty window, imagining fabrics for upholstery and drapes, and wondering how large her house would be and what kinds of carpet might look best. She tried hard to dispel dreams of helping Warren buy horses and locate a stable.

Patrick Hastings, with his wallet full of United States bonds worth close to $10,000, knew exactly what he intended to do. His list, short and in order of priority, was: purchase a house; build a sawmill; find a few men who are willing to help a Yankee cut down the timber groves in the Great Dismal Swamp.

The first week after they watched the train pull away from the station, the members of the Ashmore household—from Jessie's parents down to the most recently hired maid—were in shock and in mourning. No matter the preparation, regardless of the rituals of leave-taking, in spite of all their efforts to explain this to themselves, Jessie's family—the whole gathering of the people with whom she had lived—was bereft. Frank wondered how, after all, he could find any reason to continue. Gus understood completely, felt much the same, and never felt hurt by this. Cook spent every free minute at the stable, helping Ethel. She tried once or twice to go upstairs to visit with Alice but found herself angry at every change Alice was making in Warren's apartment. So she gave up and just stopped going.

And what about Clarke and Alice, Jessie's former lover and her sister, these two people whose lives and emotions were so wrapped around hers? They missed her terribly, but they were so unexpectedly happy, so much more delighted with each other than they had imagined, that her absence was an ache rather than an open wound. Three months after Jessie left, Alice knew she was pregnant, and she and Clarke started looking at houses. With permission from Gus and Frank, and the promise of help and supervision from Cook, Ethel Elkwood, driver for the Ashmores of Society Hill, prepared to move into Warren's old quarters. It took months, but Gus and Cook finally talked Mrs. Elkwood into walking with them from her cabin to Society Hill to share the occasional meal with her granddaughter.

Sarah and Eleanor, lovers for more than a decade, had waited for this life they now shared, had waited and dreamed about just this small set of rooms. With her confused expectations, her sharp eye for the truth, and her straight talk, Jessie had called everything into question. It had made matters infinitely worse that both Eleanor and Sarah had, at some point, wanted to take her to bed. When Jessie left that last time, they had been angry—obviously angry with Jessie—but, as the conversation that began that day revealed, also furious with each other.

When the door closed behind Jessie, for a terrible few seconds the two lovers were paralyzed and, for one of the rare times in all their years together, neither of them could think of a word to say.

The few feet between them stretched into a great abyss, and there was no way across. And then something happened that was so unlikely, such a surprising shift in the very foundation of their relationship, that it opened the door for a great many of the changes that would come in the years ahead. It was a simple thing, really, nothing unusual in the annals of lovers, but for these two it was a revolution. Eleanor Harrison looked at Sarah Portman, sat down on the dreadful sofa, put her head in her hands, and began to weep.

The travellers were not destined to stay on that comfortable train for long, nor would they reach their destination within the month, although their prediction that it would require a combination of rail, stagecoach, and steamboat was accurate. It was only after a journey marked by every imaginable difficulty and delay that they arrived in

Norfolk, Virginia, on the tenth of November 1865, two months after they boarded the train in Philadelphia and six months after the surrender at Appomattox.

They took rooms at the Atlantic Hotel in downtown Norfolk, an establishment that had been advertised in *The Norfolk Post* as having carriages ready for guests to use and a "bar and table" supplied with the best food and drink. Not that a woman would be allowed near the bar, but the description, prominently displayed in the local paper, had sounded like exactly what they needed.

From Jessie's Journal
On Going Home
April 1866

I am more tired from the journey than I expected. I guess I really do have some limits. But, tired or not, my excitement is growing as I contemplate what lies ahead. Patrick and I struck a fine bargain when he asked and I said yes. I know I have signed on for a great deal of work in the coming years, but I have always been a hard worker. And this time, I will not be working alone. I will be part of a team, forging ahead in harness with a man I find myself loving more every day. The entire thing is quite remarkable.

I am getting to know this new husband, and one thing I learned early is that my happiness makes him happy. He does really seem to love me, and he is pleased with himself when he can make me smile.

And, just for the record, he makes me smile often—in the bedroom as well as the parlor.

I believed that marriage and adventure could never come together. I was wrong.

I believed that adventure and a husband would have to come looking for me. And they did.

I do not know what the years ahead will bring. I can hardly imagine tomorrow. I hope I will have time to write in this journal. I expect that whatever comes, knowing me, it will be worthy of comment.

The sequel,

Jessie: The Further Adventures and Insights of a Nineteenth-Century Woman, The Virginia Years

Is now available in Kindle eBook or paperback on Amazon

ABOUT THE AUTHOR

Dean Robertson is the author of Looking for Lydia; Looking for God (Koehler Books, 2015) and half of the writing duo "Patricia Allison." The complete list of their books is below. Ms. Robertson and Ms. Daniels hope to be co-authoring another novel soon.

Visit Patricia Allison's Author Page on Amazon.

Available from Patricia Allison on Amazon:

- *Memory Is the Seamstress: The Story of a Family* (Robertson and Daniels)
- *Fortune's End* (Daniels)
- *Jessie: The Adventures and Insights of a 19th-Century Woman* (Robertson)
- *In Sycamore Hall: A Deke and Loomis Mystery* (Daniels)

- *Behind the Curtain: A Deke and Loomis Mystery (Daniels)*
- *Jessie: The Further Adventures and Insights—The Virginia Years* (Robertson)

Take a look at Dean Robertson's blog at pdrobertson.com. There are several long posts about this collaborative writing experience.

—

Printed in Great Britain
by Amazon